"Johnnyboy - What I Love About Your Writing:
To hear your resonate voice telling your stories
Stirs up memories long forgotten
Your writings are compelling, captivating
A page-turner that can't be put down
Eccentric characters and their names are unforgettable, delightful
Adventurous and more fun than a piano hurling off a truck
Plotting suspense and tension at every turn
Making us laugh out loud and cry in secret
Your human warmth and compassion come through boldly
As you write with your heart
You always surprise and treat us
Filling our souls with yearnings for more
And you understand the top of the hill
'The Sacred Mountain,' making us soul mates."

—a tribute from Margaret Sibley

"The first sentence of Timekeeper drew me in and wouldn't let me leave until I finished this wonderful book. The writing is first rate and made even more impressive by the fact that the young Atkinson was thought to be stupid by his teachers, unable to be taught how to read like everyone else. It is a story about abuse and a boy leaving on his own at 14 to find answers, and ultimately finds redemption. I'm thankful he takes us along with him. This is a deeply moving book and you will be the better for reading it."
—**Sharon Baldacci, author,** *A Sundog Moment*

"I just finished editing Timekeeper and I cried at the end just like I did the first time, and that's a fine thing, to cry and to be reminded of how much heart, spirit, and soul fills this book. I sincerely thank John Atkinson for writing Timekeeper. His story needed to be told and now the world needs to hear it, for the Timekeeper, for the Fisher King, for Check, Chief, Mama, and even Bugdaddy, but most importantly, for the Universal Soul."
—**Jackson Fisher, editor, Fisher King Press**

"John Atkinson tells an intriguing tale of a boy's coming-of-age with this fast-paced novel that reveals the toughness of youth as well as its vulnerability. No one with any feeling in their makeup could resist this engaging young man's journey to freedom and a wild dog's devotion and uncompromising love and sacrifice."
—**Jean C. Keating, author of the** *Genna Kingsley & Sky Dog Mystery Series*

"John Atkinson's Timekeeper is an engrossing, heartfelt account of a young man's quest for self-discovery and a place at the table of life. Johnnyboy's evolution into Timekeeper will have you rooting for this engaging underdog."
—**Howard Owen, author of** *Turn Signal* **and** *Littlejohn*

"A story that is uniquely American, evoking the best of literature. This work is a coming-of-age story that shows man at his best and worst. He also manages to connect his incredible journey to the traditions of native people, a mixture that young adult readers will find compelling."
—**Lee Irby, author,** *7000 Clams* **and** *The Up And Up*

"Timekeeper is the story of a troubled young boy locked within himself. It's the story of a youngster who has no one to rely on but himself and by trusting his instincts, he meets one person after another - each one a possible doorway to a new life. True to himself, he follows his heart, gratefully using the gifts that each teacher offers."
—**Pat Adler, Publisher, Live Wire Press**

Timekeeper

BY

John Atkinson

Fisher King Press

This is a work of fiction. Names, characters, places, and incidents either are the product of the author's imagination or are used fictitiously, and any resemblance to actual persons, living or dead, business establishments, events or locales is entirely coincidental.

Fisher King Press
www.fisherkingpress.com
1-800-228-9316

Timekeeper
Copyright © 2008 by John Atkinson
First Edition

All rights reserved. No part of this publication may be used or reproduced by any means, graphic, electronic, or mechanical, including photocopying, recording, taping or by any information storage retrieval system without the written permission of the publisher except in the case of brief quotations embodied in critical articles and reviews.

ISBN 978-0-9776076-5-5 Hardcover
ISBN 978-0-9776076-3-1 Softcover
LCCN: 2007933126

Cover image & logo by Sheri Mallory
Cover & book design by Charles Thomas

To Reneé

Preface

It's more humane to face a firing squad than a classroom, humiliated because of illiteracy. One is swift, the other leads to a lifetime of isolation and hardship. *Timekeeper* is my triumph over letters. Parts of my journey are no longer clear. Forty-eight years later, I have re-imagined events that seem most consistent to my memory.

In 1959 ground swept under my feet like a starving man scrambling for his next meal. I'd fled a dysfunctional family in Virginia. I met many people along the way, but no one could compare with Chief in Oklahoma. He filled a void in me and taught me how to join together the many pieces of life. Chief wasn't surprised that I'd crossed the country at the age of fourteen. I was a big kid and had become hardened to the ways of the streets. Right away Chief understood why I didn't fit in. The main thing was, I couldn't read. He looked into my soul and saw the suffering I'd endured in the white man's world. He also saw into my future. Anyone with a lick of sense would've been frightened of Chief, an old medicine man with strange powers. But after everyone else had given up on me, he saw how I could help myself. At first I thought he was foolish as a fish flopping on a riverbank when he said I should go north to a place he'd visited as a boy. Hell, that was back before we had automobiles. But he said I would go with a great power. I couldn't imagine where the power would come from. I thought it had to be a strong car, a big Buick Road Master. Every boy my age wanted a car. But the old man gave me a name, Timekeeper. I was no longer Johnnyboy, the affectionate name my Mama had called me. But the gift of the new name stayed a mystery for forty-eight years, the time it took me to figure out Chief's predictions. For all those years I've searched for his meaning, and now I know.

Chapter 1

Veins bulged on my father's forehead while his spitting cobra stare held me frozen. He yelled, "If you leave, Johnnyboy, don't come back!" The viper was ready to strike. I didn't show fear, but I knew enough not to flinch or I would have hell to pay. Mama sat face down at the kitchen table too scared to speak. I felt for her but never more than when her Cherokee eyes met mine. Mama's eyes set me free, free to leave. I had turned fourteen the month before. With seven children besides me, she was stuck with the monster I called bad names under my breath.

I wanted to yell, *Hell, no, I'm not coming back. Mama, you leave too. I don't have a choice. Bugdaddy will kill me one of these days and get away with it. Be like me, Mama, run. Run like a wild horse. Nothing here but misery piled high.* But, like Mama, I said nothing.

My father abused the other siblings, but plain as scuffed shoes it was me he loved to hate. Mama saw that too, so she sent me away in the summers to work on a cotton farm. I was the fourth child of eight and the first to be born in a hospital. Bugdaddy argued with the nurses the day I was born that I wasn't his child. He said I looked like a monkey because my arms were too long and claimed the hospital had given him the wrong damn baby. The only thing I had in common with Bugdaddy was neither one of us could read. Trying to please him only made matters worse. At one point, I too thought I was from another family. This heartless man couldn't be my father. He was cruel. He started taking me out of school at the age of ten to work with him. By the time I was twelve I was forced to labor alongside lowlifes who had nothing to live for but their next bottle of booze.

Newt, a brother five years older, and I shared an army cot in an eight-by-eight unheated shed where Mama washed clothes on a scrub-board. The room's dingy gray walls had no windows. What light there was came from a pull chain fixture in the center of the ceiling. When it rained, water came up through the cement floor drainpipe. The door didn't hold off bad weather either. Sometimes we'd wake up to wet shoes. Nevertheless we thought it was worth the trouble since the room gave us a little space away from Bugdaddy.

Everyone had chores. In the winter Newt and I switched turns every other day filling up the coal bin. I remember the night Newt forgot it was his turn, and the fire went out in the furnace. We couldn't tell there was a problem because our room was detached from the main house. We only knew something was wrong when we heard our father throwing chairs out of his path as he charged toward the backdoor. He was spewing foul words that cut new depths of fright into my soul. I heard him yell my name. Earlier he had come home drunk, but now the good glow of alcohol had worn off. That always made him meaner.

I held my breath when the backdoor creaked. He was coming closer and closer, making time crawl. In a split-second he kicked our door open with the rattle of wood splintering the doorframe. *What did I do wrong?* I thought as chips hit walls, floor, and bed. *Is it me he's after?* I tried to hide my head under the bedcovers to become invisible. *Oh, Moses, help me, please.* But he snatched me from our cot and dragged me outside in my underpants into the snow. I couldn't imagine what I had done wrong but I knew what was coming. I could only hope that the weapon he used wouldn't be too harsh; a stick, his belt—but my luck had run out. He held a fan belt, the most dreaded whip of all.

Yelling was pointless so I gnashed my teeth and waited, but not for long. The belt squalled like a demon. A deep moan warned of its punishment as it cut its way toward its target; bare skin. The pain began like giant bee stings. After so many lashes I couldn't tell when the stings turned into a raging fire. I begged to know what I had done, but he wouldn't tell me. Before I blacked out, he mentioned the furnace in his ranting. "You let the goddamn fire go out. I ought to kill you!"

"Oh, I won't forget again! I promise I won't forget again! I swear I won't!" I had to stop playing into his hands. *Moses, I've got to quit yelling but the fire is too hot. Oh. Moses, please help me.*

I wouldn't tell on Newt because he had taken a couple of beatings for me. We had to hang tight against our father. Telling wouldn't have done any good anyway—the old man was out to get me. There was no escape from the hurt. Peeing was my only relief from the torture. He would only stop when the pleasure of hurting me had faded in the night's winter air. I don't remember him stopping or walking away. The snow silenced his footsteps and I lay still. The cool snow relieved some of the fire on my back and legs. Folks lie when they say you can't remember pain. I remember pain very well. I remember pain that can only be described as burning hell. Snow could help pain like that a little, but snow could never help me forget. Only death could do that.

While I was outside, Newt had started a new fire in the coal furnace and made out like he was busy until Bugdaddy was out of sight. I was too scared to get up so I stayed put until Newt thought it was safe. That beating left me with a rekindled hatred of my father. It's not good to want to kill someone, but the hatred helped take my mind off the hurt, the raging hell on my skin.

After Newt went to sleep, I lay on bloody bedcovers on my side of the cot, thinking about the day I would leave. I was too young to know there was another world out there, a much kinder place. I only knew something had to change. *I'll be fourteen come spring, maybe big enough to get away. Oh, Moses, let that day come.*

Snow was blowing around our room so I put the chair that held our clothes against the door. Still, tiny flakes came through a broken panel. Newt shivered in his sleep while I watched snowflakes swirl about. It came to me that they were like friends visiting a lonely soul in the dead-quiet prison of a room. I didn't say a word to them . . . just watched the specks searching for places to land until I was swallowed to sleep by the sight.

It took spring a long time to come, and the abuse never stopped. My father would shake his penis at me and tell me, "Look at your daddy." He'd say, "Johnnyboy, you could've been shot up a nigger's ass." That spring, after I'd turned fourteen, a little stray dog started hanging around the house and took to me. The words, "He's my friend," slipped from my mouth in front of Bugdaddy. Right away I knew I'd made a terrible mistake. Using hand pliers and copper wire, he tied a tin can with gravel to the small dog's tail. Then he beat the little dog bloody. The bad man laughed when he turned the dog loose, saying he would run himself to death. I wasn't strong enough to stop him and I couldn't have hated him more, but I could leave and choose better company.

Bugdaddy fancied himself an Old Testament man. His favorite quote was about work. He'd say, "If the ox is in the mire, get him out." That meant I had to work Sundays too. I'd learned about Moses from Sunday school. For a while, he was a make-believe friend. I knew about Jesus, but I thought He had His hands full helping so many people, so I used Moses to pass on the little I had to say to the Big Guy in heaven. I would say, "Moses, tell God if I've got to live with Bugdaddy another day, just strike me dead and send me on to hell. I don't care. That man needs to be shot with sheep shit and sent to hell for stinking. Got that?" I listened but I never heard a word back.

Bugdaddy had me sanding a car to prepare it for paint, but after the dog beating I couldn't do anything right. I'd wanted to help my little friend but I'd done nothing. Now only silence came from the woods where the poor innocent pup had run yelping. I couldn't stop crying inside but only Moses knew that. I stopped sanding a second to listen for the dog hoping the can had come loose. Bugdaddy yelled, "Johnnyboy, don't make me tear your ass up. Get to work!" I got back to work, but I never stopped listening for that little dog.

A neighborhood bully, three years older, heard the old man threatening me. He said, "Let me handle him. I'll beat his ass for you." Bugdaddy gave his blessing and, like always, began rooting for the other guy. But this time was different. I told the old man that I aimed not to let anyone kick my ass again. And on that day, I didn't. When the bully finally staggered off, badly beaten, I saw fear, something I'd never seen before on my father's face. I liked seeing his fear. That sight was the turning point in my decision to leave home.

I waited for dinner to let everyone know what I was fixing to do. After I had crammed in all the food I could eat, I said I was leaving for good. Bugdaddy said I'd been eating white bread. That meant I'd had it easy at home and it would be real hard out there in the cruel world. He was trying to scare me, but he could see it wasn't working. That's when he yelled for me not to come back and I would burn in hell forever. Mama looked at me with loving eyes, the blessed glance I'll carry to my grave. She couldn't have said it with words any better than this, "My Johnnyboy, it's time for you to go." From her eyes she gave me the strength I needed.

I wanted to hurt Bugdaddy so he wouldn't be mean to Mama, hitting her with a fly swatter. I wanted to spit on the floor in front of him to get things started, but I didn't. I'd never spit on Mama's floor. She scrubbed those floors on her hands and knees. All I could see were her kind eyes, eyes that always taught peacefulness was better than hatred. With her love in mind, I slipped out the back door.

The minute I was outside I spat the hatred for my father onto the ground, and stomped the spot with my feet like it was his body being ripped to pieces. Then I ran for all the good I had in me. I needed a head start and Mama had taught me not to take anger along, especially on a journey to find where I belonged. I had run away before like a baby bird trying to leave its nest and had wandered back after a few days, but this time Johnnyboy would fly. It would be my last goodbye to Mama. I had the clothes on my back and 38 cents in my right front pants pocket, the one with no holes in it.

Why hadn't I left sooner? That thought kept reverberating in my mind as I put one foot in front of the other. *No matter. Now I can be anybody I want and nobody will know the difference. I'll call myself something good, not Johnnyboy, a foolish pissy-ass name.* But I couldn't think of one right yet.

I thought about stopping to say goodbye to some neighbors when I passed their homes, but I kept going. Unlike my family, they had good jobs and decent cars. I didn't mind though because they were good to me, making up for my father's ill treatment. They liked me because I was a little bit like Mama . . . willing to share what I had, my labor. I didn't want them to know I was running away. I had tried to leave so many times before and failed. Maybe they were tired of hearing about it. *Just get the hell away from here, Johnnyboy. Worry about that kind of stuff later.*

When I passed the dreaded school bus stop, I recalled some of my teachers talking about me, saying how I couldn't learn to read and never got anything right. *The Atkinson boy has taken me to the brink. What's wrong with him? That child is condemned to a life of menial labor. What a shame he's dimwitted.* I defended myself like always. *Who are they? They don't know anything about me. I'll prove them all wrong. Moses, tell God to damn them all. I hate their guts.*

Bugdaddy always said something was wrong with me too. My school grades were F's and, compared to my siblings' grades, proved him right. No doubt something was wrong with me. It didn't help that I couldn't hear in one ear because he'd popped my eardrum with a hard slap. My left ear never stopped ringing. If any outside noise came along while the teacher was talking, I couldn't hear what she'd said. I could only hear one thing at a time and, if three people talked, it sounded like gibberish. Nothing made sense. I didn't like classmates whispering about me. *Nobody had better call me names again. Saying I'm stupid. I hate that and I'll hurt 'em if they say bad things. I'll do hard labor . . . anything as long as it gets me the hell away from Glen Allen.*

But where would I go? I didn't have a plan. I needed time

to think, so I hid in the woods about a mile from our home place. I knew those woods better than anyplace, yet I felt lost, so lowdown lost. I needed someone to talk to, a true friend who would take me as I was. Then I remembered old Chicken Bone, a black man who lived not too far from where I sat. With my head slumped between my legs, I jumped to my feet and headed for his shack.

Chapter 2

It was dark as a condemned man's heart when I got to Chicken Bone's place. His oil lamp was burning bright and I smelled the kerosene when he opened the door. I'd met him through my best friend, Frank. Folks called him Chicken Bone because he could stick a whole drumstick in his mouth and pull out a clean bone. One time he got upset when I told him about Bugdaddy beating me with a garden hose. He said, if he were white and younger than his eighty years, he'd face the vile man and put a stop to his sinful ways.

Chicken Bone asked me in. He was glad to see me, but I felt bad because I didn't have anything for him. Frank and I usually took him a jar of homemade wine Frank's mama made. Chicken Bone liked that. His shack was tiny, not much more than a tin roof overhead. The four walls were stuffed with newspapers and covered with pieces of cardboard. Two milk crates, one stacked on the other, were used for a table. The place always smelled like hard labor, a manly sweat odor, but it didn't bother me. An out-of-date calendar, stuck on February 1932, hung on the wall. Somehow it saddened me because this was May 1959. Frank had warned me not to ask Chicken Bone why he kept his calendar that way. I trusted Frank so I didn't, although the picture on the calendar showing the first V8 Ford and an attractive blonde-haired lady with big breasts was reason enough.

The last time I was there I'd built Chicken Bone a bed out of throwaway lumber from the sawmill across the railroad tracks. Before that, he'd had a hard time getting up from a mattress on the floor. He felt he owed me, but still asked if I was running from the law. I told him no, that I just needed a place to stay for the night.

    Chicken Bone heaved a long sigh. His face was kind looking, so much so I thought he could have been Jesus come back. His snow-white angel hair was long for that time. He had a kind way like Mama and I liked his blackness. Newt said it was something wrong with my head because I refused to think one color skin was better than the other. In mid-summer mine was darker than the ones mean people called niggers. With Chicken Bone, all I could see was his goodness. My head would have to just stay messed up . . . I didn't care. I sat on a rickety chair and he asked me had I seen Herman, an old black man born a slave. I told him yes and that he was doing okay. Herman's house, a converted chicken coop, had burned down some time earlier. I was scared of Herman because he was a giant, about seven feet tall, big hands, big feet, and the biggest head I had ever seen on a man. That's what frightened me. He had a face that looked just like President Abraham Lincoln's, the one on the penny, a big mole on his cheek in the same spot. Chicken Bone said Herman's master had left Herman's folks a plantation, a big mess of land in my neck of the woods but Herman didn't like the way things were being handled. The man looking after Herman would sell off tracts of land to take care of the old man's finances, but churchgoing Herman was always somehow penniless.

    I liked that Chicken Bone and I talked about serious things, things that could get us killed. Frank had told him that he could trust me. I told Chicken Bone, according to gossip, somebody had set fire to Herman's house. With all the new white people building houses around him, maybe they didn't want to see his old chicken coop anymore. Chicken Bone agreed with me. He knew it was the truth.

    Later, as I leaned on the milk crates across from him, he began talking about the old days when he was the best muleskinner alive. I really liked hearing how he snaked logs out the woods with his team of mules. They'd get stuck in creeks. Sometimes logs got wedged between trees, and he would tell me how he got them out. I loved hearing how his mules got other muleskinners' logs out of trouble after their mules had given up, and how he could fix things without putting a scratch on his team. Everybody else used a whip, but not Chicken Bone. He would never raise a hand to harm an animal.

Chicken Bone had a favorite mule named Kate who did everything he said. It was like Kate knew the English language and loved Chicken Bone so much she lived just to work for him. I could believe that because he would share his last cent with a stranger. I thought he was the coolest guy, not like anyone else. That mule, Kate, must have thought so too. When he talked about Kate, he rubbed his hands in mid air as if stroking her like she was still alive. That was something to see. It left no doubt that Kate was his one and only love. I'd have to look away when he got to the part where Kate died because it was nothing he could do to save her. It was hard seeing the old man cry and shake. I'd stare up at the old calendar. Maybe Kate died in 1932 and that's why he kept that calendar on the wall. Maybe his life just stopped right then too. I didn't know much about love but I'd bet my life Chicken Bone loved Kate. He'd say, talking to Kate, "Now step easy, Kate. A little gee, girl. That's it, you sweet thing. Let's show 'em how it's done, lady." I pictured Kate's head dropping lower and lower under the strain, but old Chicken Bone always made sure she never overdid it.

That night, before he blew out the oil lamp, he told me to take the side of the bed against the wall because he had to get up a lot at night to pee. He said I was young and could hold my water all night, something he couldn't remember doing. I took off my tennis shoes and slept in my clothes. The bed smelled strong with urine but I felt safe, something I'd never felt at home. I never knew when Bugdaddy would strike. Besides the beatings, the fear of his punishment was constant mental torture. The anguish was so bad I couldn't think straight most of the time.

But Bugdaddy wasn't in the little shack, and Chicken Bone was seeing to it I had a good night's sleep. He told me to say my prayers and I did. He liked me talking to Moses but told me not to use bad words like got-damn-it that he'd heard me use that night praying against Bugdaddy. He said his prayers out loud for an example. It was similar to Mama's prayers, beautiful and no bad words.

I'm glad I stopped at Chicken Bone's place that first night to hear again all those stories about the old days. He told me to always be like Kate and I said I'd try. I'd be smart and make my own way. I just didn't want to grow old and live the way Chicken Bone did. He had worked hard but had nothing to show for it and he was lonely with a broken heart over Kate. It wasn't right him being old and not having his mule to talk to. It would have been better if Chicken Bone had died first and set old Kate free to roam the hills and valleys just like Johnnyboy was fixing to do. Hell yeah, Johnnyboy would go places holding onto a brave heart just like Kate. He would see things that no one else in his family would dare. Flat ground, pungent smelling swamps, mountains that take one's breath away would pass before Johnnyboy's eyes. Folks would love him, hate him, but most would never see the invisible man-child hidden in the shadows of life.

For breakfast Chicken Bone shared canned beans. They felt good on my stomach, but what mattered the most was Chicken Bone, my friend. We shook hands and said goodbyes like a father and son should do. Before I could turn and walk away, he reached out and pulled me to him. He hugged me and held onto my arms while he searched for my eyes. He wouldn't turn me loose until I looked him straight in the face. I spoke to get the intimacy over quick. "Good Lord, bless you, Chicken Bone," I said, not accustomed to such affection. I wanted to flee, but he held me and squeezed me a second time and we looked again into the windows of our souls. He said, "Johnnyboy, may the Lord bless you too." The *too* dragged out his mouth as long as a freight train hauling coal. I wanted to run but he wasn't ready to turn me loose. He was strong. He searched my face a long minute. I saw tears well up and stream down his cheeks into the white angel hair on his chin. Endless as the freight train word seemed to be, that was the last word spoken. He released me and I ran like a wild rabbit, a fox two feet behind.

Why are you running so hard, Johnnyboy? He's your friend. I ran not understanding how Chicken Bone knew we would never hold face on this earth again. If I could only go back and tell him about the affection I felt in my heart . . . that I love him. *Moses, will you take care of that for me. Much obliged if you would.*

I don't know when my friend died so I could never mark a calendar. No matter, Chicken Bone will be with me always.

After I left Chicken Bone's, I worried myself nearly sick. Plodding mile after mile, I'd wonder if I could make it alone. Frank had showed me so much about the woods but now things didn't look the same. *Oh, Moses, please help me. I'm scared. No doubt about it, I'm scared to death.* I couldn't afford to be frightened. I wanted to be brave, but I wasn't. I had already forgotten about Kate. *Get your ass going south, Johnnyboy. And don't be a thinking too much.*

I crossed farms and fields until I came upon an old wooden bridge with pipe railings, all rusted. In places where dirt had collected, grass grew in clumps over the planks. I crossed the bridge several times, not knowing which direction I needed to go. So, for a while, I abandoned my flight from hell, not worrying about food and shelter and what could happen to me. The water beneath the bridge looked dark and still, like shining enamel painted over black granite. I changed that with one well-placed stone that shattered the tranquil water and left waves that would ripple forever.

Then I saw a water spider. "Hey, spider this could be war! Bombs away!"

I threw stones at the tiny spider until I had to stop and wipe sweat from my forehead. The spider went about his business as though nothing had happened. I thought the tiny creature good-natured because he ignored my bombardment. I tried to imagine what the spider was thinking, which plunged me deep into the world of dreams, a place where I went often. Deeper and deeper I went until suddenly, as swift as a slap to the face, I fell into a cage of fear. Dreaming had always been a fun thing to do, an escape, but not this time. Thoughts of Glen Allen had me trapped, not able to flee. Bugdaddy's face rose before me, and the fear in the pit of my stomach held stubborn as a tree stump in hard ground. The bad man was coming after me holding one of his favorite whips, the green garden hose. *Have mercy. I'll be good.* I wanted to yell, but my tongue was tied. *This can't be real. Moses stop him.* Bugdaddy hissed like a snake and the whip moaned. On and on the phantom beat me, making me feel the pain of burning hell. The nightmare finally stopped after I peed. *Oh, Moses, look what's happened. I'm all wet.*

My pants were washed in the dark water and hung over the pipe guardrails to dry. But the storm in my mind was over. A breeze stirred branches of a big tree on the bank of the creek. Somehow it reminded me I would be free from the hell I'd fled. Sunspots the size of my hand filtered through the foliage onto the plank boards and danced holding me in their sway. I could feel myself rocking like a mother would rock a newborn baby. For the moment I was content to be with the beauty of lights and to dance with a stranger.

"It's done by the hand of God," I said aloud, admiring the sunspots. Soon I relaxed my forehead against the rails of the bridge and closed my eyes to peacefulness, ever so aware of the wind that moved the world around me. Then, as faint as a baby's breath, I heard someone singing, *Jesus Loves Me.*

I know the voice, I told myself. *It's so young, sweet and tender.* The voice grew stronger. I turned and looked around. "Where is he?" I said, thinking I would see Baby Jesus. But I was alone and naked on the bridge. *Jesus Loves Me,* the voice rang out louder and louder. *Jesus loves me, for the Bible tells me so.* I yelled, "That voice! I know that voice!" Yes, I knew that voice well. The voice was mine, the singing in my head.

The reality of what I was doing, running away, set in like the pungent odors from the dark water below. I looked down. My reflection revealed an uncertain boy trying to look responsible, the kind of looks I'd seen on others. *Just look at you, Johnnyboy. You're down the road all right, but your mind is still a prisoner back there. Damn you. You left your Mama in that hellhole. God will punish you for that. You just wait and see.*

Mama knew I wasn't like the other children, so she dealt with me on terms of the People, her Cherokee ancestors. She never made me do anything I didn't want to do. I was her Johnnyboy. Maybe it was her way to get even with Bugdaddy for his brutality. I didn't know, but she had managed to pass on her deep spiritual recognition of life. That was against Bugdaddy's wishes. She had told me about Grandma Tippy Toe and Grandma Flat Foot, that they were good and kind, and it would be wise for me to follow their lead. I was prone to fighting but Mama showed me another way. I'd seen her hold grain out in her hand, and wild birds would feed from it like it was a trough. I'd take a step toward her, wanting to do it too, but the birds would flutter away. Mama said I needed peace in my heart to feed wild birds. "You can't be angry and do that," she'd say, so I gave up trying when I was small. Fighting worked for me and wild birds would have to look out for themselves.

Nobody will miss me but Mama. Maybe she'll worry herself sick like she did before. Moses, I hope not. Tell her not to, hear? Oh, hell, forget it, I'll tell her my damn self. Don't worry, Mama, I'll be all right. I'll come back someday rich and buy you nice things. You won't have to worry about paying bills because Bugdaddy stopped at a beer joint. You won't go around in second-hand clothes, wearing someone's throwaway shoes that make your feet hurt. When I come back, I'll protect you from that evil bastard. I'll take you far away into the land of Moses, a land of milk and honey, I swear. So there, no more worry, you hear? Johnnyboy loves you, Mama. Never forget that, you hear me? I love you a whole lot. So Mama, stop your crying, please.

She couldn't hear my thoughts. The only thing that eased the sick feeling in the pit of my stomach was the sound of my feet taking me southbound as fast as I could go.

***

Many days later I knew it was Sunday when a bell rang in a

familiar tone. It was a big bell like the one back home. The sound cut through the morning fog as well as through my hungry soul. I'd been traveling afoot a long time in one direction. Back home the bell was a call to church and the ringing had always beckoned me to a white steeple building where cookies and grape juice awaited young ones. When I showed up at the front door this particular morning, a sharp-dressed, bulldog-looking man greeted me with, "Boy, you can't come in here looking like that." He pointed at my dirty blue jeans with holes in the knees. I hadn't taken it to mind about the way I looked, but the man's voice was so forceful I knew better than to challenge him. Standing there, I could smell the wonderful fragrance of ladies' perfumes coming through the doorway, which he defended like an angry dog. I said I went to a church like his. He growled from one side of his mouth so no one else but me could hear. "If you don't get moving, you're going to get hurt." I backed away but said, "I thought church folks were to pray together." That did it. His face turned red as a pokeberry. He spoke over his shoulder to two well-dressed men who suddenly appeared from behind him to catch me. When they flinched, I ran like a deer.

Go in proper dress, Johnnyboy. Put money in the shiny silver looking plate, but don't dare ask for anything. That was the deal for a ticket to heaven. I needed to overlook what had happened, but my hard working Mama came to mind, scraping up her nickels and dimes so I would have something to put in the little wooden piggybank that looked like a church. I wondered if she really knew how things were and if she would be angry at the way they treated me, dirty clothes or not. I had the greatest urge to tell Mama to keep her coins and use them for food, but how could I? I was aimed toward the south like a runaway train. I was near beaten down, my pants belt up to the last notch. The further down the belt notches went the more unwanted I was, the way I saw it. My mentor, Frank, had warned me not to stand out in a crowd. Blend in, he would say. Well, I couldn't get much farther outside from the well-dressed church folks than I was. I was a stranger and didn't belong there. But I was hungry, nearly starved.

At first I couldn't see what had made the bulldog man so angry. Then it hit me like a punch in the nose. It wasn't my dirty clothes that bothered him. Hell no. This was the south. It was my too dark skin, most of which was road dirt. After I figured that much out I tried to let my resentment toward him go. Maybe not being angry with those self-righteous fools would free me. Mama said every bad deed goes in The Book of Life in heaven. That's what poor people say when they don't stand a fighting chance.

There were more good people than bad ones who gathered in church, according to Mama. I had my doubts about that. She also said the Lord worked on the streets for the ones who needed Him. I didn't have any trouble believing that. I remembered the Bible story about the man who was robbed on the highway and left for dead. A Good Samaritan came along and helped him mend his wounds and put him in a room, even gave him spending change. That's what I needed. Mama would have said the bulldog man was an exception, not the rule. She always tried to smooth things over and was usually right, but not this time. Granted, I was still alive by the goodness of others, be they churchgoers or whatever, but not this day. I couldn't see a tomorrow. I would have to live with being lost, lonely, and desperate for a friend and food. *Church people? Damn them. Got-damn them all.*

CHAPTER 3

The next day I was aware that every face would be a stranger. I met a drifter who wouldn't say where he was from or where he was headed, but he shared his food with me. After that we talked about his tattoos. Then from out of the blue he said it was okay to be ignorant, but not stupid. I didn't know the difference. He said you can fix ignorance but stupid stays with you for life. "What does that have to do with tattoos?" I asked. "Everything," he said. He had marked up his body and that was stupid, something he had to live with. Right then I knew I'd never get a tattoo. I didn't want to do anything stupid. I wanted to be smart. I asked him how to stretch food to hold off hunger, and he told me to take French bread and dig out the inside and fill it with canned beans. He said in a pinch that would hold me two days.

Like so many people I met along the way, I took bits and pieces of advice from those who offered. Some advice was good and some was not. In order to survive, I became street smart in a hurry.

Telling myself that better times were down the road, always, I kept walking and hitching rides south. In South Carolina on old U. S. Highway One, I got a ride with an ex-Marine, Sergeant Wells. Wells was twenty-one and looked like Adolph Hitler, mustache and all. He was celebrating his release from the Marine Corps and was heading to Texas in a hurry. He drove a red hardtop with a high-powered police interceptor engine under the hood. He bragged that he could suck down a twelve-ounce beer in six seconds and could outrun the devil because he had learned to drive hauling moonshine for his dad.

I was having second thoughts as to why I was riding with Sergeant Wells. At speeds over 100 miles per hour, the Georgia State police were chasing us. Wells managed to lose them by driving across a one-track train trestle. The police didn't follow us. They had better sense. I saw a train approaching the trestle from the other side. Wells whooped like a cowboy riding a wild bull, holding the steering wheel with one hand while he lit a cigarette that hung in the corner of his mouth with the other. "You got-damn fool," I yelled. "If we make it, I'm going to get the hell away from you." Right then I knew the man was foolish as a fish-eyed fool—a crazy person with a death wish. I had to do something to save my life so I did what came natural. I called him names: "Hey Fish-eyes, won't this car move any faster?"

Wells floored the gas pedal and the car surged ahead, shuddering as it jounced over crossties. Sand and dust bounced up from the floor onto my lap while the ashtray tossed out cigarettes butts like popcorn from a hot pot with a loose lid. I screamed, "We're going to die!" Wells smiled a foolish grin, something like I had never seen before. He sucked in smoke from his cigarette without putting his free hand on the wheel. I felt sick when I saw a glint of pleasure in his eyes. "Get ready," he yelled, the tobacco smoke from his mouth escaping out the window. I thought about the farms Mama had sent me to as a small boy. They'd be a welcome sight now instead of a train, its one bright light warning anything in its path. "Here I come, ready or not," the train seemed to be saying. *Red Rover, Red Rover, let me cross over!* I knew for a fact right then and there that Mama had sent me to those farms to protect me from Bugdaddy. *Mama, send me to a farm now. Please.*

"Oh, Moses, we're going to hit the train," I yelled. "We're going to die!"

Wells heard me over the noise and replied, "Yeah, it'll be fun."

"Fun for you, fool, but not for me!" I searched out the passenger door window, looking for a way out, a place to jump.

But in the middle of the trestle, there was none. Far below was a muddy river. If I jumped, the fall would surely kill me. I fell back in my seat in a cold sweat. *Dear Moses, what the hell is he thinking? I'm a goner. I'm trapped.*

The engine was wide open, but the car felt like we were crawling over crossties. I figured we were going to collide near the end of the bridge. If only we could gain more speed. "Go faster! Go faster!" I screamed.

Wells yelled for me to hang on. His words stuck in my mind like chewing gum on the bottom of a shoe. We were ten feet from the end of the bridge, the train about fifty feet ahead. What would the guys back home think when they found out how I was killed? They'd laugh and call me stupid and there wouldn't be anything I could do about it. They were right. I could hear my teachers scolding me: "Sound out your words. Don't act like a clown, Johnnyboy. You can't be tardy and expect to keep up. Pay attention! Do your lessons."

A blast of the locomotive's air-horn brought me back to reality. Blinded by the light, I hoped that the pain of death would be short when I felt the car swerve sharply to the left. The grinding of metal on metal was followed by a sudden jerk as the train scraped the rear quarter-panel just behind my door and ripped off the back bumper. Diesel fumes filled the car. Had I reached out my window an inch or two, I could have touched the steel wheels as they zoomed by, taking my breath with them.

The impact knocked the rear of the car off the rails, straightening it to run along side the train. Dust blew up around the car as Wells fought to stay away from the tracks. I listened to clatter of the bumper being pushed across the trestle by the train. I rubbed my eyes and called Wells a fish-eyed fool again. I told him if it had been a passenger train we would be dead. He laughed insane like and said that we had plenty of time—at least two seconds to spare.

Later, I did what Bugdaddy would have done—drank beer. Even six bottles didn't relieve my tension. *Oh, Moses, I hope I'm not getting like Bugdaddy. Hell no, that could never happen because he's a coward. He doesn't have enough nerve to go out on his own. I'm not like him.*

The early death I had narrowly escaped rushed through my head, mixed up with crazy memories of home. I thought about my best friend, Frank, and the dangers he'd put me through. One time Frank had talked me into riding in a pram down the steepest hill anywhere. It didn't matter that a boy had broken his arm going down the hill because his bicycle tire blew out from going too fast. Hell no. That was the reason Frank had wanted me to face that hill, for the danger. Frank said getting hurt was the mother of all invention.

I wasn't a stranger to doing crazy things. Frank told everybody I could jump a drainage ditch knowing very well it was impossible. He'd put me on the spot with a bunch of boys so I'd give it a try. The guy who loaned me his bike cried because it was destroyed. Frank told him anyone with half a brain would have better sense than to loan me a bicycle, and that I could break an anvil. That made me swell with pride.

Frank showed me how to be cool and not let things get to me that could spin out of control. If I hadn't learned that kind of stuff, I'd been killed years earlier. Little did I know that the crazy things Frank got me to do back then were preparing me for what lay ahead. I found some comfort that I was the man Frank had said I was, that I could face danger and be cool about it.

But I wasn't too cool with Sergeant Wells because I had no control over the car, the train or him. My mind kept drifting back to the train trestle, thinking that if we had been a few seconds slower the train would have struck on my side, killing me for sure. I could imagine the crushing of my body. The big iron monster didn't care about me because it would travel on to towns and places I would never see. Nothing could relieve my worried mind but time and I didn't know how much I had left. Later when Wells bought more beer, the store's owner said he had heard about us over his police radio. He told us to get what we wanted and get moving fast. He also said the Georgia police had friends in Alabama and they would soon be on our trail.

Wells thanked him and ordered two cases of beer to go.

Sometime the next day we crossed the Louisiana state line, drunk. Wells and I parted company in New Orleans, the Big Easy, where he drove away with another hitchhiker. He wasn't the craziest person I met that year. There were those who were more direct in attempting to kill me. I represented something they could not face in themselves . . . they could be me, a worthless bum—a drifter whose name didn't matter one cent.

Chapter 4

After Wells, I was lucky to meet a Jewish couple in New Orleans. I walked the sidewalks for two days without much to eat, digging through trash cans behind supermarkets. I needed a day job where I got paid the same day, but I was having bad luck with that, as my clothes were dirty. That was a serious problem. I saw this gray haired man come out a grocery store wearing a soiled white apron. I told him I was hungry and needed work. He smiled like we were old friends and said to wait a second for him to close up. He said we would go home then because his wife, Minna, had cooked us a great meal.

I thought I was in one of my daydreams, but he asked me to hold the door open for him so he could get the little sign with the daily specials on it inside. He had the kindest face, topped with a smile like I'd just told him a good joke. He locked up the place and, before we took a step to his car, he turned to me with his hand out and said, "I'm Simon." We shook hands and I said the first name that came to my mind, Billy. I didn't want to take a chance as I was wanted by the law because I'd ridden with the fool Wells. Billy was an easy name to stick with.

We walked to the back of his store to his fancy new car. He had the biggest car on the road . . . a new black and white Cadillac with more chrome than two cars could hold, and he asked me did I have a driver's license. I would have lied about that too but the car's beauty took me aback. I said no and he said it was too bad because he was going to let me drive. *Damn*, I said under my breath. *I blew it.*

Simon was kind but Minna was a lady with enormous love. I'll never forget her. When I came through their front door her eyes lit up with joy, like Simon had brought home the President of our nation. She threw up her hands and folded them to her chest like she was hugging something tiny before the first word came out her mouth. "Who do we have here, Simon?" she asked. I wasn't used to anyone making over me like she was doing. He told her, Billy with no last name and added I was hungry. She said to him like he had said something stupid, "Of course he is. Wash up, Billy. Dinner is ready."

"Thank you," I said sheepishly. I couldn't get over how nice they were to a stranger. Minna must have known how hungry I was because she handed me a piece of bread from the table to take with me to the bathroom. I swallowed it before I was out of her sight. She yelled down the hallway for us to hurry before the food got cold.

I knew about roast beef and potatoes, carrots and onions in gravy. Mama fixed it on Sundays sometimes. That's what Minna had. The more I ate, the better Minna liked it. She watched me eat and Simon had to remind her to eat. But she didn't because she was only concerned about me. I got full, then sleepy at the table. Minna asked me did I want to watch a little TV after dinner. "Why not," I said, as I had her figured out.

Everything was great so far so I may as well light up a smoke. She got an ashtray and made over me with that too. Later, when I said I'd sleep on their porch after they had offered me a room for the night, she shed a tear but tried to keep it hidden from me. People can't do that because I read faces. But she was crying from happiness. I liked that a lot because that was something I seldom saw, folks being happy.

The next morning Simon asked me to help him in the store so I could earn some money. This couldn't be happening to me, I thought. I'd always had to struggle for every damn thing, every penny I made, like picking huckleberries for fifteen cents a quart. The customers wanted to know if there were any green ones in the damn free Mason jar that came with the berries. This was on the left side of the scale of life. There had to be a hitch with Simon and Minna, there just had to be, I thought. Why the hell were they being so good to me? I hadn't done anything for them. I was a drifter without a job, without an honest name. I called myself Billy, Billy Barlow, the travelingest man alive. Minna was smart not to ask me about where I was from and where I was headed. I think Simon had warned her about that. If she had, I was out of there because I couldn't answer those things.

I had fun working in Simon's store. He taught me Jewish sayings. I liked the one, "It's better to work a man who's willing but not able than to work a man that's able and not willing." Maybe he thought I needed the wisdom. Sometimes I'd daydream and stand like a stone statue but it didn't bother him like it did my schoolteachers or Bugdaddy. Only one time did he ask me what was bothering me. I didn't know how to answer him so I went back to my task. I learned neat stuff that I thought were secret things. Simon showed me the Star of David on canned goods. That meant they were kosher, that Jewish folks could eat them. I wanted to be a Jew and do secret things and have a good name like Berger.

After a few days at work and stuffing myself with Minna's cooking, I told them I was ready to move on. Minna didn't take this well because she had a reason for wanting me to stay. She begged me to go upstairs to her boy's room. It was very nice with a big bed and banners on the wall from where he had gone to school. Minna said the room was mine if I wanted it. She picked up her boy's picture and held it to her chest. She looked at me and said they had lost their only son in the Korean War. Minna would have done anything to get me to stay. I felt this the first night I was there but at that moment I knew all things came with a price. I needed to find myself, who I was, and to be proud of myself. It may have been a mistake not staying, but if I had stayed one more night I think she would have become too attached, and I don't know what would have happened. It was hard enough to leave good folks who showered me with love like one of their own. It was a wonderful feeling having that love. At the front door she pinned ten dollars in my watch pocket. I'll never forget her crying and her trembling fingers as they fumbled with a safety pin. She didn't want me losing the extra money. Simon put my pay in an envelope and I stuffed it in my front pocket. He had to pull her from me and hold her when I left.

Oh, Moses, what is this? Minna suddenly thought I was her son who had come back from the dead and I had no idea how something like that could happen. I hadn't cried for a while but to see Minna fall down on her knees and beg me not to go off to war caused me to weep. Such a sight from when we first met three days before, her sparkling eyes, and arms flung upward and then falling across her chest like she was hugging something soft.

"I'll come back some day," I said. "Don't worry about me. I'll be all right. Don't worry, Miss Minna. Please don't cry. Please!" But she cried until my walking took me far, far away. I heard her cry all the while. Sometimes late at night I heard her calling me Billy. Billy, please come home.

I'm sorry, Simon. I'm so sorry, Minna. I'm sorry I didn't tell you that something was missing in me. And I wish I hadn't told you that one lie. My name ain't Billy. But the way you said it, Miss Minna, makes me wish to God it was.

I walked with my head down until I was nearly out of New Orleans. I could only see the expansion joints in the sidewalk pass under my feet. The mother-of-pearl in the cement sparkled like jewels. The glitter was in everything made of cement—fences, sidewalks and streets. I didn't look ahead and I didn't look behind. I watched the cracks and heard Miss Minna cry. I heard her cry, cry, cry with her heart broken as I walked east out of town.

I knew plenty about crying. It bothered me more than I could stand to hear my Mama cry. She hid when she did that, but I always snuck up close to her door to make sure she was okay. I didn't like to hear my brothers and sisters cry either, but I wanted to die when Mama wept. Her sobs were soft and low and I had to listen real hard because I only had that one good ear. The sound of someone crying got to me, especially my

Mama because it melted my heart like crayon on a hot radiator. I always wanted to say, "Don't you cry, Mama, it'll be all right. Johnnyboy loves you. Please don't cry."

I couldn't stand by Minna's door and listen to see how she was. Even though I was weary, something in me drove me onward without rest. *Sing, Johnnyboy, sing a song. Don't think any more, Johnnyboy. Just sing.*

The song *I Am Weary, Let Me Rest* came to me like an old friend. The song triggered a long forgotten memory of a black man singing in a cotton field. I first heard him sing the tune as a boy of ten. His face I don't remember well, but his sorrowful voice is imbedded in my mind like a tombstone on hard ground. A dozen black folks and one misfit, me, listened as we thinned newly planted cotton plants. Cottonseeds are very small, so they sprout out the ground in bunches. Before I knew the song, I'd repeated under my breath, two and three, two and three for hours, chopping away excess plants with a long handle hoe, which left only two or three plants standing. I almost lost my mind from the task, the boredom. The song was welcomed by everyone there but especially by a young boy who needed to be a part of something and to have a name other than stupid. I was lost in a world of little understanding. I couldn't get along in school, and being on a farm in North Carolina to get away from Bugdaddy didn't help one bit.

What do I do after he's finished singing? I asked myself. *Do I clap because his words bring thoughts of Mama? I see he loves his mama too. I want to lay my head on my Mama's breasts. She'll kiss my forehead and tell me she loves me. But that's never going to happen. Hell, no. She sent me to this farm because I couldn't do good in school. I'd just as soon be dead as to go back there. They made fun of me, called me dummy. I'm not dumb, damn it to all. Oh, Johnnyboy, why don't you forget about all that and listen to the pretty song he's singing? What should I say to him? He's a big man, and he sounds like he's crying inside just like me instead of singing happy tunes like they do on the radio in the living room come nights around here. I know exactly how he feels–longing for love and rest. He might think I'm crazy if I ask him anything. Who cares? I'll tell him I like his song and ask him to sing it again. I'll ask anything that will take my mind off this got-damned long-ass cotton row. Anything, I swear.*

I worked along with the crew and kept my mouth shut. Sometime later the dinner bell rang a half-mile away. Leaning against my hoe, I wanted to lay down where I stood but a crew doesn't leave a field hand behind. I became part of that gang when a skinny black field hand led me away from the dreaded cotton rows.

At meals I didn't get to eat with the black folk like I wanted. They ate on the screened-in-porch at picnic tables pushed together covered with red-checkered cloths and lots of food. I had to eat in the kitchen where it was hotter from frying chicken.

The lady of the house would pull out one white breast at a time to feed her baby as I watched in amazement, the baby sucking like a piglet. That was okay. The meal was over not long after the baby was full and asleep in her arms. Her husband took the child from her while she washed her breasts with a washcloth and tucked them back into her button-up denim shirt. The crew headed back to the field of endless cotton rows. I followed, dragging my hoe behind me like a plow.

Sing that song, I said to myself, talking to a world that didn't know me. *Let him sing that song I Am Weary, Let Me Rest, dear Moses.*

But he didn't sing that song again that day. The crew sang another one and then another one and the songs took me far away from the despised cotton field. They sang about heaven and cool rivers, a home with Jesus where everybody's faults were forgiven because Jesus did it all for us. No more hard labor in the hot sun, but a place where folks have everything they want. Jesus was waiting for the faithful servants. I knew why they sang and I hummed along. My humming stopped my repetitive counting, two and three, and carried me to that far away place in the mind known as the Promised Land. My black brothers and sisters bestowed all those sweet sounds in my head.

That summer I saw a woman have a baby in the field and I thought I knew then all I needed to know about life. She looked pleased after she gave birth to a white ghost-like baby boy who turned darker as laughter rose from the women field hands standing all around her keeping the men folk away. They didn't push me back. *New life brings joy,* I thought. *Now let's sing the happy songs, the ones about being in love and making babies. Sing about anything but being in the cotton fields. Got-damn cotton, got-damn school.*

I ran away twice from the farm that summer. That made matters worse. "What are we going to do with Johnnyboy," they barked. "He's headstrong, determined to have his way." I knew what they were doing. They were trying to smother my will. That wasn't going to happen because when you're dumb like Johnnyboy, you've got to be tough. I wouldn't let them get to me.

My mind was back on Minna's tears.

When I'm cornered, I still hide inside those songs black folk taught me. It works. It will for you too, Minna. So, please stop crying, Miss Minna. Just listen to the song I Am Weary, Let Me Rest. Hush, hush yourself, I'll sing it for you right now. And I did all of that day.

Chapter 5

My second brush with death was in Florida a few days after leaving New Orleans. Following the Gulf Coast, I hitched a ride with a trucker. Along the way I saw chain gangs wearing broad black and white striped clothing with balls and chains attached to their ankles. The driver said that happened to drifters like me. The prisoners were cutting tall cane on the sides of the two-lane highway. Every few miles the scene repeated itself with ten, twenty, sometimes thirty men swinging sickles as armed guards with shotguns stood over them. We were into what I thought was the panhandle of Florida. I couldn't believe there were so many prisoners, most all black men. I vowed under my breath that I wouldn't be taken alive to do something like that. Having a chain around my leg would be horrible, but to be linked to someone else was beyond all that. I needed space to roam and plenty of it.

The driver's name was Ely. Even though he had given me a ride, I didn't like him. I saw something in his face like I saw in Bugdaddy's expression. That scared me. He was hauling live oysters bagged in eighty-pound hemp sacks and very hard to handle. Ely needed someone to transfer some bags from the rear to the forward axles before we reached a weigh station. I wasn't a stranger to work, so I jumped inside the trailer and moved the sacks the best way I could. It was a two-man job because the sacks were awkward and dangerous to carry. Oysters are sharp as razors on the edges and, before I knew it, I was bleeding from my forearms. After about an hour of moving bags, I had the weight shifted forward. But I was covered in blood and oyster slime. I needed cleaning up because no one would give me a ride looking like I did. As nasty as I was, Ely let me ride in the truck cab until we reached the first truck stop about ten miles up the road. He said he would pay me for my hard labor after I got cleaned up.

The truck stop was busy with lots of people, and I was in a hurry to get bathed. I rushed into the men's room to wash my face and then started on an impossible task of making my clothes presentable. As I took off my shirt and started washing it in the sink a black man came out of a stall. He stared at me and seemed agitated so I spoke to show I meant him no harm. He said that I was in the colored bathroom and he was concerned for my safety. This was the Deep South. I didn't want to put my shirt back on dirty because it was bloody. The black man said I should climb out the window as soon as I could. He left. I thought he meant black folks would hurt me because I used their bathroom. I didn't know until I had left that it was the whites he was warning me about.

No sooner had I stepped into daylight than someone yelled, nigger lover, and a brick came whirling past my head, only missing me by an inch. Let's get him was the next thing I heard. Thank God I was young and very fast on my feet. Six or seven men, maybe more, rushed toward me. But like Mama used to say, there's always one bad apple in the bunch. I believed this to be true, but I didn't have time to find him. A mob of angry men hurried my way. I didn't wonder why they were after me because I had lived among the prejudices of my time. This was insanity, spawned by fear. You'd think I'd done something real bad to have men with the determination to kill me. Yes, I used the colored bathroom, an act of treason to them. I didn't want to live in an America under these conditions, but there was no time for explaining all that. No matter if I wanted to or not, it was fight Johnnyboy or die. No talking them out of their hatred because things were moving too fast for that.

One man thought I'd stand there and let him hit me with his fist. I ducked and landed a punch to his jaw and he went down like a sack of dry grain. They tried to back me into the colored bathroom but I knew that would be the end of me if they did. I had to do something unsuspected so I attacked like a wild animal, screaming and chopping with my open hands and making an opening in their ranks. Once on the other side I had room to run, but not without more violence. I hit men as men hit me. If I went down it was over, my being at the mercy of the mob. They wouldn't let me walk away. Another man was down but more men were coming from the direction of the gas pumps. I didn't know if they would help me or side with the angry ones. Mama always said, when it rains, it pours, which meant things would only get worse, and those men coming toward me were my foes. I got close to an eighteen-wheeler and, after slinging myself free from a good old boy who held one arm, ducked under the trailer and rolled in a flash out the other side and onto my feet. That taste of freedom gave me what I needed, a chance to sprint. My tennis shoes hissed under my feet like angry cats and the wind in my face told me I was in full stride. Faster and faster I picked my feet up and put them down. Nothing afoot could catch me now.

Tall cane was not far away and the chatter behind grew faint. I crashed into tall brush three or four feet over my head braking me down into slow motion. But I was determined to flee and I waded as hard and fast as I could. I heard gunshots and bullets cut tiny paths through the weeds all around me. I dove down like I was diving into water face first. I couldn't make much headway but the eerie sound of bullets kept me moving, digging with all fours. From the good treatment I received from Simon and Minna, this was the opposite of that.

As it began, it ended. Voices turned the other way and the silence of the guns brought on sounds of the rustling weeds all around me. I lay on my stomach thinking how things happened so fast and then, like the morning sun had suddenly popped over the horizon, I knew the driver Ely had set me up. During my struggle, nothing mattered but my freedom, and a face is only a face, two eyes, a mouth and a nose along with swinging fists. As sweat flooded from my pores, Ely's face came to me from the mob as one of the attackers. He didn't want to pay me for my work. But not just that, he wanted me dead. That's what I had read on his face. He was a bad man like Bugdaddy and I was lucky I came away with my life.

With bird songs comforting me, I thought about my next move. Folks don't like you nasty looking. I needed to clean up and move on. I made another major mistake that day. I moved deeper into the weeds, thinking I would come out on another road. Instead I found myself in a knee-deep swamp. For two days I struggled to survive. I was never sure that I held one direction during daylight. I had the stars at night but I was too afraid to move because I'd become a meal to a hungry gator. And, if a snake bit me, that would be it. I didn't have so much as a pocketknife to bleed the poison out, which was the thing to do at that time.

I was in hell because of the things that went on, not around me, but in my mind. Raw fear. It was the worst thing that could have happened to me. Nights, I slept around trees while the mosquitoes ate me alive. If I wasn't eaten, I believed that I would die a slow death wading through water that had a lime green cover thick as a blanket. I would get sick from some disease. The swamp was more than I could take. At one point I wanted to die so I could escape. The pungent odor was riveted in my memory forever. The stench became the doorway to a heartless death cycle, void the loving hand of God. It's not a place for man. I made it through the ordeal by thinking about home and Bugdaddy's will over me. He had toughened my spirit. But whatever there was embedded in me, I made peace with the alien world. I kept my thoughts on two very nice people I had met. I thanked Simon and Minna for the money in my pockets. I could buy new clothes when I made it out the swamp.

I came out onto the same road I had fled. I was wiser to the natural world but still not able to feed wild birds like Mama. But now I would become smarter to the ways of man. Life was compressed while traveling on the road. There were rules to follow and I needed to pay attention to that. I might ride high in the cab of an eighteen-wheeler, and I might find myself in a swamp hugging a cypress tree for safety, all in the same day. Things moved that fast. When you ride with someone else, you ride with their luck, their karma. I made that rule number two. Rule number one. Learn to read people's faces better, Johnnyboy. Learn or die.

Chapter 6

I covered a lot of ground searching for what was missing inside me. It seemed to be my mission, going in one direction instinctively like a goose goes south before winter sets in. In about a month I had thumbed west as far as Oklahoma. And Oklahoma is the state where my life took a turn that changed Johnnyboy forever. I met a cool old man, whose name was so foreign from anything I'd ever heard, that he let me call him Chief. Chief offered me a ride without me sticking out my thumb. He said he thought he recognized me from my gait. I thought that was a setup, a strange thing to say so he could learn about me. He wore an interesting hat with two feathers, one split in half. I found out later that the split feather meant he had been wounded in battle, but he never said where.

I wanted to know about Chief once I had read his face that held peaceful intentions. He wanted to help me by giving me a ride. That's all that mattered at that point. I'd heard his noisy pickup truck long before I turned around to look. The old man was dressed fancy in home-style clothes, tan gun-barrel pants and boots with pinched-back heels. His shirt was long sleeved in bright colors with tassels on the arms as well as the body of the shirt. I don't remember folk's clothing, but Chief's was so different it impressed me, especially the hat. It was black with a high dome and wide brim straight and flat as a mud pie.

The old truck didn't match Chief's apparel. I got in the cab and kept quiet, which was the right thing to do. The truck had a new smell, mesquite. After he shifted the gears, Chief started probing me with where I was going and where was I from—stuff like that. I couldn't say I was drifting around, so I told him I was going to see my Aunt Midge in Utah. He seemed concerned for my safety. His mannerisms were different from anyone I had met on the road and I was drawn to him without knowing why. A little later it hit me. He acted like my Mama's Uncle, Powell. The knockout punch was that Chief said he was a medicine man, and he shared things of the mind. He spoke another language, but his fractured English came across good enough. He said that he had been away on spiritual business. I thought that was a good thing to be on.

We talked maybe an hour on our ride. He was very kind and honest, but another knockout was, he just up and said that he could see into the future. That excited me. He said there were things I had to confront but only after I got the great power. I liked that great power stuff because that could only mean one thing in my young mind. I was going to get something, maybe a car. Chief had a way like Frank, teaching me good stuff, but Chief was a hundred times better at it.

He said things that Mama wanted to, but was afraid to because of Bugdaddy. Somehow I knew Chief was one of her people. Mama must have spoken to him, because he knew things about me no one but Mama knew. He said I was doing right by journeying into the land of spirits. That shocked me because that was news to me. I didn't know that's what I was doing. But after thinking about it I said that I was trying to find my aunt and myself too. He grunted, knowing very well I was lying through my teeth about my aunt. I was drifting, but thank Moses, in one direction. That was in high favor with him, keeping one course. Chief said that showed who I was as a man, spirited.

Chief talked and I listened like never before. Nothing could interfere with what was coming out of his mouth. The things he said made good sense and I was intent on catching every word like they were bits of steak for my hungry stomach. Right away, so focused I thought I could hear him in my bad ear. Maybe he was speaking to me in another way than by mouth, like messages are sent through a radio. When he talked, a bomb could have gone off and I wouldn't have flinched or turned away from him. My schoolteachers would have jumped for joy if something like that had happened.

While riding along he said my skin was darker than his. I thought old people said odd things, but still it made me feel uncomfortable that I was different. I wanted him to be my grandfather, my mother's father. He said I was summer burned. Laughter followed when he mentioned my sun bleached curly hair. I told him about Mama's blood, that she was half Cherokee. To my surprise he said I didn't need to tell him because he could see for himself. All the uncertain feelings in the cab of his truck faded away, and I felt good again like we were kin. Nothing would be better than to be around Mama's people, my family, where I'd feel safe enough to take a long rest. With Chief headed to his village, I could be around my family. When I could hear only the road sounds, I daydreamed the native peoples would love me and welcome me to my new home.

When my daydreams were over, I wanted to tell Chief something was wrong with my head, but he kept me busy answering questions about other things. In the back of my mind, Chief reminded me of Mama. At one point I caught myself staring at him to see if he looked like her. His hand gestures were the same. It was like they had grown up together in the same house. "Yes, Chief must be Mama's father," I believed. I could learn a lot from him because he was old and wise. I'd be respectful no matter what and see where that led me. After riding for several hours north, the wrong direction that I was headed, we pulled into a small village with a narrow dirt lane and tiny houses lined on either side. It was close to dark. He invited me to come in his house. He said, "You're my guest, Timekeeper."

I knew he liked me listening to him from Texas to Oklahoma, and that merited the invitation into his home. But him calling me Timekeeper took me aback. What did I do to deserve that? I thought maybe he just made up a name like I did. That was okay because I was tired and hungry. My main concern was that he might try to sexually assault me. He was a bit strange compared to most, but it was as plain as peanut butter on sliced bread that Chief meant me no harm. I could read it in his deep wrinkled face. So I put my concerns aside for the moment as we stood outside of his house. There, Chief elected to let me call him Chief. After all, he was a medicine Chief.

In the back of my mind I could hardly wait for the next day. I wanted to see everyone, my new family. Mama's people were much different from how I was raised. Now I had a chance to learn how they lived. I didn't understand anything about prophecy or prophesizing the stars, rocks that talked or plants that showed the way to some place mystical. All those things were funny and fun was in short supply. Chief spoke of these things on the way to his house. He liked that I was traveling alone because that took someone special, he said. I didn't tell him how scared I was at times—scared about my future too. He said I was on a vision quest, and it was his job to help me get on the right path. Once I had things figured out between us, I could play along, with nothing to lose and everything to gain.

Standing beside his old truck, I believed Chief's lodge was on an Indian reservation. The houses in the neighborhood reminded me of the ones in the Deep South where the poorest of the poor folks lived, whites and blacks. Chief's neighbors didn't take kindly to me. Harsh verbiage came from windows and doorways. Thinking that everyone would welcome me with open arms, that hurt a lot, but I tried not to show it in front of Chief. He said they were a clannish bunch and suspicious of outsiders. He avoided them when we crossed the yard to his front door, but I couldn't. I felt their eyes locked onto me like I was a mangy dog, and Chief was doing something wrong by bringing the flea bitten critter home. All the daydreaming about finding where I belonged ended with his neighbors' profanities in broken English.

I learned later they didn't like Chief because he was a man of the world, the white man's world. He was savvy to the white man's ways and those things had almost no value in Indian society, at least not there in the tiny village. Chief avoided talking about his neighbors when I asked why they distrusted me, that I hadn't done anything to harm them. He didn't answer or say much after we went inside . . . just pointed at a bunk in a room the size of a walk in closet. The smell of mesquite was strong in his house too. He handed me a strip of beef jerky and an Indian wool blanket and said, "Sleep, Timekeeper." That was simple enough as I gnawed on the piece of meat. Never mind the trail dust or my broken heart over Mama's people not liking me, just pull the blanket over my hard head and get some shuteye. The food tasted good and I was soon asleep in spite of eyes that burned from silently crying.

The next day Chief was more interesting than ever, and that made up for his unfriendly clan. In the back of my mind he was still my grandfather on Mama's side of the family and nothing had happened to change that. I knew he really wasn't, but that's how my mind worked. I needed a father, someone to look up to. I wouldn't let Chief know about my feelings on this matter, but I suspected he already knew. The man was clairvoyant.

After a breakfast of beans and eggs, he started saying strange things like: "Timekeeper, listen to the wind, it whispers many secrets. Spirits journey riding the wind through sagebrush looking for lost loved ones. Learn what they have to say." I figured Chief was trying to make me smarter for the road. I liked that he cared. But it was much more than that. Chief was teaching me a way of life, something that had been lost. He explained that it was up to me how I reacted when I first met someone. This was a test of spirits and a most important one. He said in the old days a man carried a shield over his chest for all to see who he was. That was long ago and now good men did what I did, read faces. He knew right away I had a special gift for that. One thing I came away with, there's no accident in people you meet. This is the Great Spirit's work. Bringing folk together.

On and on Chief talked and never stopped teaching me until I was smart to his ways. He said it was his pleasure to teach me. It was who he was, a man of medicine.

Chief had a kiva about a hundred yards beyond the privy in

the back of his house. He used the kiva for religious ceremonies. It was round, something like an igloo with no windows, and a small hole to enter covered with buckskin. After a week of resting and learning his ways, he invited me into the kiva. He said he wanted to open my mind by ingesting mescal buttons. This was a special ceremony, my vision quest. This wasn't another knockout punch from him but an earthshaking event. By this time, if Chief had told me to take a dose of poison, I would have gladly done so.

Chanting all the while, he lit a kerosene storm lantern and the light made the ribs of the kiva feel like iron bars keeping us safe from a wicked world outside. Chief's chant was soft and low, something like a murmur coming from a brokenhearted maiden, her man died at sea. The sounds came from deep within and the back of his throat, guttural with much crying. He spoke in his native tongue and handed me a few mescal pods. "Chew Timekeeper," he said. I chewed them while he made a tea. *Oh, Moses, they are so bitter.* I wanted to spit them out but I kept chewing. After the tea was done he spoke again in English, more broken than before.

"Timekeeper, think of death and resurrection. We journey now," said Chief, warning me how awestruck I would become. We drank the cactus pods tea together until I saw things that weren't there. Chief said that those things were in my head and needed to be confronted. He moved stones in a circle, four bigger ones in opposite directions, which stood for north, south, east and west. Then Chief scratched a circle on the ground inside the stones, a Medicine Wheel, and explained the four directions, what they meant for the powers of animals great and small that worked in harmony with laws of nature. He said man had to learn those laws, but animals came into this world with the knowledge and we had to learn from them.

Chief said I was out of balance, not in harmony with the universe and the wheel on the ground was going to help me. He lit an open flame lamp, a bowl like thing similar to an old-timey whale oil lamp. Then he blew out the storm lantern. The new light had blue in the yellow flame, which waved from side to side of the bowl making the shadows shift about the kiva wall like hidden secrets in the cosmos.

After chewing many bitter buttons, I could see anything Chief suggested. At this point I had no choice but was along for the ride of my life. I got scared. I felt drunk, and sick to my stomach. The hallucinations weren't nice to watch, like a dog eating another dog. Chief told me that those things were inside my head and to look beyond all the trash known to him as fear. He said he understood my fear because I just had my mind opened for the first time. He said I needed to weed through the fear and look for good things like, peace of mind and the heart that's willing to learn. Maybe that's why I couldn't hold wild birds like Mama did. My heart was filled with anger. This was my chance to fix all that, I thought. This was what my ceremony was all about, to clean my head out, Chief had said.

After the fright had subsided, I listened to Chief and tried to catch his every word. At this point, most of the things spoken made no sense at all. I was tripping on the drug. But what's new with Johnnyboy, had he overdone it again? Yes, and I was getting angrier by the minute because I felt cheated from Chief's lesson. But Chief called "Timekeeper" out loud and my anger went away like in a puff of smoke. Then again he'd chant his native language unless it was something he wanted me to know. I asked a hundred times why he called me Timekeeper. He'd answer in his tongue, which only kept my head spinning. Then he would stop chanting and turn to me looking serious and tell me my questions would be answered after I got to the Sacred Mountain. *Oh, Moses, where the hell is that?*

But Chief said enough to make me follow his way of thinking that night in the kiva. I was enlightened to things inside me that before I never knew existed. They overwhelmed me and I got swept away with Chief's powers. I fell asleep with Chief chanting soft and low like the loving voice of Moses singing me a celestial lullaby. I could have slept in the kiva for days, I don't know. I awoke a different person. That's the way I felt. I can't explain it, but I thought of myself as being new, lifted up and given a boost in life. I'd lived with low self-esteem so long that this was a taste of heaven.

A few days later Chief warned me not to take the ceremony as being fun. He said the things that had taken place in the kiva would take time to unfold, to understand. The ceremony was a serious matter balanced between life and death. After I understood the importance, I paid close attention to his warning. I never knew the unfolding would take years and years. Being young, Chief must have known I would want instant gratification on the visions I had. Chief elected not to tell me the duration of the entire lesson because youth are not willing to wait very long. Chief was a wise man on that.

One day from out of nowhere he said it was time for me to go on my vision quest north. It was just like that, abrupt. It didn't bother me because I knew he liked me a lot, like a grandfather should. I was more secure now and ready to meet the world head on. We locked eyes the way my schoolteacher would have wanted them. His eyes were kind and I knew he was going to give me something of great value. But he handed me some buttons in a cloth tobacco pouch. *That's it,* I thought. Gee, what a let down, but I stuffed the pouch in my pants pocket and tried to be of good cheer. Things got better when he said I was going to meet a great power. He said at first I wouldn't recognize the power. He said I'd bed down and sleep with the power and not know it. He said by the time I learned the truth about the power I would go to the Sacred Mountain. That would change my life for the good. Of all the serious things Chief talked about, that seized in my mind like a rusted plow bolt.

When he finished explaining, I felt a chill come over me, the uncertain man-child, Johnnyboy, was losing control again. But my life needed changing. He said for me to use the buttons like he showed me. "Listen carefully, Timekeeper. Do exactly as I tell you. One wrong move could cost you your life."

I saw how important his message was. I answered him that I understood. Then he made a prediction for me to take along with the buttons in my pocket. He said I would do right for myself this time. That felt wonderful to hear him say that. They were the sweetest words I ever heard in my youth.

I told Chief I'd come back some day and he said he would give me a new name when I did. Timekeeper was good enough for now, but it didn't have any lasting meaning. Because I had a gift to receive, the great power, I was ready to go. But I would hold Chief in my heart until I returned like a hungry man holds his last sip of stew.

Chapter 7

I left Oklahoma in a hurry and backtracked to New Orleans. I couldn't go north without money. I knew where to get dough fast . . . at the loading docks. I had worked there before under bogus names. When they needed help they'd do anything to get it. I knew how to work and pull my load, and I got on great with the other workers. But Mike, a tall lanky fellow, seemed to have a problem. He looked like he wasn't doing as much as everyone else. I thought he did okay, but the crew didn't see it that way and they complained. They thought he was a slacker. Everyone's money was divided equally when the job was done. But something went wrong. The crew, that is everyone but me, beat Mike to an inch of his life before the money was issued. The fight started and ended on the loading dock behind an 18 wheeler loaded for New York City. I didn't go to Mike's rescue because I had learned you don't fight somebody else's battle, especially living on the road. It was three against one.

You followed the boss's orders. If the boss wanted the fight stopped he would have said so, but he was throwing a few punches too. Later when he doled out our money, I had more than was coming to me. I didn't think much about it. Mike was at a good distance away licking his wounds, I was told by the boss. It never crossed my mind Mike's share was divided between us like thieves. I thought the boss was happy because we had done good, worked hard, and he had given us a bonus.

Loaded with money, about a hundred dollars, I bought new clothes, blue jeans and a blue cotton flannel shirt. I transferred the peyote buttons in the sack to my new pants. I wanted to see the Big Easy again before heading out of town. I had a room not far away from the loading docks, but I felt antsy to get moving to find the great power. I saw the old French Quarter and the bars with adult things going on inside. I didn't chance going in a bar because I didn't have an ID to lie about my age. But I could peep through the swinging doors. The women were dressed in what looked like bathing suits with feathers in the right places. They slung their arms and legs and other parts around with the music and it was a soul-shaking tune that made me want to move my feet about too. I wanted to lean back, hands holding my side and rock to and fro like marching to a heavenly band. I couldn't help myself and I wasn't alone on the sidewalk with that feeling. There were street dancers making smooth dance moves with the joyful sounds coming from a club. Although I never met him, I had heard about a dancer named Bojangles who danced his way around the Big Easy. They said he had been in the movies with Shirley Temple, but I didn't know who she was. I wondered if he might have been this black guy who danced on the sidewalk right beside me and looked like he was floating on a cloud.

The next thing I knew a man stepped out of a bar with women hanging on his arms. I never saw a long tailed suit on a man before and I asked the guy standing next to me who the dude was. "Why, that's King Creole," he said like I was stupid and had been left in the swamp all my life. "A king, huh," I said under my breath. "I didn't know we had kings here."

By nightfall I was tired of roaming the streets . . . tired of everything but the music. I could never get tired of that. It was fun but I wasn't going to be a dancer. I wandered back to the docks headed to my boarding room. I had plenty of money left as I didn't spend more than two dollars. A fog had gathered and the air felt thick, hard to breathe. When I got to an alley between two smelly buildings, I looked down and saw someone digging through trashcans. I knew about that because I had rummaged a few. I stopped to get a closer look and the person's movements looked familiar as he went from can to can. It was Mike looking for food the dockworkers had thrown out. Thinking a second or two whether I should call out to him, it hit me that he was out of money and hungry, a pain one never forgets. I figured he had been robbed of his cash or he had blown it on wine, women, or gambled it away in a craps game. It didn't enter my mind that I had some of his money in the pocket of my new blue jeans. I called his name and he looked my way. Even in the fog and the dim alley light I could see how badly the crew had made a mess of his face. He came toward me without saying a word and I stood on guard, ready to defend myself. But Mike was friendly and said he knew who I was. Mike told me what I already knew about the beating, but when he told me they took his money, I was knocked for a good loop. How could this be that my friends, my coworkers, our crew could do something like that? Stupid Johnnyboy. I'd missed what really happened that day. The crew had stolen Mike's money and the no-good boss was in on it. I felt bad, a dimwit for not knowing all this.

I told Mike he needed to take care of his wounds because he was having trouble breathing through his nose. Some ribs were broken and his nose was clogged with blood. I told him I knew they had beaten him because he was a slacker, but I was dumb about the money part. We talked a while in the alley and then I bought some food and we ate together in a hamburger stand about a mile away. After we ate, we walked a ways to a cemetery where tombs were above ground. We sat on a bench and I had a smoke. I thought about sharing my buttons with him to heal his wounds but had second thoughts, the Chief's warning.

Mike said he came from a well-to-do family and that he was educated. It had to be because he could say more with few words than anyone I'd ever met. I never talked much but Mike made me feel free to speak, bad language and all. He came there to practice his religious beliefs, try to be like Jesus. This shocked me. Why would anyone want to be beat up or hung on a cross? Wasn't life tough enough as it was? It seemed Mike was looking for trouble. If that was true you didn't have to go far to find trouble in the Big Easy.

Mike was my opposite when it came to faith. He believed if

it didn't fit don't force it. It didn't take me long to find out what his problem was. He was too nice a guy to work with hardened men. I tried to tell him what I did . . . fight like hell when somebody wronged me. I tried to incite him to anger, to get even with those bastards who took his money. Right there as I ranted, it hit me that I had his money too. I knew about bad luck, and dirty money wouldn't get you anything but trouble. I said, "Mike, take half of what I've got," just like old Chicken Bone would've done. Mike refused it and started talking about his deep spiritual beliefs. That's what really bothered the crew. It wasn't about work. Hell no. It was his faith. Maybe I minded my business too much that day. I should've paid more attention like my schoolteachers had said. I was so angry with the crew I jumped to my feet and told Mike that I kicked ass for shit like that. "I'll find them and do it for you!" But he wouldn't hear it.

Mike showed me by example that there were different kinds of people in this world, different in their thinking and in their actions. I knew sometimes I overreacted to situations. If only I had been slow to act, things would've gone smoother. I was hard-wired with a short fuse. Mike wasn't angry with the crew and he proved it. He believed that to carry any ill feelings for anyone was a sin. I figured if he'd had a father like Bugdaddy he'd be dead and never have gotten to see the Big Easy. His ideas didn't carry far with me. "Mike, you want to be like Jesus? Look what they did to Him. Are you blind, man?"

Finally he took some of the back pocket money with the idea he would pay me back. He was giving most of his money to charity anyway. I found that out from one of the crewmembers after I threatened to put the fear of God in him. A lot of good that did. I knew it wouldn't be long before the streets would eat Mike alive. If a man didn't know how to fight, he'd better know how to run. Mike would do neither. He said he took his orders from the good Lord, not man. Mama would have loved his thinking, but not me. I had to fight my own battle without a soul in my corner. Mike had Jesus, maybe Moses too and neither ever took up for me, not one damn time. I'd do the right thing though because of what Mama said Jesus would do in a certain situation. It was Mama's love, her quietness in the face of hell that kept me glued together.

Mike and I shook hands in the cemetery and parted. I never saw him again. I headed west toward Brownsville the next day thinking things would be better. Now that I had money on the hip I could look for the great power.

Chapter 8

New things down the road kept me moving. The great power Chief spoke of was constantly on my mind. Good things were waiting around the bend and over the next hill. I needed to be sharp and recognize those things Chief talked about. I felt better with money in my pocket, but still something was missing inside me. Always uncertain at the end of the day, uncertain of a future, I needed something more than money. It was about time I learned what it was I needed. I needed someone who understood my lost soul, understood my being in a struggle to find where in this old world did I fit in. Money can't buy that. I needed to share the load I carried with someone special. Chief said the great power would come to me like a soft wind whispering through the pines. It would just be there before I knew it. So on the way to Brownsville, I looked real hard.

In the countryside, I met a gray dog. I believe I was still in the state of Louisiana. The dog was in a cattle pasture, the woods about two football fields away. I hopped the fence at the edge of the road to get a better look at what he was sniffing out. He acted strange, shy like, and that's what caught my interest. I didn't know if the dog was good, bad or just mistreated and distrustful of strangers, only that he was different from most dogs, the way he moved, the way he checked me out. Something had happened to him, maybe the loss of his hunting companion, his master. He didn't have on a collar. He wouldn't come to me, yet I felt we could become friends. *He could be the power.* I took in a deep breath. The dog knew I was checking him out and he didn't run. He returned his nose, waving high and low, his muzzle taking in my scent. I moved closer and he vanished into the brush.

Was that the wind in the pines? Oh, Moses, I want him to be. I moved away and like magic the gray dog reappeared. One glance my way and I felt a kinship. But his shyness said no. How could something so shy possibly lead me to the Sacred Mountain? At the moment it didn't matter about a gift coming to me because I wanted to be like Mama feeding wild birds. I wanted the gray dog eating out of my hand. But no matter how hard I tried, he wouldn't take part so I put bits of crackers on the ground and backed away. He sniffed the air and after a long minute took my bait. I said, "Check," calling out a name to him and he raised his head. Check, my protector. Things were right for him to be my friend. He took my food but things didn't go as planned. I'd never seen a dog act so un-dog like. I had to know more about Check.

Friends? Check thought it was a mistake on his part because he let his guard down by allowing me to see him. With my Mama's charm in me, he got over that soon enough. Maybe he was lonely too. Late in the day I got a good look at Check. He was muscular weighing around fifty pounds. Check was square headed with two big bulging blood veins that came down the sides of his muzzle like a horse's. That's what caught my attention. If he weren't gray he could have been an Australian dingo. Of all his features nothing could match his eyes. They were yellowish golden, depending on the light, and when he got angry they turned black as a hundred midnights. When our eyes met close up for the first time we saw into each other's souls. No matter what anyone says about that, I know dogs have souls. Mama believed it too, but I learned it for sure from Check. In a matter of just a few days I grew to love him more than life itself, just like old Chicken Bone loved Kate.

Check was like me, wild and free to search endless lands to find where he belonged. I had to win him over. I knew about his problem. He liked me but Check didn't know how to make friends. That was okay because I was like that once and I had outgrown some of the fear. Chief helped me with that. Check needed time to learn that I meant him no harm. Every time I'd get within thirty feet he'd show his teeth and snarl for me to stay back. He wasn't mean or anything. He just needed his space, and that was something I understood very well. I needed that too.

I carried cans of sardines in my back pockets, sometimes two to a pocket. They were convenient and didn't cost much, about ten to twelve cents a can. If things got tough and both pockets were filled with sardines, I had food for four days, one can per day. I don't remember seeing sardines in anything but oil back then and I ate every drop by licking the can clean. I felt I could invest in a can as a peace offering to Check. My jacket pockets were stuffed with fried chicken. The grease had soaked through and the smell had attracted Check to come closer. I held out a piece of chicken to tease him. I'd take a bite and wave it so the aroma would drift his way. He looked starved, but he wouldn't warm up to me, which made me respect him even more. I had to have Check.

Much later and, tired of trying, I opened a can of sardines and left it by the chicken bones I had gnawed clean. I moved away to rest for the evening under a giant live oak tree draped in Spanish moss. It was about a hundred feet from where I'd eaten. At the edge of dark I saw Check creep up to the food. First he crushed the chicken bones like they were straw. Then he ate the sardines, licking the can clean just like me. I cursed him affectionately. "Damn you, Check. You ate my food. Now you be my dog, you hear?" Check looked at me the way cats do when they don't want to have anything much to do with you.

During the night, I felt Check wouldn't be far away looking after me and I slept better than usual, without the nightmares of school and Bugdaddy. Stuff like: Look how stupid Johnnyboy is, he can't spell beans. No one wants a desk next to me because I'm a loser, a dimwit. I wore the same clothes to school for a week. The other kids had too many clothes because I had two pair of pants, two shirts, and one pair of shoes. How much more would a boy need? I never knew kids had chest of drawers that were filled with clothes because Newt and I used a chair. But the lack of clothes is what made me leave the church. Boys made fun of my clothes, but not to my face. On the road it didn't matter because I was among people who didn't know me and didn't care but so much. It was up to me to blend in and not stand out. I had good clothes on, money in the pocket, and maybe a friend on the way, Check dog. As I slept, I shoved the bad things aside and thought about Check, the pretty gray dog. I saw something about him. Like Chief had said, the Great Spirit crosses our paths. And Check was out of place and without a friend. No doubt folks would read him wrong, maybe they'd think he was mean. I couldn't figure out why I felt so close to him, a kinship. Soon enough it hit me like a brick on a toe. Check was a reflection of me. He was frightened and had every right to be. Even though Mama taught me to believe in guardian angels, I never knew if I'd wake up and be alive or have my throat cut in the night. As a team, we could change all that. No more bad dreams and no more fear of the dark.

CHAPTER 9

The next morning I was ready to get moving. Back at the loading docks I had heard how nice it was in Brownsville, Texas. I wanted to see for myself. I looked around for Check but he wasn't in sight. I meandered to a creek that cattle used for drinking water and washed my face. It was quiet and I listened hard for the dog . . . not a sound but bird songs of early day. My investment hadn't worked. I felt a little sad and the gnawing feeling of fear of the darkness was still with me. It would be so nice to have a traveling pal, the smart gray dog that didn't trust people. No doubt he was my kind of dog. Maybe it was the smell of the mosquito repellent I bought at an Army Navy store he didn't like. I cursed myself for using that damn repellent. I splashed water on my face and drank some from cupped hand. The wooded taste of the dark water wasn't that good; maybe I was drinking cow piss. But it gave me the sense I needed, the sense of freedom. But without Check, freedom wasn't all that great. Something was missing in my heart. Why couldn't we be friends? Why shouldn't I have a dog just like any other boy my age? Bugdaddy wasn't around to stop it.

Suddenly, as sharp as a snap of a twig in the night, there stood Check upstream just looking at me, yellow eyes bright as the morning sun. *Oh, Moses, there he is.* Check was looking into my soul and me into his. We stood motionless, staring at each other not more than ten feet apart. I felt a primitive sense coming from him, something I had never felt before. Should I turn my head away and let him think he was better than me, more of a man, better at staring? He was strong. I couldn't let him out do me, intimidate me. Hell no, I'd die first.

I spoke to lighten the tension. "Hey, Mule Head, I guess you're looking for the rest of my chicken, huh?" I said, or something like that. It must have insulted Check because he turned and disappeared into the brush, just like the day before. I yelled, "Go the hell on then. I don't need a nasty dog anyway." Of course I lied. I needed him badly, but I had pride. I would move on but first searched the grounds around me for the gray dog.

It was a good day for walking. I must have covered six or seven miles while my mind daydreamed about what had happened while on the roam. I was searching for something and didn't have a clue as to what. Except for the road before me, I was lost to the world. While examining who I was, only a few cars passed by, in a hurry for parts unknown. Finally I reached a small settlement with a few houses, a post office and general store in the same building. The screen on the door had a picture painted of a larger than life loaf of bread with two slices laid outside the wrapper ready to be eaten. After pulling the door toward me, it squeaked and slammed shut with an un-likeable pop when I stepped inside.

I replaced the can of sardines and bought a pack of Pickyung regular cigarettes. They came in three grades, mild, regular, and strong. I had tried the strong but they were too much. One puff left my head swimming. I told the storekeeper where I was going and asked if there was a busier route so I could hitch a ride. Like I had put him to a lot of trouble, he said, "When you get to the junction, make a left and stay on that road until you come to another junction." His attitude was worse than Check's. He wouldn't look at me after the money exchange. He must have thought I was riding in an automobile because I didn't reach that intersection until many hours later. I almost missed turning left, but I did turn and walked on to twilight. Not more than a few dozen cars had passed me the entire day and trouble was on the way.

A storm came from behind and fear of the night heightened.

Lightning flashes ripped horizontally through a mean looking dark cloud. Each time I looked the black wall was growing higher and higher. Wind pushed me along. Plant debris rushed past like they were fleeing the darkness too. I began to sprint for cover. Afraid of being struck by lightning, I tried to outrun the leaves. Never before had I seen darkness come up so quick. I had to trust my feet where they were landing.

From a lightning flash I saw an old broken-down barn in the distance, nestled in a knee-high cotton field not that far away. That was like a Motel 6 because icy raindrops had started peppering my face. Sprinting, I prayed to Moses that the good Lord above wouldn't waste lightning on me because of not being worthy of a strike. I was very scared at this point. I pushed myself faster and faster toward the barn and harder and harder the rains came. Now I needed the flashes of lightning to see where I was going. In one bolt I saw Check about fifty feet to my right just ahead of me. At first, I thought I was daydreaming. But no, it was the gray dog and he was headed for the same spot. He beat me inside by a few paces. He went to one corner and I stayed in the other, both at the same end of the barn. The other end was damaged and exposed to the elements. At that end of the roof there was a hole you could drop a car through. From the flashes I could see raindrops splattering on the ground. I couldn't figure out how something like a big hole in a roof could happen when the rest of the barn looked strong.

Even though I was frightened of the storm I pondered the dog's stealth. How could he have followed me the entire day and me not know it? I grew up in the country and was savvy with the ways of the woods. Frank had taught me plenty and few things could go on around me I didn't know about, things like rabbits squealing and the language of the crow. I was impressed with Check even more than I had been with Frank. But lightning struck close and brought me to my senses about the danger we were in.

I looked around. Some of the siding at the other end of the barn was missing but there was enough shelter overhead to keep the rain off. Lightning flaring through the hole in the roof with the water pouring down appeared as stage lights and a spooky play was about to start. I waited in a balled knot, my chin resting on my knees, my butt on the ground and back against a wall. Each time lightning lit up the sky it showed what was going on upon the stage, not much, yet.

But God vented His anger with the wind, rain, hail the size of golf balls, and one lightning strike after another. The Big Guy was warning me to be a good boy, not to steal, and to obey His laws and the laws of the land. I made a solemn oath I would do right, just like Chicken Bone's Kate. I wanted to ask Moses to make the storm go away but Mama said you should sit and be quiet. She'd have us sit still and not say a word. I sat motionless and my mind returned to Check. In pitch darkness I waited for the blinding flashes to see him. He was in the next corner, huddled like me, watching the play on stage at the other end of the barn.

Mama wasn't around so I started a one-way conversation, turning on my charm. "Check dog," I called. "I don't think it's a good idea to get too close to one another, do you? Mama said dogs attract lightning." I figured that was a dumb thing to say. I needed to flatter him, not insult his dignity. I made it right. I told Check I'd never known anything that could do what he had done, track me. I told him how far we had traveled, something like thirty miles. Told him I wanted what he had, a secret way of moving about.

Lightning struck close, the ground trembled and pieces of barn fell from the weak end. Back up against the gable end of the barn, I felt a tingling in my haunches like electricity was trying to climb up my spine. I leaned forward, away from the logs, and talked to Check trying to take my mind off the worst storm I'd ever seen. Hurricane winds rushed outside. I told Check I prayed our end held together. The air got thicker. I couldn't handle that, so I lit a cigarette to calm my nerves. The flair from the match revealed nothing but trembling hands. Later a lightening flash showed Check on his feet, ready to bolt. I felt something bad was going to happen. If he ran I was going to scramble out too.

"Come here, boy, I'm scared," I yelled with certain fear in my voice. "I'm not saying you're scared, but I don't want to die alone. Please come to me."

I looked again and Check was three feet away. He had never seen a storm like this either. His eyes had dilated to two black pools, looking as if they were seeing into the depths of something from long ago. I imagined him seeing into my heart. He knew what I needed. He knew how afraid I was.

"Come here, Check. I won't hurt you, boy."

He sniffed the air so I took a whiff too. I could smell the storm, a mixture of plants and ozone like from an electric motor. I tossed my smoke away because I thought it might bother him. Lightning flashed like machinegun fire. Check searching me out was something kind of spooky. His head moved high and then low, like in a too slow silent movie, but always his eyes on me. Those eyes held the power of heaven and earth. No doubt he was looking into my heart, to see if I was good or bad, if I meant him harm. In those moments of fear, anxiety and a kind of eternity, we settled our differences and accepted each other as equals.

Check wasn't the kind of dog one could boss around. No, he was like me, his own man. Through his windows of the world, in that moment in time, I felt he took me to his way of being, an animal consciousness. I couldn't stay there long, but I was with him. It was wrong for humans to turn wild, I thought, to change the rules. Maybe I was dreaming but I could feel the gray dog walking me through green fields with sunshine on my back, showing me that only the strong ones survive. Check was so powerful. But a sharp crack of lightning near by awakened me from the trance, staring into the tar pools of Check's eyes. Something else was happening. I needed Check because Bugdaddy was coming after me. But Check stayed put and wouldn't come closer. I didn't want to pee in my pants. It had been a while. So far so good, but I heard Bugdaddy calling Johnnyboy. I had to do something to stop the bad man.

I talked to Check like this; "It's real bad when it takes a disaster to bring friends together, huh? Truth is, I'm scared and

I'm glad you're here with me. I won't have to die alone. I'm not saying you're afraid Check and I know you won't tell anybody that I am. We'll just be friends. That's that."

I talked in a tone that Check would know I liked him. Minute by minute the fury outside worsened. I started telling Check about Chief in Oklahoma. I talked a long time, maybe thirty minutes, and Check got closer and closer until he squatted on all fours and finally laid his head on my leg just above my knee. I knew better than to touch him, but I really wanted to. I felt so peaceful with him there. I thanked Moses that Check saw me as a good guy. The dog was something special, something I had no words for. He was like the power over all things that were out of balance inside me . . . like I need not to worry about the storm, peeing in my pants, or Bugdaddy. God would get his ass some day. Check's warm chin made me know to never look back at the bad people who mistreated me. God would get their asses too. The warm muzzle was peaceful yet it held a fury of fire that could spring upon a trespasser as quick as the lightening flashes outside. I felt like I had a future, the looking ahead to good things was to come.

I thought about Chief in Oklahoma. He'd had a way about him that made me go on looking ahead for new days because he had the power to see into the future. He'd mentioned a great power, something in-between heaven and earth. Chief was a wise man, a shaman, and I'd felt I'd known him a long time, maybe from another life, like we had lived together in another world, grandfather and son. Chief's powers awed me but the warm spot where the gray rested had the middle ground between heaven and earth. I could feel his might on my leg stronger than if lightning had shot from his jaw. Thanks to Chief, I was wise not to confront the gray dog because of my fears. Thanks to Chief, I was beginning to see Check was the power he'd talked about. I was happy because I'd made the right choice, something I'd rarely done. But good can't stand alone. I thought about the things I feared, things in school I couldn't escape.

"Johnnyboy, can you point out the subject and verb in the sentence?" My teacher held her finger on the blackboard just below the pretty script that had flowed from her hand like summer wine.

"No, ma'am. I can't."

"Give it a try, please."

"I don't have a clue."

Laughter rushed through the class like angry waves crashing on shore.

"Quiet class! No, no, no! You managed to have your mind closed. How can you be so stupid?"

No matter now. I had the gray dog resting on my leg and he would lead the way to better days, the Sacred Mountain. As the storm raged on, I fell in and out of sleep, dreaming, not knowing what was real. I thought I was back somewhere near a small town, Alva, Oklahoma, face to face with the shaman, my dear friend. Chief's face was serene and his body movements were smooth, absent of strife. His peaceful voice spoke, explaining the world of visions. In the dream the old man was right there in the barn, telling me what to do next with Check. Chief had wisdom to carry a man far. He had the greatest way of showing me what should be done. I felt the peace of his wisdom. Chief called my attention to Check, the mighty gray dog. "Timekeeper, he's the great power." Chief pointed a knotted finger at Check with an expression of astonishment as though it was his last excitement in life.

Lightning struck close and I jerked back into the nightmare going on outside the old barn. From the flashes, I saw other animals had taken shelter—raccoons, rabbits, and even a gray fox at the bad end of the barn. Because of the storm, we were not enemies or a threat to one another. I was cold and my body shivered from being wet. I might have had a fever. But Check was still with me, breathing calmly. I backtracked in my mind to the last camp where I had slept and then it happened. Oh, my God! Why hadn't I paid attention to the indentation on the other side of the tree? How could I have not known that Check had slept there? The shaman's voice came to me again, "Timekeeper, you will sleep with the power and not know it."

Check. The gray dog was the power.

Suddenly, I felt the world could come to an end and it wouldn't matter because I had Check with me. I wasn't afraid any longer. Check was what Chief had told me I would find, a great power. Now I would learn about life, why I was here and how I was to act in a world so strange I never felt I belonged. There could only be one place to learn all that, the Sacred Mountain up north. "You'll know the Mountain when you see it, Timekeeper. Go north." The shaman's voice faded into the raindrops that fell on the tin roof above. I didn't care about what came next with the storm. With Check at my side, I could find the Mountain. Yes, I had Check, and I was young and strong and able to withstand much. No more thoughts about seeing Brownsville, Texas. I would make my way north no matter what. Mama said I was the most determined child in the whole world and that I would have my way come hell or high water. Now with Check, I could go to the ends of the earth. Nothing could stop me. Nothing. Nothing. Nothing.

Chapter 10

Awaking the next morning, I was alone. You could see on my blue jeans where Check rested his head. The storm was over and clear skies brought on new rules. The animals that had spent the night in the barn were gone and so was Check. I wasn't about to leave without him. Hell no. I would drink water from a mud hole and eat the cans of sardines before I went anywhere without Check. He wasn't far off. I could feel his big yellow eyes watching my every move. Those eyes would strike terror in the hearts of my enemies. To look into his eyes was a direct threat, a challenge to war. Only a fool would do that. His eyes reflected power and a will to win. With Check, all things would be equal. I would be patient and win him over. I took the last piece of chicken from my jacket pocket and waved it while I spoke like Chief did, soft and low. "This is for you," I chanted. Normally I would have moved on. There were places to go and things to see, but nothing would be worth seeing without the gray dog. The world would see us as a team, fearless and courageous. I imagined what Check and I could do together, more heart than a book of faith had.

My willingness to wait paid off. Later that day the mystery dog showed himself from afar—near where the edge of the cotton field met the woods. His head bobbed up and down like the handle on a pitcher pump as he studied what I was doing. I bit the chicken and started chewing. "This is for you, Check," I said, inviting him to dine. I stood sideways showing him I respected who he was. He weaved in and out the cotton field and the woods, moving closer and closer down the line toward me. Soon enough our eyes met and they locked in a struggle for who would be the dominant one. Instinctively, I knew there was no other way in the animal world. I'd learned about dominance when I fought. Somebody had to be boss and hold the upper hand. It's a primitive language looking into the eyes of an opponent, seeing the power, and I wasn't about to give in. All would be lost if I did. I faced Check and chanted softly and offered him the meat, never turning my eyes from his. He bluffed with a deep growl, and his hair bristled down the ridge of his stiffened body. He looked much bigger and I had second thoughts about who would be boss. Maybe I had made a mistake. Check was wild and he could eat me alive if he chose to. But I believed Chief and I mimicked the shaman's way of talking, smooth and low, a chanting of love. Check wanted a friend too, just like Chief had said. After several long and grueling minutes, Check turned his head ever so slowly away from me until the weight of his power moved toward the old barn where we had slept. He seemed to remember that we stayed the night. I rewarded him with the chicken by laying it on the ground and backing away, never taking my eyes off him. All this left no doubt that Check was truly wild. When he crept up to the food, his back still bristled. I was a little wild myself and I could see this readily. One thing we had in common was we were lonely and needed a partner but didn't know how to go about getting one. He accepted me when he dropped his head, not looking at me. He raised his lips exposing huge teeth when he crushed the bones like they were striped candy canes and swallowed them with a few licks of his muzzle.

"Was that good, boy?" I asked like a friend. Now his look was one of respect. He knew I had given him the food willingly.

We could take on anything. We were so much alike. Check liked to travel and he didn't trust people. He could read body language as well as regular people could read a newspaper. Check was amazingly fast. He could run at lightning speeds and for long distances. He could sense danger before we confronted it. For the first time in my life, I was truly happy. Check gave me what I needed, a friend for life.

We ate all the food, which was the way of the animal world just like Chief had said because there are no tomorrows when it came to food.

There was this one strange thing about Check. If I left him for more than a day, we had to reestablish the pecking order. For more than two days I had to use fried chicken to be in his good graces. Chicken was his weakness.

The gray dog with a soul was walking, eating, and hunting with me. We were a team. If I had been a year older, things most likely wouldn't have worked. I wasn't that much interested in girls. I wanted Check's company because we were wild and free. To change that meant only a broken heart.

We would go north like Chief had said to search for the Sacred Mountain, a place that would set me freer than ever . . . a place that would give me answers to life's taunting problems. I had plenty of those when it came to society. The main problem was why I couldn't read. But I didn't care about all that stuff at the moment. I had the power. I had Check.

Check and I became partners as though God was running things from above, our union preordained. The Great Spirit could have said, "All right, you two, hang tight and you'll get rewarded." I guess God knew my heart and what I was after, even if I didn't sometimes. Mama had said the Great Spirit knew when a tiny sparrow had fallen. God had eyes for everything. But Check and I were sure enough hanging tight and nothing was coming in-between us, not even food when we were hungry. We shared everything. Check seemed to know that as long as I was alive, he had the best chance for life. I felt the same way about him.

I had gotten lots of wisdom from Frank about the woods and was using it too. On the move for about three months since I'd left Virginia, I was plenty much wise to making distance in a day. Check and I had been together for about a week going north afoot. I'd let him know how street smart I was whenever the opportunity arose.

I would talk to him something like this; "Check, Mama said the safest place to sleep is in a cemetery. That may be true but I'll never sleep in one. I always walk light on my toes and hold my breath when I cross a grave. Frank showed me that. I don't like to step on graves out of respect for the dead. You member that, hear?"

I was learning new things every day. Things like, when funeral processions passed on the road, drivers, who had nothing to do with the procession pulled their cars onto the shoulder, took off their hats and waited until the line of cars with headlights on had passed. I didn't know what they were thinking when they pulled off the road but I thought about the departed, who he was, and what life he led. Was he a good guy or a bad man like Bugdaddy? I doubted if anyone would be at his funeral.

I talked to the gray. "Check, in New Orleans families pay folks to march in the departed's funeral. They cakewalk down the street to the graveyard like they are in the Macy's Day Parade going down Fifth Avenue in New York City. I ain't never been to New York but I heard it's something to see. Now that's going in style—that cakewalking stuff."

The first time I saw dancing in the street I didn't have a clue what was going on. I couldn't stand still with the Dixieland music rocking my soul. I danced on the sidewalk like a lot of other folks did. After the procession had passed, I found out from the happy crowd that it was a funeral. Most didn't know the dead person, but they were moved by the music and the idea that the departed was headed to a better place. I liked that idea too. It was happy like.

While Check and I were still in Louisiana, we came across a graveside service. We kept our distance so as not to show ourselves, but we listened to a man in a dark suit preaching the things I'd heard in Sunday school. After the preaching, I wanted the sugar cookies and grape juice they gave us kids.

"I can taste those sweet cookies in my mouth right now, Check." That's what I thought about until the man threw some dirt in the hole in the ground. Everybody looked sad and I was too. I wanted to tell them about doing the cakewalk and being happy but knew better. They needed to get out of the cemetery because it was a lonely place to be. They should go to the place where food waited, cookies too.

"Check, I wish me and you could go. But we wouldn't know how to act, would we? You would gobble down your food like it was your last meal."

That's the way Check would be, but if they got sad and somebody started crying, I would cry too. I can't help that I pick up on stuff like that. Mama said I was just like that, that I had an oversized heart. Frank called me a touchy feely kind of guy. He said that would save my life some day because when bad people had ill intentions, I would know it.

"Look at 'em, Check, standing around the grave like they're waiting for their turn to jump in the damn hole. Ain't no hole in the ground going to get us, huh?" Check didn't look at me, just kept his head on his paws pointed at the graveside service. He was watching folks like a guard dog watching sheep. He knew more than me when it came to the dead. Chief had said that animals knew the deal, life and death, and man had to learn the best way he can, from animals.

"I want a cakewalk when I go, Check. You see to that, you hear," I clamored with a chuckle. "I want folks laughing, happy, and having fun. None of this sad stuff."

A small child stepped forward to the hole in the ground and tossed in a flower. I wondered why people left bunches of flowers on top around the grave and only gave the dead one in the hole a few. This was one of the many mysteries I came across. Another one was some people would say one thing but mean another. Mama said she wanted her flowers while she was living. She also said that dead people don't tell lies, but if you listen real hard they'll speak in the wind coming through the pines.

"Check, what's that dead man thinking right now?" I asked a stupid question not knowing if the departed was a man or a woman. I knew Check knew, but he wasn't giving up any secrets.

"We need to head north," I said. Check stood, ready to move out. I looked again at the crowd of people for one last time. We slipped around the sad souls who were holding each other's hands and no one even knew we were there. I was good at stuff like that . . . Check even better. He could move without making a sound. Sometimes I'd step on a twig hidden under leaves and it would snap. Frank was the best person for quietness in the woods. Lots of times I wondered who taught Frank the things he taught me, how not to be noticed, and to go about undetected. Check was proud of me because I already knew that stuff too, thanks to Frank. Hell, I could sneak up on a crow if I wanted to. I was at my best leaving the graveside service. I knew Check was real pleased I didn't make a sound. Later on he jumped up to my chest, punching me with his paws, and that was his way of saying so.

Chapter 11

North wasn't always true north. After walking most of the time, any ride west was okay. I could get Check into beds of pickup trucks without too much trouble and sometimes automobiles, providing the driver was a lady. Check hated the smell of men folk. He didn't mind women, but he would let me know when someone was coming long before I could see or hear them. But ladies were scarce when it came to rides and the struggle for rides was as endless as the roads that lay before us. Check had learned to tolerate a lot from me, but he demanded space. He didn't like being in close quarters. When he was boxed in, things could go wrong. Pickup truck beds were one thing, but the front seat of a car was another. Sedans would work. Legal ownership was Check's once he entered a car. I had to get in first to maintain control over who was going to be the boss. If he got in the front seat before me, then the person behind the wheel had to prove his dominance. That wasn't cool. One time Check ran a man out of his car when the fellow raised his voice at him for soiling the seat covers with his paws. I had to use a treat to get Check out the car. Another time a lady accused me of being nuts for having a mean dog and she threatened to call the police if I didn't get Check out of her tiny sports car immediately. She opened the door, not me. Nothing doing that time. Check liked the perfume or some other smell. Every time I got close to the tiny car, he would show his teeth to let me know it was his ride. At that moment I was out of the pack. And if she'd been willing to go along with him, they would've teamed up leaving me on the side of the road. The lady held the steering wheel stiff as a crow bar too scared to look Check's way. Thank God, I had a can of sardines to bribe him out. We had to hide in the woods a while after she pulled away screaming like she had seen a spitting cobra. I was afraid she'd call the cops. From then on I didn't stick my thumb out when I saw tiny cars, no matter who was driving. I had to work hard and pay attention to get things right. If someone opened the front door to his car, it was a scramble to get there first. I would laugh silently inside when a driver questioned why I closed the front door and got in the back seat. I would think to myself, mister, you really don't need to know. Check would curl up and go fast to sleep, providing I wasn't alarmed about the driver. If I showed any concern, he'd pick up on that and would sit up watching every damn move the man made.

Check's grayness attracted curiosity with animal lovers. When he was clean, his fur reflected a silver bluish tint especially in the bright sunlight. Also, there was a faint tiger striping deeper down in his coat that was attractive. But he was much more than fur. He had his own way of moving about like he was modeling his muscles. But Check had a way of dealing with the world and sometimes he could be too much for strangers. He was the great power, something to be in awe of. I focused on Check and avoided looking at myself. I didn't see myself as handsome because I was right beat down. The ladies would sometimes tell me I was, but like schoolwork, it didn't stick in my head. They described Check's golden yellow eyes, his gray coat and his proud stance. Well, I knew the guard duty stance was for me as Check was always protective of me. Ride after ride, I had to say we were going north to see an old friend. I got good at figuring out why they stopped to give us rides. Lots of people just wanted to help. Some had minor reasons like being lonely, some were just curious. In less than a minute I could tell why they'd stopped and Check would go straight to sleep if things were okay. When folks were nice, Check would relax enough for me to touch the top of his head. That was one love touch, no more than that or I'd be looking for another ride.

After many days of thumbing, mountains finally came

into view. When I first saw them, I was shocked like someone had sneaked up on me and hollered boo. The hills were overwhelming, not like the ones on the east coast. They were rockier at the tops, with not so many trees and undergrowth at the base. They really took my breath.

Chief's prediction came like a voice in a dark alley. He said, "Your eyes will know the Sacred Mountain, Timekeeper. Trust your heart, not your head."

From excitement I started talking to Check like he understood the foolishness I carried on. He would cock his head and search my face for meaning. Oh, Moses, that was so much fun. I'd talk and he'd tried to talk back. I believe if Check had had vocal cords, he could have talked. I laughed until I started coughing. I told Check I wasn't laughing at him but he didn't care anyway. He liked it when I laughed. I guess he'd figured that as long as I was laughing there was nothing to be on guard about.

Things didn't go as fast as I wanted. I wanted the Sacred Mountain on the first day I saw hills. But days passed and I was running out of supplies and money. The Sacred Mountain would have to come soon or we'd be in trouble.

"North, Check. Let's go. My tennis shoes are about gone." My shoes weren't real solid, just canvas sides and a glued on rubber sole. I'd bought the old PF Flyers because they'd advertised you could run faster and jump higher. No matter if it was true or not, I liked them. I could go barefoot, but I knew better. Society frowned on that. It was also getting colder the higher we went. We needed supplies but I wouldn't steal them and risk going to jail, or losing the best damn dog in the world.

"Check, I've got to take a job for a few days. We need money, boy."

He seemed to understand. If a person was willing in those days, he could get all the work he wanted. The pay wasn't much, but a dollar felt very big in the pocket. My specialty was manual labor. I had a natural talent working with my hands. I could do carpenter's work without thinking about it. Also, in a pinch, I could help lay brick and block. No problem. What to do with Check while I worked was the thing. If a mason took a cinder block from me, Check would think he was taking something that belonged to us and instant trouble would be there. I pounced on the jobs Check and I could do alone.

Folks in the great northwest were very friendly. I would fix a gate, paint a barn, anything outside where Check could go around and pee on everything another dog had peed on. One job I had to abandon because Check and a German Shepherd wanted to pee on the same spot at the same time, and I didn't have the money for a vet. I got plenty pissed off about losing that job, and Check stayed out of my sight as long as I cursed him for his aggression. He knew when I was angry and knew how long to stay away. But there was always more work and another day, never another gray dog. We were together again before sunset, me loving him as much as ever.

With money in my pocket and food in our stomachs, it was north bound or hell to pay. The mountains ahead were growing taller. Now and then I'd search my backpack to see if the peyote buttons Chief gave me were still there. They were, so onward through mountains that were breathtaking. After many days and to my surprise, I stood in new boots before Alberta, Canada, I think.

"Oh, Moses, we crossed America and now I'm looking at another man's land." I stood there telling Check over and over that we were looking at Canada. I kept thinking how we did it. It was all the same to Check. I said, "Check, don't it mean anything to you? I can find what I need . . . you can too. That should make you happy." But moving was what made Check dog happy.

Being a free spirit, I didn't give it one thought about asking permission to enter Canada. I was in search of the Sacred Mountain and I didn't have time for a permission slip. We crossed the border without a hitch and folks were friendly. They didn't think twice about Check and I traipsing around like two squirrels searching for nuts in the fall. Of course Check stayed out of sight most of the time when someone was around. I had accepted that he would always be smart, just like that.

A few days later, before dusk, it came to me like a fist right between the eyes. There it stood, the Sacred Mountain, just like Chief had said. *How can this be?* I asked myself. *I've never been here before but I know that Mountain like I know my new boots.* Excited, I started talking to Check.

"Let's make camp and tomorrow we'll climb at first light."

Later, I couldn't sleep because my mind raced. "Hey, Check, wonder what tomorrow will bring us? Looks like it's going to be a long night."

The air was clear so, lying on my back, I searched the heavens. I loved to talk about the night sky to Check. "Check, it's quiet enough to hear them stars moving around up there, wouldn't you say? Maybe we can make it to the top of the Mountain we saw . . . you know that tall one that holds the secrets of the world and maybe the moon and heaven too." I laughed from the excitement. "Hey, boy, Chief said rocks, trees and water can talk on that Mountain. He said that I would know it when I saw it. He was right. Funny thing, it looked like it was beckoning us to come on right then, remember? Oh, it could have been shadows that caused things to move, but I don't think so. It beckoned us all right. Things will be great from now on. Just you wait and see. We'll live happy ever after. We can hunt forever without money and stuff. You wait, Check. You just wait and see. Maybe I can learn to read you a book, a big book. We'll see, huh?"

Check wanted to move on in the dark and he could've done it too. It was too dangerous for me stumbling around in a deep forest with wild animals looking for their next meals. A cut and the smell of blood might give a timber wolf encouragement to get me. I wasn't stupid when it came to the laws of nature. I could hear wolves calling one another like they were lonesome or maybe hungry. I wasn't but so scared because I had Check and he could take 'em in a fight. It was better to stay put and keep our scent in one place so I did without much sleep.

I would talk to the mighty gray dog, switching subjects, like a rabbit hopping cornrows. "Big Sky Country was something, wasn't it? How about the look on that construction worker's face when you took his sandwich and swallowed it whole? He shouldn't have waved it around while running his big mouth. You thought he was giving it to you, huh? Too bad I never taught you table manners. Check, I'd like to put one of them fancy cloth napkins around your neck one day and make you sit up straight, just like Mama tried to get me to do at the table. Fat chance on that, huh?"

I thought about Mama and what she was going through living with Bugdaddy. "Oh, Mama. I miss her a whole lot, Check. When I get things right on the Mountain, I'm going back and save her life. I can't talk about that right now because I miss her too much. You know how I am about looking backward—Bugdaddy and all. Night, Check. We're going to the top tomorrow, no matter if hell comes."

That's the way it was when I talked to Check. He moved to a new spot. He turned around a few times making himself a fit bed. I was getting cold and I needed him to sleep near me for his body heat. I started talking again.

"I put up with your shit, now you're going to put up with mine. I bet nobody except Chief would believe how we live, how we hunt. You and me know that animals talk, but trees and rocks? That's crazy, don't you think? Sounds to me like Chief was drinking too much of that funny tea."

I was talking just to hear myself because I couldn't ignore the wolves howling in the far distance. Check howled like they did sometimes. The first time I'd heard those bad boys, was about a week earlier. I wanted to learn their howls like I had learned the crow's call. Somehow I had tuned out the wolves by running my mouth to Check. That worked. But suddenly, and as clear as drinking water, Chief's voice sprang up from nowhere and ran through my mind like a child romping through a house. He said, "Take these, Timekeeper. Chew on the buttons while you make the tea."

In a panic I searched my pack. The bulging lumps were still there. I thought about many things that Chief had talked about in the kiva and passed them on to the gray. "Check, how can a person be a buffalo and a man too?" Me and Chief had tripped that night, got real crazy, too. I thought about what I saw through the drug and figured it was a good thing Check wasn't there when Chief opened doors to my mind. Moses only knows what Check would have done to Chief the time he'd grabbed me by the arm to get my attention.

I flung my arms around my body. "I'm cold, Check. Come over here and keep me warm, boy."

It was rare but my nagging worked. Check got up like any normal pet would do and snuggled up to me. "It's about time, Mule Head." I went to sleep dreaming about the climb to the top of the Sacred Mountain where I could get answers to life's problems. We were so near that first night I could hardly rest. *Oh, Moses, we're in another man's country but still in God's world, that much is known. What can stop me? Why shouldn't I have what I need? Aren't I someone God could love? Damn straight. Then why was I treated so bad back in Glen Allen? Why did I not fit in there? Most importantly, who's the man-child in the reflection? What is his name, Stupid?*

I'd heard about people losing themselves in books, but that ain't spit for me. I'd heard about folk losing themselves in other countries, and even in drugs and alcohol. But I was in some nowhere-place in-between life and death. No matter now. Come tomorrow, all those things would be answered on the Sacred Mountain. "Night Check."

CHAPTER 12

It was just before daylight. Check was ready to go and it didn't matter if it was up the hill or down. He started out sniffing and running off in one direction and then doubling back to another. He'd found a new scent and I hoped it wasn't a brown bear, the kind I'd seen in a store all stuffed inside but standing tall, claws out, and a big mouth, ready to bite heads off. A bear of that size would have needed a hundred pounds of meat to fill its stomach. That's a lot of meat on a plate.

I had to wait for more light to head in the right direction. Chief had said the plants would show me the way. Sounded crazy, but he was right. The low-lying brush had an opening, a path, and I would follow it. This was a place one could get lost and never find a way back out again. This was a path that had all the dangers in life. Maybe if I'd stood there and thought about the bad things that could happen, I would have turned around and fled. I didn't do that. I had the faith of a child. Also, I had Check and I needed things cleared up in my head before taking a step in the go-back direction. In the birdsong morning, I could hear ringing in my ear, the one that took the blows from my Bugdaddy's hand. If I closed my eyes, I could see shaking fingers of teachers scolding me. "You're not listening to me! What's going on in that head of yours, Johnnyboy? I'm losing my patience!" I heard that. *To hell with them.*

I didn't really have a choice. I had to go up the mountain and free myself like I'd done with Bugdaddy. To do otherwise would be a step back into hell.

In between Check's running fit, he'd come up to me, show those big yellow eyes that seemed to say, "Hey, partner, ain't you going to help me catch this critter?" I tried to get Check to calm down a notch but he was too excited to eat. I rolled up my knapsack and gathered our few things, food and utensils that we would need when we got to the edge of heaven.

Finally there was enough light to get myself familiar with our surroundings. With the backpack shouldered, I looked up and saw it, the Mountain of relief . . . the peak that would save me, make me a new man. I would search for answers there about who I was and about fitting into society. Having faith and the gray dog, I thought I would return to Oklahoma if things didn't turn out the way I'd planned. I felt young and very strong. Without the least bit of hesitation, I took my first steps toward the Sacred Mountain.

Check and I started out downhill, crossing small streams before the big rise began. We were either climbing or descending and nothing was on level ground. But like Chief had predicted, the path through the brush showed the way. It wasn't long before I felt the pain of the uphill climb, steady and unrelenting. Up the path a ways I found out what had made Check so excited. Thirty feet up a tree was a young mountain lion. She was beautiful, and terrifying at the same time. She wasn't afraid of Check as she was of me. When I came close she ripped a scream that sent the message I wasn't her friend and I had better listen. Check wanted a piece of the cat, but if trouble started, I would be the one to pay the bill. I had to keep a distance. I was afraid Check would bring down the cat with his taunting. My heart was pounding as I moved away briskly. At a safe distance, I could see Check had no intentions of leaving his new acquaintance. After about twenty minutes of him jumping and clawing on the tree trunk, Check ran up to me with the most disappointed look like he was saying, "Hey, Johnnyboy, you damn sure ain't going to help me, are you?"

"Hell no. I'm not getting sucked into your little game," I told Check, and then explained that he was going to be her next meal and he was ruining my plans. While Check played himself out barking, clawing and peeing on every bush in sight, I made a spear out of a hardwood sapling and reexamined the situation.

"Oh, Moses, it's been a while since I've asked you for a favor. I'll get right to it. Can things change inside one's head to make good luck? I've got a bad outlook on life and I don't know how to fix it. Chief sent me here to get things straight, but I don't know. I'm pissed off at the moment. Check has his own ideas. Being angry doesn't happen as often as it used to. Traveling has settled me down a whole bunch. That's a fact. Still, I've got a short fuse—my dog is acting foolish. I want things to be right."

In the back of my mind I was looking for magic to happen, like when Chief and I chewed peyote. I knew I was so close to the spot where Chief had been as a young man. I could feel that much. I was kind of seeing things through his eyes. No more bad luck for me. I needed the good stuff. It was as though the ground ahead was waiting for me to tread and I would get the answers I desperately needed.

"Moses, what do I have to do to be like everyone else? I want to fit in like sprocket teeth joining into a bicycle chain?"

I moved the buttons from the backpack to my front pants pocket. In spite of Chief's warning, the peyote was the assurance I needed, a warm blanket to cover whatever was cold. I could build my own world with the drug.

I flung a stick at the gray. "Check, will you please stop hassling the cat, damn-it."

I listened for sounds of automobiles, airplanes, anything, but suddenly it was quiet as a pauper's grave. My four-legged partner had left for drinking water. Now I could think straight. I thought about the long road there, the tough haul. But it was back to what was on my mind, what I needed.

"Moses, I'm not lost. I feel okay. Check doesn't take crap off nothing. Here's the deal. I'm befuddled to things most folk take for granted. Now I know you've heard this a thousand times before, but hear me out one last time. Some good luck won't hurt me. That's what I need."

It felt good talking to Moses. It was like working out a simple math problem using my fingers. And thinking out loud I was less likely to slip from the topic. "Moses, I've tried hard with the other stuff, but that didn't work. Never did. I'd go back to school in the fall thinking I could learn. Huh, I'd come away more screwed up than the year before. Oh, Moses, I hate those bastards that teased me. That runs deep. Hell, a coalmine shaft ain't nothing deep as I am with a hole in my heart. The hurt? It's downright low, wedged in tighter than a dog tick ready to pop. What can I do about it? I'm not going to get book sense out here unless I get some good luck. It's got to be magic on top of the Sacred Mountain. Dig this. I can read road signs and I know what direction I'm headed. I ain't stupid with that. But knowing the direction doesn't help when it comes to bad luck. Have I got to learn everything the hard way . . . or use the buttons that'll bring me good luck? Oh, Moses, are you listening to me?"

I could hear Check returning to the cat with a renewed fighting spirit. I kicked the tree I stood by. "Aw piss! That stupid ass dog. Moses, you ain't much help either. What kind of friend are you? Maybe you're a sissy, too damn scared to give my message to the Big Guy. He slaps you around? Stand up to Him. Be a man."

Check was back to the treed cat. Between Check acting crazy and the cat's screams, I couldn't think straight. What was left on my mind was snapped at Moses. "Answer me this, old friend. Say that God made me messed up in the head for some purpose, okay. What does He have in mind? What the hell am I suppose to do, forget about needing good luck? Don't life get worse when you get older? My schooling, am I to be punished the rest of my life? That's the main thing. Now you go and ask what's up for me or we're through talking forever. Good luck for me, or nothing, got-damn-it. Now go to it, Mr. Moses."

That was it for Moses, unless he itched another commandment in a stone like, "Thou shall not piss off Johnnyboy." I yelled to Check that I was going up the mountain and he could find me when he had finished screwing up. It must have gotten into his hard head because he followed as soon as I was out of sight. With my nerves nearly shot, I felt relieved all that cat business was over.

I climbed steadily. I thought the top didn't look far away when we started, but I'd learned about distances in Big Sky Country. What looks like snow ten miles away turns out to be eighty. That's how far I could see. But this particular mountain didn't seem so tough because I was following a path animals had beaten down for thousands of years. Check and I were just tamping down our part. We climbed until the sun was straight up, around two o'clock, but the top didn't look that much closer. The straps on the backpack felt like they had cut into my shoulders. I stopped and rested awhile against a tree without taking it off. I was tired but I felt alive. Everything was fun again so we headed up. We stopped some time later and ate like starving animals. I laughed when morsels fell from my mouth because we raced to see who would get it. Check was quick as lightning. He usually got anything that hit the ground and sometimes snapped the food in midair. He'd already finished his food. Up close to my face, he'd watch me eat. I liked that because I could let food fall from my mouth and pretend I was going for it, which made him go faster. When I'd spit a piece of meat from my mouth, he'd catch it in a flash. His muzzle popped together with such force it seemed his canines could punch holes in steel plates. One time I pitched him food in front of construction workers and that made them nervous. Check had a habit of raising his lips to show he was ready for the game to begin. His impressive teeth and aggressive nature going after food rattled the best of men. No one could play the game but us. But what really got them shook was Check would not warm up to them even when they offered him food. He was a one-man dog and no one else was invited to be part of the pack. This was good. I wasn't afraid of anyone as long as Check was around. He would teach a lesson about the rules of engagement and it didn't take but a second or two for them to learn. His massive teeth were like the teacher's yardstick, to get the attention. You had to be blind to miss Check's pearly-whites when he raised his lips.

Rested, we started climbing again, hoping to make the top before dark. I was driven like never before. I daydreamed constantly about having a world given to me that would put my head on right, to fit in with everyone else. But I also daydreamed about getting revenge for the evil things done . . . the things at home, and in school . . . being robbed of my childhood, my education. *I'll show them who's boss, who can do his lessons. The shy kid, who exploded with rage, won't need to stay in the shadows anymore. I'll be out front and center stage, cool and calm just like Frank. I won't hesitate to face them all, even on their terms. I won't worry about who they think I am, some kind of crazy kid, just because of not liking crowds and social games that make no damn sense at all. Hell no. I'll be one of them mixed in the bunch like sugar in Mama's pound cake. I'll get what I want on the Sacred Mountain.*

I couldn't wait to get there. But as I dreamed, I remembered Chief's warning. He'd said, "First things first. Timekeeper, don't start out asking for anything. Just pray and sing the song that gives thanks for your journey."

Chief had warned me if I asked trees or rocks for anything when I first got there, the Sacred Mountain would run me off. I would have to leave in shame because this was a onetime thing. He said that I would have to go back where I came from until the Mountain invited me, but that might never happen. He said I should just drink the tea and my mind would be opened for the gifts.

I don't remember telling Chief that I was a dreamer of the kind that had built a world of my own, a place where I could find a little comfort, a little safety. Starting at the age of five, I had learned how to daydream worlds of shelter. This habit wasn't leaving me but growing stronger as time went by. No matter how hard I tried to look forward, my thoughts would return to the beginning, my soul searching for something missing on the inside. I hadn't even shared this with Check. Hopefully this searching would stop at the Sacred Mountain. But for now my mind needed to go back home, to the beginning, while I climbed higher and higher.

Chapter 12

I didn't like Bugdaddy from the beginning and no one else did either, far as I could tell. I especially didn't like him feeling Mama's breasts at the stove while she made us dinner. That made me nervous because Mama would hit him and the fighting would start. *Don't hit Bugdaddy, Mama. He's a bad man and I don't want anything to happen to you. I love Mama.*

Everyone was frightened of Bugdaddy. I don't know what made him so mean all the time, but sometimes the looks on Mama's face made me stiff with fear. Bugdaddy liked to beat me. Mama said, "My Johnnyboy, you need to learn rule number one. Stay out of Bugdaddy's sight." But he had everyone huddled in a corner of the kitchen. I couldn't take my eyes off of Mama. He was yelling at her. Each time she answered, he got louder and meaner. All he needed was horns coming out his forehead and a pitchfork instead of the fly swatter and he would be the red face devil. *Be quiet, Mama. Can't you see you're making him madder and madder? He will hit you.* I cried because Mama started crying and then the Bugdaddy grabbed me by the arm and snatched me from the corner. He said he was going to give me something to cry for. His big angry hand moved as quick as a snake's strike toward my head, sending me to the floor. As he jerked me up by my arm, pain shot through my shoulder. Mama screamed that he had pulled my arm out the socket. I didn't know what that meant, only that Mama went after him like the neighbor's dog went after squirrels. Bugdaddy turned me loose so he could fight Mama and I ran back into the huddle. I hid my face in my hands, hoping Bugdaddy would go away, but I heard things breaking. The noise of fighting grew. This time I didn't think it would ever end. *Oh, please, don't hurt Mama. Please!*

Later Mama took me to the family doctor. I wanted to tell him that Bugdaddy had hurt me, but I trusted Mama who told me to hush my fuss. She said they might take me away and we wouldn't see each other again if I said anything. I didn't. I would look after Mama because she made me feel good with her smiles and peanut butter and jelly sandwiches. Mama needed me to grow up and be strong for her. Her people didn't do things like Bugdaddy did. She didn't know he was a bad man when she married him so we needed to make the best of it and stick together. Hell no, I wouldn't tell the doctor a damn thing and I wouldn't cry either when he popped my arm back in place. I was going to look after my Mama, no matter what.

Mama washed our clothes by hand on a scrub board. I kept sticks on the ground and waited for her to dump the gray water so my stick boats would float to far off lands, far away from Bugdaddy. "Are you ready, Mama? My boats are. They want to go away. I'm in a hurry. Please dump the got-damn water."

I could cuss like my drunken father and Mama would get swelled up like a propane tank. Sometimes she would snap a word or two at me but that only made me laugh. Mama loved me because I was like her people. She said so lots of times. "Oh, Johnnyboy, you are a hard one," she would say. Having my way, she'd say was a bound-to-be. That's why she called me her Johnnyboy. Sometimes folks outside the family called me that name. I got used to it. I got called other names too, names that stained my mind like blueberries on Sunday's white shirt. Stupid was the worst name, and my brother and sisters called me that one lots of times. I didn't know how to deal with that name. My brother and sisters were real keen with school lessons and I listened to them showing off how smart they were with their studies. I'd think, if you don't know which way the wind blows, and where to find a hen's egg, all that schoolwork stuff don't matter more than a pile of poop. They talked to me about school only to tease me. I'd listen to their teasing and their long list of names but when it got to stupid, I was out of there.

Mama would say, "Go play outside, Johnnyboy, and make yourself happy." I'd go off to myself, deep into the woods in the back of our house. I had hiding places no one knew about. If I could have figured out how to feed myself, I'd have never gone back except to see Mama. She never called me bad names and she talked to me when no one else was around. She made me feel good and that made Bugdaddy mean. He'd make things harder for Mama and me so we got smarter about talking. At the table she'd give me secret looks while my brother and sisters carried on. Bugdaddy caught on to this so Mama got fast with it. She taught me to read her face in a flash. No one else could do that but me. I could read Mama's signs. Bugdaddy loved it when my siblings called me ugly names and he had figured out the one I hated most. It was funny to everyone when I hid my face in my hands. They joked I'd be sent to a reformatory when I started school. I thought that meant jail, and I swore I'd turn things around and be just as smart as they were. My brother and sisters said I was in the habit of running away. I guess that was true but something was wrong inside me. I was messed up in my head and no one had an answer for that.

My back-in-time dream took a rest. Check and I were still climbing. I thought about names. *Who wants to be called bad names? Stupid. Dimwit. Not me. I want a good name, something honorable. I'll get that on the Sacred Mountain. But there's more to deal with before I take another step toward the top. No need trying to stop it. It's a festered sore and needs to be popped.*

The sore to be worked out was about my broken arm when I was five. I'd fallen from a pigeon coop in the top of the garage and grabbed a bucket filled with cement to stop my fall. The bucket followed me down landing on my right arm. After being strapped down in a hospital bed for a good while, maybe months, I don't know, I never was the same inside my head. I remember the doctors argued over taking off my mangled arm. They thought I was knocked out under a drug but somebody forgot to give it to me. I fought them with all my might. But I woke up in the burn ward at Medical College of Virginia with my arm the size of a basketball and hanging in a sling from the ceiling. They kept me in a sterilized environment. I was used to running around, playing in our woods, with no restrictions on how far I could go from home, trying to stay within yelling distance so I didn't miss Mama's jelly sandwiches. We had wild animals like rabbits, squirrels, red and gray fox and even bobcats. They went well with Mama's cooking. Now suddenly I was in a strange place and didn't know a soul. Being used to freedom, I didn't like using a bedpan so I held nature until two ladies gave me an enema. I was big for five years and the bedpan really hurt my dignity. The nurses warned me they would shove a tube up my pee-pee hole if I didn't pee. The threat worked. I peed.

The only boy in the burn ward was much older, a bad kid, about twelve. The doctors were making him a face using skin from his butt. After we'd been in the ward a long time, I asked would his face stink. Others overheard me and made a big deal about my question. They all laughed. But the big kid didn't like it at all and got real mad. I saw this in his face. I told him I was sorry, but that didn't help. Later that day he tricked me into trusting him. He led me to the basement where cadavers were kept and said they were getting ready to come back to life. The big boy turned out the lights and locked me in the room with dead people. I started searching for the light switch to see a way out but couldn't find round buttons to push, one pops in and the other pops out. Not like Mama's wall switch that clicked up and down. My tiny thumb could only cover about a third of the huge button I touched in the dark. Maybe I could have gotten the lights to come on if I'd used my strong hand but it was in the sling mending. My left hand was weaker and not accurate to work light switches in the dark.

I could only search with one hand. The wall felt cold, colder than any wall I'd ever felt before. I had to look out for myself but I was getting too scared to go on searching. I needed help but I didn't want to yell and get a beating. Maybe a dead person was searching for me like I was searching for the switch and he would find me first. I had to hurry. I wasn't here for this to happen. I was Mama's little man. *She needs me at home to get her things from under the sink. Mama is having it hard to reach with a baby in her stomach.*

I didn't think about death or why, just that the dead people wanted to get me. I didn't think about what they would do after I was caught, just that their beatings would be worse than Bugdaddy's. *Mama, Mama. Everybody has forgotten about me. Oh, please, Mama, come get me. I'm scared.*

I yelled, but it sounded different, not like wanting to have my way. My yell was loud but only in my head. Nothing came out of my mouth for anyone to hear. Only dead people could hear me scream and from the darkness they were coming after me. I slid my back down the cold wall and sat on a cement floor, waiting, waiting for a cold hand.

Things hummed in the dark, big refrigerators, electric motors. I gave up my search for the light switch. It was better to take what was coming without looking any more. The dead people had taken my voice. They liked darkness, but I never ever did again.

Some time later a blinding light flash. I covered my eyes with my arm. The door across the room opened and a nurse pushed in the big light switch button. She was glad to see me, but I needed my Mama. The bad boy, who was my brother's size, had gone to freedom after he locked me away. But freedom wasn't enough for me any longer, not the nice lady holding me. I needed something I had no name for. Now something felt wrong in my stomach, in my soul. Johnnyboy was the same. The boy who tried to yell for help and couldn't wasn't the same person. This boy was new-born with a yearning, a look-see, condemned to search for a way out, a roaming in his mind, searching onward and onward for a safe place like Mama's arms. There she could find the light switch for him. But Mama wasn't there.

Mama wasn't there to hold me, to protect me from dead people. Even though I was in the arms of the nice nurse, I felt small comfort. I needed to push in the button and make the lights come on and chase away the un-living who were after me. I didn't want the nurse to put me down. If only I could speak I'd ask her to let me push in the button, then I could go back to being Mama's Johnnyboy. If only I could have found that button but I never did. Instead, I was left with a relentless search, which left me wild, restless, always on the prowl, searching for a cold, unkind wall for buttons to turn on lights.

The good folks at the hospital didn't say anything about what happened to me. That was because my family was very poor and a charity was paying my tab. I didn't know about things like that. But I knew no one in my family came to see me while I was there. Mama was big in the stomach and had her hands full. But still I felt she had left me to fight for my life.

Nobody at home knew about the un-living and I could never face things to tell them what had happened. All I knew was, I didn't like being closed in any room no matter how big it was. It smothered me. I avoided closed-in places at all cost.

Mama could reach me at times but it didn't seem to bother her that I was out of control. I was simply Johnnyboy, the wild child, and she had other kids to consider. At school is when trouble began. They said something was wrong with me, things as plain as dirt under fingernails. They said things like this, "That boy has a loose screw. He's not normal."

They thought I was so distant they could speak in front of me and I couldn't hear them. Doctor Mac said the only time I acted like a regular child was when he pumped me full of painkillers. Doctor Mac gave me something in the form of a horse needle and I saw colors flash before my eyes like big city lighting. When I wasn't grabbing at the strange world others had a handle on, I was busy looking for a hiding place away from all. That was the epic struggle of my youth. To escape, I'd beg Mama for paregoric, a cocktail of milky looking opium. Sometimes I'd get my way, which was considered a well-deserved vacation for all.

The first day Mama took me to school, she tried to explain how I would go off and hide in the woods for hours, and how she'd tried everything to get me to sit still but I'd only gotten worse. She told the school about a neighbor who kept me sometime and how I would run away from her too. Mama told them I lived in an imaginary world. She was doing a good job explaining but they didn't listen to her. I fled school a few minutes after Mama left. I did this for three days in a row. Mrs. White, my schoolteacher asked me what would it take to get me to stay, and I said she had to leave the window open. She opened it, and the smothered feeling left enough for me to stay.

Right away the school board knew something was wrong with me. I was too shy to tell them what I had been through with Bugdaddy and the damn hospital. I figured no one cared but Mama, and she abandoned me to a worthless schoolhouse. Mama was getting big again in the stomach.

Bugdaddy's side of the family had a name for the way I acted. They called it the Mackness. Mack was a bull-headed uncle born in the nineteenth century. Bugdaddy said I was like Uncle Mack. Never mind which direction to follow, just go fast and far as hell, and worry about the consequences later. That was me, that's what I did, and they called it the Mackness moves. Bugdaddy hated my guts, no doubt about that. Punishment didn't work because I was willing to take brutality to get my freedom from the smothering feeling. So, from time to time, I would feel Bugdaddy's frustrations. He would use whatever he could get his hands on to beat me. Blood would fly. When his fit was over, the word Mackness spewed out his mouth along with other cuss words. I thought Mack must have been a cool guy, and I wished from time to time that Mack was my damn name instead of Johnnyboy.

On the way up the Sacred Mountain I reverted my thoughts toward Check. I talked to him. I'd rattle on even when he couldn't hear me. I did this something like Mama did talking to blue birds. I'd unload troublesome things on my mind to loosen the weight of the backpack straps cutting into my shoulders. Check didn't care that Bugdaddy hadn't made it through the third grade. I'd heard Bugdaddy brag about that lots of times, so why should I hang around school? I was much better with hands-on things like horses, rabbits, dogs, chickens, squirrels, cats, hammers, saws, stuff like that. I needed to touch things, to breathe fresh air, climb trees and fences, and throw rocks. I didn't answer my teachers. I was too busy searching for my next chance to flee. I needed to escape the closed in feeling that left me without air to breathe. And if I couldn't get away, I would daydream I was somewhere else. That's what I did and as time went by it only got worse, not better. I failed every grade like Bugdaddy and they held me back, put me forward, sent me home, or made me stay after school. Everyone could see that the school system didn't know what to do with me. I charmed the teachers and they laughed, they cried, took me for treats, took me home and got upset in front of Bugdaddy. He would beat me after they left, but they didn't know about that. Finally,

Bugdaddy got tired of them coming around and got tired of beating me for a worthless education. He said educated folk had ruined this country and I agreed. I wanted to go fishing and that was worth a whole lot.

After running away those first three days, the school sent a nice man to pick me up at home. He volunteered to take the problem child to school and to sit with him to make damn sure he didn't run off. I was a quiet child and thought to be dumb. A person had to hard press me to say anything. Mama wished the nice man good luck and off we went. Down the road a mile to an intersection he was to take a right, but he turned left and took me to the wrong school. I wanted to tell him his mistake but I thought he would act like Bugdaddy and explode. Down a strange hallway, the nice man searched for a room and found one. We went in and stood by the door a long minute. The class was in session but all eyes were on me. The teacher was nice too. She had the janitor bring in two more desks.

After we were seated, it wasn't much going on, just books with the alphabet we could color. When I didn't do any coloring, the teacher and the nice man figured something was wrong. She asked me lots of questions but I was too scared to open my mouth. I wanted to tell that the nice man had taken me to the wrong place but could only think about how I could escape. They began a discussion about me being deaf and dumb right there in front of everyone. The nice man had never heard me speak so he figured I couldn't talk, and he could tell something was wrong with my head, which hung down.

The teacher took my chin to draw my eyes to hers, but I pulled away and stiffened. I figured if I didn't see her, she wouldn't slap me. I searched for an open window, one I could dive through. I couldn't breathe right. While the other kids stared and the two big people worked out what could be done, another man came in excited. He told them I was at the wrong school and everyone in the right school was sick that something bad had happened, maybe a car wreck.

During our ride to the right school, the nice man wasn't happy anymore. He said I'd made a fool of him. He asked me if I could speak but I didn't answer. To talk at that point would be the worse thing I could do, so I made a plan to stay silent no matter what he did to me. My mind was running faster than Newt's bicycle because I was planning to escape after I got to the right school. The nice man said I needed my ass whipped. I knew plenty about that so I didn't look at him, in fear he would strike me with his hand like Bugdaddy did. That left my ear ringing and I didn't want to lose any more hearing than I already had.

At the right school I wasn't received well. The principal wanted to take me home to be punished. He wanted answers but I wasn't talking. Luckily, Mrs. White was a wise lady. She gave me a treat, some penny candy. She made me feel like I was special, just like Mama did, and then we had a talk. I didn't say a lot but it was enough for us to go back to her classroom. I sat at her side after she opened the window so I could have fresh air. That ended my fourth day of school, but not the compulsion to flee.

If it hadn't been for Mrs. White, I don't know what would have happened. It was her last year of teaching and she had dealt with all types of children. She told me that I wasn't like anyone she had taught before, and I took that as a compliment. She gave me things in secret besides penny candy. She was a pretty lady with white hair, always smiling at the class but especially at me.

Year after year I was placed in classrooms where I didn't belong. But what were they to do? I was out of control, a daydreamer with my mind miles away and not on schoolwork. Around twelve, I had earned a reputation of being a lost cause. Not a bad person but one who was lost to academics. Even when I told them what was going on, about the daydreams, it didn't matter to them any longer. My confession either left them laughing or crying. Seldom was there anything in between tears and laughter.

The last days of school were eventful. I understood what a bull's eye meant better than most boys. Instinctively I could hit the bull's eye with ease. When I did, I'd yell, "Bull's eye!"

like I'd just won a whole dollar and a dollar seemed as big as a blanket. That was always fun yelling bull's eye. One day the principal was in a bad mood. For the life of me, I could not do the English lesson he gave me. He grabbed me by the ears, face to face, and had no intention of turning me loose. It wasn't a big deal to be there because I'd had a desk in his office since the first day back from summer break. All the guys thought it was funny, me having a desk there. The teacher just didn't know what to do with me. The principal didn't either. He should have let me go fishing because I was good at that. Day by day tension was building between us because he couldn't get his way. I tried everything to make him like me, but the more I tried, the more uptight he got. Nothing worked. He was a doctor of academics, and I would be educated even if it killed him. I was afraid of him. He was a big man and had played football as an offensive guard or something like that in college. This day he hit my desktop with his open hand, trying to get my attention, and my desktop snapped like a twig. Now the man held my ears with a death grip and wouldn't let go. He was way beyond being real pissed off, more like treading the grounds of insanity.

Earlier that morning I had noticed one of his wingtip shoes had been cut away, and a white bandage poked through where his big toe was. Old Dr. Mac who had mended me many a time, had operated on the principal's ingrown toenail. That's what his secretary had said. Maybe that's why he had a short fuse that day, I don't know. Times before, he would have set me free by slamming me down in my desk and shaking a finger in my face. But now he yanked me back and forth, trying to tear off my ears. This was a new painful thing and I wanted out in the worst way. I felt smothered like the time in the hospital. His big toe, wrapped with gauze and white tape, was an easy mark. I didn't have to look, I knew where it was, so I stomped the white bandage with the heel of my brogan. His blue eyes swelled and then rolled back in his head. I was okay with that, but what scared me was I never knew a man could suck in so much air. It was like he took in all the oxygen from the room and left me nothing to breathe. As his hands set my ears free, he fell over backward like a tree falling, stiff as a board, until he crashed on his desk like a dead man all rubbery like. His secretary screamed and I did what came natural, ran like hell. The boys said I yelled bull's eye when I stomped his toe but that's not true. I didn't say anything, just busted through the big front door like a wild horse out of a burning barn. The guys thought it was funny when I got in trouble. They lied all the time and they lied about me yelling bull's eye that day. That added to their jokes, but this time it wasn't funny. I was in serious trouble.

That evening the principal came to my house with the sheriff. Good thing the sheriff liked me. He drank Bugdaddy's homemade beer. The sheriff bragged there wasn't a man in Glen Allen who could drink down three long neck bottles of Bugdaddy's beers and walk away. It was true. I would tell Bugdaddy when the beer was ready for capping. After a few weeks of fermenting, I'd sampled it every day and knew better than anyone when it was ready for drinking. Bugdaddy didn't mind me having a taste because it slowed me down. I hid outside the house while the three men made their plan to graduate me from school altogether. I heard everything. The principal wanted me locked up where I couldn't hurt anyone else, but the sheriff wouldn't hear of it. Bugdaddy was leaning toward the principal's way of thinking. I knew he would because I was getting too big to manhandle. Bugdaddy had seen me fight the week before. My arms were 37 inches long, shoulder to wrist, and I could deliver blows like a mule kicking. A big guy in our neighborhood said that's what it sounded like. I'd busted a lot of my opponents' ribs and closed their eyes. After treating me so awful over the years, Bugdaddy might have figured he had it coming. I was leaning toward his way of thinking too. But the sheriff got his way. A few days later I told my school I was not coming back. She, my regular teacher, wrote something on a piece of paper and said goodbye. I stayed out of the principal's sight.

"Hey Check, I went farther in school than Bugdaddy did. They sent my records to Henrico Middle School. If I weren't so wild and hell-bent on having my freedom, I could have made the grade there. I always wanted to change classes, but I didn't get that far. Who cares anyway?"

Something was wrong with me. That's why I was headed up the mountain, why Chief had sent me. All that stuff would be fixed and it was time to stop daydreaming. Check and I rested but we needed to climb to make it to the top before dark.

"Time's here, Check. I know you heard my mind spewing brain burps. When we get on top of the Sacred Mountain, I'll get everything cleaned out. It's time to move."

Chapter 13

We were near the top of the Sacred Mountain. I couldn't tell if I was at the right place because it looked different from what I had seen down below. Check was ahead with plenty of fire left in him, but I was slowing down and taking short breaks every few minutes. Suddenly something told me we were there. I yelled for Check to make camp. There wasn't much daylight left. We stopped at a small stream, one you could jump across. I drank from cupped hands and cooled my face while Check lapped and put his paws in the icy water. Not having the backpack holding me down, I felt like I would rise up in the air like a gas balloon. On my knees, I looked around and felt a strange feeling come over me. I didn't know if someone or something was watching us because that's the way it felt. A puff of wind brushed by my wet face as though to say, "Timekeeper you are home."

"Oh, my God, Check." I yelled. "We're here! We're here!" Check came over to see what was wrong. He had never seen me like this, crying from excitement. Cocking his head this way and that made me stop my whimpers and laugh. I tried fake crying to see if he would do it again, but he was onto my tricks. He had all the secrets of life and I couldn't fool him. In a while I gathered my senses and started on what I was supposed to do, give thanks. While making a fire I was so conscious not to ask for anything I forgot to chew on the buttons. Did I ruin everything like usual? I was always getting everything wrong. Gee, I hoped not.

I told Check that I would get it right this time and tossed

buttons in my mouth. They didn't taste the way they did the first time, not as bitter. At Chief's, I'd wanted to see what the juice looked like so now on the mountain I spat on the back of my hand. I couldn't see a color. The juice looked clear as water so I chewed on and made tea. Things were going right. Check had settled in for a rest.

"Drink the tea, Timekeeper." I sipped the hot juice and it burned a layer of skin from the roof of my mouth. I didn't feel any pain, just the dangling membrane above my tongue. Something was happening to me but I had Check to explain it to. Chief said I would know everything in due time but things weren't moving fast enough. But something did happen. All of a sudden I got angry with my Christian God, and for no-good reason. It was the devil asking me, how was this life fair to one person and yet another person starved from lack of food and medicine? "Damn the Christian God," I said, but didn't really mean it. Mama would fall dead if she heard me say that. I was ashamed it flew from my mouth. It was as though two people were inside; one angry and the other awed with life, the surroundings and what lay ahead, the quest for a future.

Check moved a few feet away. My negative ranting bothered him so I stopped when Check finally rested and blinked his yellow eyes at me. His eyes seemed to say, "Be still, Johnnyboy. Calm yourself." And suddenly another voice appeared . . . it was Chief's. He said I would go through many forests to get to the right place. He said to keep moving until I come to the Sacred Mountain, a place in my mind. "There, Timekeeper, give thanks to the ones who will bring you gifts."

I started seeing things just like I did at Chief's . . . animals of all kinds. They didn't bother me, but I got scared when my hearing became acute. I could hear Check breathing like a freight train rushing down the tracks. The stream fifty feet away sounded like a raging river. There was an overwhelming feeling to jump around like a monkey and slap my knuckles on the ground. But that didn't happen.

Hunched over, I started dancing around the fire like I was another person, maybe Chief. I didn't care at first about the dance. I just did it without knowing why. But then it felt fun, very fun. Check moved to another spot but kept a watchful eye on me. He looked pleased because I was having a good time. I couldn't stop dancing, laughing and singing.

Strange animals came to our campsite, but I knew they were all in my mind. I saw wolves with their heads low to the ground and tails between their hind legs. I knew very well that I was hallucinating about them because Check didn't move and didn't worry about protecting us. I laughed and danced without getting the least bit tired. On and on I reeled at such sights like a baggy pants elephant rocking to my voice. I went through this phase until I came to the new forest Chief spoke of. I wasn't scared because I figured I had everything to gain.

Standing in a strange drug induced wonderland, I would speak a word and it seemed to fly out my mouth and fall down to the ground and bounce back in my face. I could feel the vibrations hitting me. Some words felt different, stronger in force. This was funny so I crammed in more buttons, chewed, sucked the juice between my teeth and swallowed it down like I was thirsting to death. A rock I'd placed around our campfire spoke to me and I thought it was normal, just like Chief had said.

But everything wasn't fun. Later the earth moved beneath me like an ocean wave knocking me off balance onto the ground. I couldn't get back up because the surface drew me down like steel to a magnet. I was scared because the fun was over. I got even more afraid when I heard human footsteps. I wanted to flee with all my might but I was stuck like a fly on sticky paper.

Be wary, Johnnyboy, danger is on its way. Get your ass up and run, boy. But it was too late. A figure appeared wearing a long black coat with a hood raised over his head. He looked like the Grim Reaper, the one I had seen in a comic book. It seemed the earth, which held me, and the hooded man worked together to keep me trapped on the sticky paper. I rolled about trying to find something to right myself. I grabbed at branches like a drunk, missing and falling back stuck again.

"What the hell is wrong?" My brain shook like milk in a

coconut. "Check, help me. The hangman is here." It was all a bad dream, yet my plea caused the strange figure standing in a shadow to come closer. He refused to show his face. *He must be awesome,* I thought. Brown braided rope lay around his black boots like obedient snakes while he adjusted the knot in a henchman's noose. His bony fingers moved like spider legs wrapping its prey with its web showing he had done this task a thousand times before. The Grim Reaper didn't have a reason to be in a hurry. The job will be done, the hanging of Johnnyboy, no matter what. I yelled, "I haven't done a fucking thing to you, man. Let me go."

The hooded beast without a heart never stopped fumbling with the rope. *Let's see your face. Who the hell are you?* I tried to scream. But my voice was mute, only thoughts sloshed about in the coconut juiced head.

He wore a black trench coat that draped to his boot ankles, hood stitched on with rawhide strips and human hair. Why should I give a damn about that? Because Chief wouldn't wear something like that, and I wouldn't either. Only a man from hell would.

Relax, Timekeeper. Be cool. It's your imagination. He's not real. Check would be on to his ass if he were.

Those thoughts weren't convincing enough to hide my fright. Perhaps a dare of some sort would shake the ghost's determination to hang me. *Oh, Moses, help me stay cool.*

But I was far from calm and Check seemed unconcerned. Then the dark figure turned its hood facing my direction. *What the hell?* It was blank, pitch black inside without a face. A voice welled up from the dark void. "Johnnyboy," he said like the sound came from a deep canyon. "Listen, Johnnyboy. The wages of sin is death."

No one but the angel of death would say something like that. *Oh, shit, Moses. Help me. I'm scared.*

This was it, the test to find out what I'm made of. Was I a coward? I stared at the messenger of death and yelled at the void in the hood. "No. To hell with you, man. You are sin."

Anger had replaced fear. On my journey I had learned that some people were compassionate for reasons unknown. On the other hand some hated me and that too had no reason. What the hell did I do to them? The thing that kept me from harm was my ability to read faces. I had a knack for healthy fear. One couldn't always sidestep danger. At those times, fear needs to be met head on. Anger comes when things don't go right. The bullheadedness arose in me because the death angel's hood was empty and there wasn't a face to read.

"You win. Kill me you son-of-a-bitch. See what that gets you, oh, boy."

I was satisfied with my decision to challenge that evil thing. I could no longer be afraid and death could be my only choice. I would face whatever I had to face on the other side. But the hooded monster took his rope, turned away and faded into the brush, leaving me ready to fight. I waited for the next forest, or fool thing to come. The peyote was not going to wear off any time soon. I tripped a long time at Chief's with only half of what I had eaten on the Sacred Mountain.

I thought I knew enough about the peyote ceremony to do it alone. It wasn't safe with only Check watching over me. I figured Check would stand guard like he'd done in our journey there. After all, he was the great power. That was plain to see. But the evil ghost that had appeared was inside my head and Check knew nothing about him. Check was ready to bed down, everything was calm to him.

"Check, I'm under a spell," I said, complaining. But he didn't come to me. As with Chief in the kiva, I knew something would happen, a dream that was real as could be. I spoke to Check again. "Why can't somebody goofy come along? He could smash a toe and make me laugh at him hopping around holding one foot." Check didn't move and I could feel the drug's effect getting stronger. Things were changing all around me. I knew when it happened . . . the peyote entered a certain spot in my brain that controlled colors. Everything turned to shades of bronze. It was beautiful, like a heaven with streets paved in gold. I was in awe at the sight, but I didn't have time to question what was happening. It ended with many different colors exploding before me, a vivid world with patterns that were not natural in any environment known to man. This was a prettier place by far than the natural world.

Possibilities were endless with the drug flowing through my veins. I moved into a world of competition, dreaming I was in a foot race, the goal line only two strides away. But my body would only move in slow motion no matter how much effort I put forth. Wildlife had the same desire to cross the finish line first. Somehow I knew they were far behind me moving forward fast without problems. I was so close to the goal . . . with only one step to go. I couldn't let them catch me. "Check, Check! Set me free! You have the power!" But my movements were like pouring cold molasses. The harder I strained, the slower I was.

What the hell is going on? I looked around and I'm in my school's auditorium. I'm in the center isle headed uphill to the exit. The race was still on, but behind me in the lead of all the other animals was a silver back gorilla. He didn't care about the finish line. Hell no. He was after me. If I could get outside of the auditorium I'd be safe. But the monster was gaining while my legs moved like a minute hand on a wall clock. I was more frightened of the gorilla than Bugdaddy. Things couldn't be any worse. The big ape's breath was hot on my neck ready to take its first bite. But he didn't touch me. I was back in the foot race again and a half stride away from victory. I relaxed and like butter left near a wood cook stove my leg sagged, and my toe touched the goal line ever so lightly. I heard creatures stampeding by, stirring up a cloud of dust that was thick and hard to breathe. With the sound of hooves, the cloud became a red, roaring, swirling flame, engulfing me in a fire. I worried but not about the big gorilla. Would I be burned up never to see the green forest again? I didn't feel any pain. Would I be separated from my beloved companion, Check? Suddenly the foot race held great concern. *Dear God, for the love of Moses, did I win?* Somehow I knew a creature had crossed the finish line before me. I had the feeling of losing, the one feeling I knew, oh, so well.

CHAPTER 13   117

"Johnnyboy, you sorry-ass kid. You can't do one got-damn thing right. I ought to do the world a favor and kill you, you sorry ass."

"Who's there? I didn't do anything wrong . . . did I?" I yelled, playing innocent to that and whatever other charges could be brought against me. "Don't hurt me. I came here to learn—for a new name. That's all."

My fear didn't matter because the drug moved me to another forest, one I couldn't sort out. If only I had my Mama. She would soothe me. "Johnnyboy, go outside and play. Make yourself content. I'll be right here if you need me."

"Mama, I need to figure out this stuff. You have any clues?"

You're playing with fire, son. Leave it alone. Mama placed her moral issues right in my face and I knew them well. She would rather talk to an animal than someone with riches. Life was so confusing.

What was I thinking? Mama wasn't around. *She's back in Glen Allen. Check's it. He's got the answers.*

"Check, was I born a failure? Chief said I wasn't. He said I was put on the wrong path. Did Mama do that? Chief sent me here to straighten this stuff out. He said I was taught to accept failure without question. He said I'm brainwashed not to win. You think I'm that way? Who did this to me?"

Check didn't budge as he was resting peacefully. I sniffed the air, and the ground below me smelled like something good to eat. Check had eaten odd things at times, but he knew many secrets I didn't. I had to learn on my own, so I licked the spot where I had stood. I was wishing for Mama's bread pudding, the one with raisins and lemon sauce, instead of what tasted like rotten wood. "And you like that crap," I said to Check, wanting to involve him. "Tastes horrible. I'm hungry, but that can wait. Damn, lets hope for something not so scary."

With no control over my mind and body, I squatted and my arms went down on all fours. Like a dog, I circled the campfire spewing that I could smell everything in the vicinity, including

Check. Check didn't like this one bit so he moved back, cocked his leg on a bush and peed.

"Am I crazy, boy? Have I lost my mind? Me and you are friends for life, right?" Check blinked and I knew he meant yes. I stood up again but with a calm I had never known. I wasn't angry with anyone. Not God, Moses, not even Bugdaddy, no one. I looked down at the fire and the rock around the flame became a mouth. It said I was special, just like Chief had said I was. "Okay," I said, "I can dig that." I laughed and mimicked a wolf's howl. I did that a long time. This was good because Check got real interested and watched me like I was the king of the hill. In the wolf's call is a sad cry I called high-lonesome. Once I hit that note it caused the wolves to answer with the same sound, which invited all to join in the chorus.

After the wolves, I believed that I was a grizzly bear and moved about clawing at the sky and trees and the ground. That was fun. Then I became an elk for a while, then I was a crawling king snake, could hiss like an alley cat. Then I was back to being a wolf. It was a satisfying feeling and Check mimicked me. He howled and I listened and heard him speak a language far, far older than anything I'd ever heard before. The Great Spirit of all creation gave Check a soul, and he could speak to me, and I knew what he was saying. I spoke to him in his language and I howled our brotherhood was forever and things would never be any better than the way they were at that moment. I wanted to pop my teeth together like Check did but couldn't stop howling long enough to try. This went on a long time and I wasn't tired one bit. When I did stop, I heard howls of high-lonesome coming from every direction. Wolves were telling us that they were there and liked what we were doing, what we'd said. The wolves honored me the way I was. They didn't have to tell me that I was a danger. I knew enough about that, that I could be a formidable creature with weapons that kill. Wolves were the best hunters but men could be bad. I said I was sorry because I would be a man again soon thereafter. I might be like Bugdaddy, a soulless person from hell. But I was a wolf that night. And I promised to watch my step and not become a bad person. I said I didn't want that to happen. I assured the wolves my mother was blood of this land and I was her son, not his.

The great power Chief had talked about went into action. Check dug his paws into the ground and strutted around the campsite showing me that he was the boss. He raised his head to give thanks for his life. Then, his nose dropped near the ground before it snapped back up toward the heavens. He had a song to sing. *Oh, Moses, this is wonderful.* Check's howl started out sounding a little low but more vocal cords charged in until they brought on a primitive sound like none I had ever heard before. The sound was so high-lonesome it cut through me like a radio wave and left something deep in my bones. That's what it felt like. I was so proud of Check, to be with him as an equal. I cried, I was so happy. The night was a night that opened my mind to the animal world of long, long ago, Mama's world.

As the years go by, I still feel those vibrations in my bones and the residue of some color-like touch that was painted inside me. Those high-lonesome cries can still bring on a chill, a smile. I got my degree, my education that night. But I'm still learning from the magical things that happened on the Sacred Mountain. Things I saw in visions are still unfolding. I had the gray dog, and he was at my side and I could do no wrong. Not like in grade school. I was one hundred percent right with nature and that was where I belonged. Oh, Check, the greatness, my soul mate, where would I have been without you?

Chief was right. The Mountain took me to a special place in the mind and I found some peace. The search to find myself stopped for a little while. I had left good people behind like Simon and Minna because I was so restless. Like the love I received from the loving couple, I held onto that place of wonder like it was gold in the hands of a beggar.

The Sacred Mountain, in its beauty of rock and trees, cast long shadows. Those shadows led the way to far off worlds of imagination. I found myself drifting farther and farther away from the hardship it took to get us there. The journey had been worth every bruise, every blister and every hunger pain. Taking in the holy ground made me feel special. I felt privileged Check and I were guests. Out of respect I held my breath as long as I could. But the thought of getting what I wanted had its effect on me. My body felt relaxed but my mind sped faster than ever, jumping from one desire to another. I imagined seeing animals roam on the very spot where I stood, animals that don't live on earth any more. Chief said to weed through that kind of stuff and look for buffalo grazing. That would be a good sign. I looked into the mouth of our campfire and there they were, roaming peacefully among the embers. I looked at Check and one glance from his golden eyes told me what I needed to know, that he was with me all the way.

Minutes later, I looked beyond our camp into the darkness and was frightened. "Check! See! There's Bugdaddy. He's a bad man. Get him, boy!"

When Check smiled I knew that I had nothing to be afraid of, not even the ghost of my father. I didn't have to worry about his cruelty or peeing in my pants ever again. No more beatings, no more insults, no more him making me feel small and dumb. One glance at Check and the world was well. But inside my head a tug of war was still raging. I needed to be connected to the ground but I felt I was drifting into space, away from the Sacred Mountain, away from Check. Maybe I had held my breath too long. I staggered backward and reached for a branch but missed it when I fell to the ground like a drunkard. I heard the thud of my body, yet I didn't feel the fall. The Campfire light was gone. I saw stars between branches where I lay. Check suddenly appeared and licked my face. I rolled over and sat up, the world spinning. I asked Check, not the mountain or the rocks or the trees, "Check, what's life about? Is this God's way?"

Check didn't answer, just licked my face to make me feel better until I pushed him back. I crawled back to the campfire with Check at my side wanting me to stand. He'd never given me so much kindness, so much attention. The Sacred Mountain was a magical place, making all that happen. But my restless mind hadn't found the final peace it needed. My thoughts raced back to the hell I had left behind. *Why can't I forget my past? Why must I take it with me to every corner of the earth? Ain't that what I'm running from, my past?* I felt sick. I needed a comforter. I teased myself in a drunken stupor. *Johnnyboy needs his Mama's titty.* Even though I was sick to my stomach, I laughed about my tease. With my mood swings, I needed that look Mama always gave me, the one that made me love her. I glanced at Check and he had the same expression Mama had. Hell no. I wasn't losing my mind. This was real. I was beginning to feel like a new person.

I chewed on the buttons that were stashed in my cheek. Check moved to get a better look at me and made sure everything was okay. I was doing everything right. I was the smartest man on the Sacred Mountain and we had the spot that had magic.

Visions kept rolling by. Some made me scared and some made me want to stay like it was the only place for me. Who wouldn't love a cool stream of water where you could dangle your feet while the sun warmed your naked body? I imagined that, my head resting on a warm sandy bank, Check at my side.

"Check, this ain't the stuff I learned in Sunday school. I ain't supposed to ask for nothing here."

The Sacred Mountain had me dreaming like never before, and I didn't reject what I hated the most, school. Like a wild horse, I had always buck jumped everything off my back when it came to education. Frank always said I could do what I wanted. All I had to do was make up my mind to do it. But that's not true. I never saw it that way because I thought I'd tried with all my might and failed. I couldn't, couldn't, couldn't. I couldn't read and I couldn't take the taunting from my classmates. I couldn't make people see me in a favorable manner when it came to learning school stuff. They thought I was stupid, wild and crazy, so I gave them just that, crazy, what they wanted. On the Sacred Mountain I didn't have to play that part any more. Something had happened; a door had opened before me. I stepped through, looked around and saw another campsite, like Check and I were in another world, another time. I wasn't divided, looking in one direction and then another.

"You can do it, Johnnyboy. You can be like everyone else."

Frank yammered.

Yes, I could put together the pieces my schoolteachers had tried to do. I wanted an education. *Oh, Moses, how many times have I said that? But all I have to do is ask for it and the Sacred Mountain will hand it over, me all smart in the head.*

"No, no, Timekeeper. Stop," I yelled at myself because I remembered what Chief had said. Don't ask for anything. Pray and give thanks. But this was my chance to get even with all those assholes who had laughed at me, mocked me. They thought they were better than me, so smart. One gift from the Sacred Mountain and I will be free from all that. Free from being a knucklehead, a shit for brains. No more standing in the corner or in the principal's office. I wouldn't have to stomp my reader to pieces either. One gift and I could get even with my teacher for embarrassing me to no end. One request from the Sacred Mountain and Frank wouldn't have to forge notes saying why I missed school. Inside this great doorway, I could ask for anything and it's mine, mine, mine.

But Chief's warning came about that things come with a price to pay. *Don't do it, Timekeeper, you'll be sorry. You'll be very sorry for the rest of your life.*

"Okay, okay. I hear you. I have the great power anyway. I can look straight ahead and do what Chief said, not ask for one got-damn thing. How is that, Check?"

I gazed at the stars that twinkled above. For me this was new, but the Sacred Mountain had seen those jewels billions of times before. I thanked the Mountain for being there. I didn't ask for one tiny thing. I was obedient. Check and I stayed on the Mountain for two days. That's how long it took to let go of the magic spell that kept me focused. Now I could continue my journey with a new outlook.

Chapter 14

I missed a few belt loops wanting to get back to Chief to tell him about what had happened. He could explain the rocks talking. He was the only person that would know I wasn't crazy because of what went on up on the Sacred Mountain. Things like me calling to a crow and the crow fussing at me because I didn't know his name. That would be exciting to Chief, but have much meaning, and I knew Chief would like that very much. He would say something like I was eating all the animals' spiritual flesh and I was to beg for forgiveness. He would be wide eyed waiting for the next word coming from my mouth like it was food for his hungry mind. Chief would wait without a word spoken because he would want to know about the great power, Check dog. That was certain. All I had to do was get Check back to Oklahoma and Chief would see first hand the power of a dog with a soul . . . a dog that had nothing alive above him. Chief would witness an unyielding spirit. He would see the million-mile depth of golden yellow eyes, eyes that could burrow into a person and know if he was bad or good. I wanted to believe Check my dog all the while, but the Sacred Mountain had enlightened me. The Mountain taught me where I stood in this world and that was oh, so, humbling. That feeling would never fade. I kept my head down when I left. Check could look up but not me. I knew better. Check had the power and I had only the privilege to see a glimpse of his world—something only Chief would understand. I had ranted out my hatred and desire to hurt those wrong doers. Check had shown me another way, one where I could be in awe of a special life given to me, a gift from the Great Spirit. The spell had taken me beyond time to a place where there wasn't a clock to mark the years, but to a spot just a step beyond the very beginning of things. Being respectful of that place is why Chief called me Timekeeper, that's what I believed coming off the mountain. Chief had been there before me and knew sanctity well. That's why he said I would know the Sacred Mountain when I saw it because of what it did for him. That much I was sure of. But Chief would want to know all the details and that made me anxious to return to his village.

In fear of forgetting some of the things that had taken place, I was in a hurry to get back to Oklahoma. I didn't want to leave out one thought. Check would ease Chief's mind the minute he flashed his powerful eyes at him. What I couldn't tell, hopefully Chief would find out from the gray might.

Check didn't want to leave the mountain. I didn't blame him at first, but enough was enough. I understood his love for the ground, but my wanting to see Chief drove me to whatever means necessary. My vision quest was over and most of all I had a new name coming, one I wanted in the worst way. Chief would be the only one who could rename me. How wonderful it would be becoming this new person, acting natural and not fabricating fake names along the pathway of life. Enlightened from it all, I could be what Chief offered.

Not following the path I had taken, I descended fast. I came across an old logging road, which helped me. At the bottom I waited for Check, but he didn't show himself. I called and called. I knew he was somewhere close, watching from the shadows, wanting me to stay. Deep down I felt the same. Had I been treated with loving arms out there in the world of busy streets, schoolteachers yelling with coffee breath first thing in the morning? Hell no.

The daydreaming started because of the downside of the drug high. While I waited for Check my mind recalled this and that. I could see my second grade schoolteacher pacing back and forth in front of the class. She held a ruler for pointing and whacking hands of students who didn't pay attention. "Where is your mind, Johnnyboy?"

"I'm sorry, I fell asleep," I'd say, hiding my embarrassment from the classmates' laughter when she struck me on the hand with the stick. I was dreaming. Somewhere else. Playing. Having fun with my best friend Frank.

Chapter 15

We headed southbound and reentered the States with no problem. I needed a car more than ever because Check was worse than before about not liking the smell of men folk. The experience on the Mountain had caused him to revert back to his old wildness. It would be rough going until I made some money. At times I lost my cool, said bad things and threw things at him. I was frustrated that he went back so far so fast, not trusting my judgment. I was supposed to be the one to say which direction to go. That was my job and he was to pay attention.

Much later, I worked near two weeks in Montana doing odd jobs and making good money. I couldn't take on steady work because of my partner, Check. That was okay. My mind was clean from drugs. I had money stashed in every pocket and was amazed how nice folks were after I had finished. They said I did pretty work and some folks paid me way more than the price I charged. One lady gave me a twenty dollar tip and the job wasn't but ten. I got spoiled on that job. She let me sleep in a spare bedroom. Just about everyone tipped me. They liked seeing Check watching me work, thought it was funny. One man tipped Check, gave me ten dollars to buy him real dog food after he saw him eat table scraps. I explained that Check wasn't a real dog, but the man looked at me like I was touchy in the head when I said I didn't know they made food for dogs. Mama had fed the neighborhood dogs scraps from the table. So, I got wise to dog food, but that didn't curb Check's appetite for table scraps.

We needed more than food. I needed to travel fast and Check knew what I had on my mind, a car. The going price of a good used car was fifty dollars. A Buick was completely out of the picture, too high. The people who had a Buick didn't turn them loose so readily. While Check watched from the shadows, I bought our first car. It was from a private owner, a black 1946 Chevy Fleetwood four-door sedan. The knee action shocks were shot but the ride was heavenly anything above walking speed. I didn't think about having a driver's permit or license plates, not anything other than oil in the crankcase and gas in the tank. I had seen plenty of license plates in junkyards so that would be a place to get one. No problem not telling the man running the yard what I really wanted the plate for. I could always take fresh paint and change the year on the plate. That's what I did. Did everything to bring our sedan, the best car in the whole world, up to date. When it was completely worn out, that'd be okay because fifty dollars could buy another one . . . I'd just switch the forged license plates. Being mechanically inclined, I could fix most anything on a car. If it had gas and a spark, I could make it go. And if it didn't have a spark, I could fix that too.

Bugdaddy junked cars and I had helped. We'd started out using an ax to cut them up. Much later he bought a cutting torch. He always set fire to a car before we hacked it. I used to dream about who owned the old car and where it had traveled like the car was a person. I thought cutting up some of the cars was a sinful waste. I'd play behind the steering wheel as much as I could before Bugdaddy gave the order to set fire to it. I had burned a hundred cars and knew the ugly sight by memory. Some of the prettier ones with shiny paint saddened me a lot when they turned black with soot. I could've really used one of those cars after the Sacred Mountain.

Our newly bought car was a home for me, and a den for Check. This was a problem. If I worked away from the car to have traveling money, I had to deal with Check who wouldn't give up his den when I got back. If I stayed gone more than three days, I had to use fried chicken to get him out in order to gain repossession of the car. Once he was outside, I would jump in and then we became equal owners. I didn't have to worry about anyone stealing our car. To be safe, I kept it hidden away from the public eye.

Check always rode in the back but moved to the front seat when I got out. I never figured why he did that. Maybe that's where I came in. Whatever, Check could have figured it was the boss' seat. Filling the car with gas was okay because I would tell him to get his ass in the back seat and he would do it right away. More time away, about an hour, made new rules. I'd have to pay a toll to get him to move to the back and threatening wasn't one. If I didn't have a bribe, Check had to leave the car before I could take over. I couldn't just hand him something inside the car and get in or move to the back seat. Hell, no. He had to leave and give up the ownership from the outside. If I didn't have a bribe to offer, well, that was too bad. I had to wait for him to go pee. One time I didn't have any food for a bribe, but I pretended I did by holding out my hand. It worked that time but never again. He'd cock his nose up and take a whiff. That was it. No more tricking him. Either pay up or wait for His Highness to pee.

There was no self-service in the 50's. Nobody pumped gasoline into their car but me. Check would try to eat the windows out to get to the station attendant. While motoring, Check was sedated by the car's motion but as soon as I stopped he came to life, wary and aggressive.

We didn't have a radio that worked and, with Check fast asleep on the back seat, I would get bored sometimes singing and talking to myself. Boredom was okay as long as something wasn't breaking down like a busted radiator hose or a generator that quit charging. With the car rocking up and down because of bad shocks, the hum of the motion, all that had a tendency to make me sleepy. Nothing could help that but pull off the road, out of sight, and hunker down. With Check, I never worried about someone knocking me in the head. No, I worried instead about someone coming upon us and not being able to stop Check from eating them alive. When I left for work, I'd leave the front door propped open, remove the dome light so the battery wouldn't run down, and leave him a little dry dog food and water. But with one sniff he could find water within a mile. I never worried about having enough drinking water with Check around. I only worried about people he could hurt.

Chapter 16

We were in Wyoming cutting a good clip, about fifty-five miles per hour. The car was rocking, one tire thumping and the speedometer wobbling with a tick, tick, tick. Check was asleep in the back as usual and the sounds and motion from the rural road rocked me asleep behind the steering wheel. I woke up to saplings beating the windshield and thinking some monster was swallowing the car whole. The stop wasn't smooth. When I came to my senses, I looked behind and saw we had cut a neat tunnel from the highway about fifty feet deep into underbrush. Check's head was cut by the right windshield and dashboard on impact. He was okay other than it put him in a bad mood. The steering wheel stopped me from going into the windshield. I wasn't bleeding like Check, but my chest was bruised and one arm was hard to move about. I had my nap all right, and now I needed to figure out how we could get back on the highway. What would I do next? How bad was the car damaged? Would it run?

It was too late for all that, red light flashed behind us. Just plain bad luck. I didn't have a driver's license. My tags were forged and, of course, I didn't have a registration to the car. Also, I didn't have a way to identify myself to the authorities. I did have a bill of sale for the car but that would be of little value in a court of law. Two policemen were headed down the freshly made path toward our sedan. I had to come up with some kind of excuse in a matter of seconds as to why the car had run off the road.

Check caught a whiff of the approaching men and the chain of events began. Blood clouded Check's vision and that made matters worse. I jumped out the car and slammed the door behind me. Check's mood turned from real pissed off to insanely mad. He didn't like me closing him in. He was trapped. I tried to calm him down by chanting soft and low like you do a run away horse but he wasn't buying it. He got to growling so loud that he couldn't have heard a civil thought pass through in his mind. The closer the police officers came, the worse Check acted. Oh shit, what could be worse? I just knew I was going to jail and Check would be shot on sight. I ran around to the right front of the car and stabbed the tire with my knife. With a flat, I could say that's what drove me into the woods. Great move, but the strange sounds of air coming out the tire caused Check to go really nuts. He started biting the steering wheel, seats, door arm rests, even the windows. Blood from his head smeared on the glass and his huge teeth chomping at the glass was like a horror movie. If Check got out he would attack the first person he saw, even me. He wanted out and it looked like it wouldn't be long before he would eat a hole through the car, metal and all.

Before they got to our car, one policeman yelled, "Who owns this vehicle?" For a policeman, he was small for the job in those days. Police officers were usually my size and bigger. Before I could answer, the other policeman asked in disbelief, "What the hell is that?" Check was going from window to window gnashing his teeth and smearing blood everywhere.

I tried to act calm so Check would pick up on that. "That's my dog," I said nonchalantly like that was the way dogs were supposed to act.

"Goddamn! We might have to shoot that thing," one cop said to the other. He was afraid of dogs and Check was really putting on a show not letting up a bit, something like I had never seen before. With his performance, it looked like I was going to jail. Let's see your driver's license and registration. I had to be quick and cool, just like Frank would be. I said it was in the glove box on the dash and pretended I was going to open the door and get it.

"Don't open that door!" the frightened cop yelled and pointed at the wild thing. I didn't know what my next move would be. I wasn't a fool. I knew they were going to shoot Check. The officer went for his pistol and I yelled, "Please, Check's trapped in there, that's all. He's a nice dog. Give me a chance to settle him down."

The scared policeman took his pistol out the holster. I jumped in between him and the car. The other cop struck me from behind with his club. The blow on my shoulder took me down to my knees but I rose to defend Check. Life wasn't worth that much without Check and I would die trying to save him. The cop, who'd hit me, drew back his stick again when someone at the mouth of the tunnel yelled for him to stop. I looked over the shoulder of the policeman holding the gun to see who he was. Lands sakes, it was the biggest man I'd ever seen bounding down the path. He nodded at the cops like he knew them. Dear Moses, the man could have been the mythological Big Foot as far as I was concerned. His words really meant something to the two cops. He spoke and they listened real hard. "Gentlemen, I've got my wrecker. I'll just hook her up."

"We're not done here, Mr. Jeff," one cop complained.

"Okay, you can come to my shop for that. Get your things done there," the huge man said. He turned to me and asked me my name and if I had any money. I told him my name was Johnnyboy and that I had money on the hip. He grinned and I heaved a sigh of relief. He said his name was Jeff and, if he couldn't fix my car, he'd sell me another one of equal value. Maybe I wasn't going to jail right away but Check was still acting crazy like. I could just see him eating a way out and ruining everything. Mr. Jeff told the two policemen to meet us at his shop, that I would ride with him. I couldn't believe they took orders from Mr. Jeff even though he was the biggest man in the world. And the cops, they had guns too. The three men went back to the road together and I tried to get Check to calm down, but he wasn't buying any of it.

Mr. Jeff dragged the wrecker cable down the path toward our car. I had started to set Check free to run when I saw him and the two cops returning. I worried they'd cut a deal with Mr. Jeff to have my ass in jail, yet I didn't run. Mr. Jeff latched the cable hook to the car and spoke to the two police officers. "Gentlemen, he's going to ride with me and that's that." Then he added much louder, "Any problems?" They said no but their expressions didn't reflect that. They wanted me. I got a little afraid because I didn't know if Mr. Jeff was going to kill me. If he chose to, there wasn't a damn thing I could do to stop him. When men with guns feared Mr. Jeff that was a sign I should fear him too. After the two police officers left, Mr. Jeff turned to me and said for me to turn Check loose. He smiled and said he wasn't afraid of Check. I felt right then that Mr. Jeff knew a lot about dogs and that he was a nice man. I told Mr. Jeff to stand still because Check was wild some. I opened the door and Check came busting out by Mr. Jeff and me, sniffing and peeing on every bush in sight. Mr. Jeff talked to Check and I was shocked that Check liked it. Mr. Jeff knew better than to try to stroke Check, yet he showed lots of affection toward him. He talked to Check while he changed the front tire. As soon as Mr. Jeff stood back from the car, Check walked up and peed on the spare tire like he was telling Mr. Jeff his handiwork was okay and now it was time we were on our way.

    Mr. Jeff walked back to his truck to winch our car out. At the first sign of movement from the wrecker cable, I opened a door and Check dove in the front seat behind the wheel. I followed afoot as the car inched out backward. Check didn't seem to mind anything, me being out the car or the car going backward, but I still worried what was going to become of us.

Chapter 17

I got to know Mr. Jeff a little with the twenty-minute ride to his mechanic shop. Things had to move fast or I was going to jail. I leveled with him, telling him I only had a bill of sale for the car and nothing else. As for being honest, this was a major turning point in my life. Making the choice to be honest saved me, not just at that point in time but throughout. I guess the Sacred Mountain did that. Mr. Jeff said he didn't care what we didn't have, that Check and I looked like we needed a good meal. With that, I nearly cried. Mr. Jeff was in my corner. He said his wife Martha was the best cook in the world and for me to take a good look at him to know that. He looked well fed all right. He said Martha would want to fatten me up too. I laughed a bit when he said she wouldn't allow dogs in the house.

Everything was cool at that point, but I knew the two cops would be at his shop wanting to take me in. Check had most likely gone back to sleep without a worry, but his partner wasn't out of trouble yet. The decision to be straight with the big man paid off.

I used mister in front of Jeff's name just like the two cops did. I would have called him mister anyway after I saw him pull the tow cable like it was a piece of twine. If the winch locked, I imagined the cable would have surely snapped, given his strength and size. Jeff would always be Mr. Jeff to me. I didn't care what other people called him.

I told Mr. Jeff that Check didn't like the smell of men folk. He laughed and said Martha didn't like the smell of him until he had his bath evenings. I laughed too but got back to my concerns, which were I didn't want to go to jail, and I didn't want anything bad happening to Check. When I showed him my money, Mr. Jeff said I surely wasn't going to jail. I was his customer and he said he would deal with his cousins at the shop. He told me not to worry about my little ole poochy. "Johnnyboy," he said, "if you got money, then you can ride." What a relief that was to hear Mr. Jeff's honesty.

I felt like I had fallen asleep in hell only to wake up in heaven. To ride again was a joy and a source of freedom. Check and I fancied our car that way.

Mr. Jeff said I was real good with my license plates forgery, said he never would have noticed if I hadn't called attention to them. I felt proud. I told Mr. Jeff that I had a knack for certain things like music. I really wanted a radio in our car so I could keep up with the top ten Hit Parade songs. I loved the Andrew Sisters and Les Paul and Mary Ford when she sang *How High The Moon*. I liked Johnny Cash, songs like *I Walk The Line, Luther Played the Boogie* and *Big River*. Elvis was cool, too. He bellowed one out called *Hound Dog*. God almighty, I nearly jumped out of my skin the first time I heard that tune. Rock and roll was it, wonderful, nearly brand new. Check and I could sure use a radio. I needed to stay awake while he slept and the latest tunes could help.

When Mr. Jeff met the police back at his shop's parking lot, he scared me because I thought he might hand me over. They talked a good while with Mr. Jeff swinging his huge hands first this way and that way. The policemen didn't look none too happy when they returned to their patrol car. After they left, burning rubber off their tires, Mr. Jeff walked up to me and acted like he had done a day's work. He wiped his forehead and said, "Them ole boys want to know how you got down in the woods. They ain't seen your driver's license and they don't know if you ain't wanted by the law somewhere. I had to do a heap of talking to keep them from shooting your dog and locking you up."

He tried to hold a straight face but I had learned to read

faces much better by this time. He hid a smile with seriousness, and said he needed to know where I was from and where I was going. I didn't hesitate. I said I was going to Oklahoma to see a friend. Mr. Jeff could read faces too. He asked me how I got my money. I said I worked for it and showed him my hands, hands that were scarred and callused. He asked me about my last home-cooked meal. I told him I couldn't remember but I thought of Minna in New Orleans months ago. When he raised my T-shirt, my stomach was sunk in.

"Martha is gonna love to get a hold on you Johnnyboy," he said releasing my shirt.

Chapter 18

I really felt safe when Mr. Jeff dumped the antifreeze that was in a bucket. He told me antifreeze would kill dogs if they drank any amount. He sure knew a lot about dogs not to have one. Later I learned from Martha Mr. Jeff's dog had recently died of old age and he wasn't ready for another one just yet. I went off to myself and cried about that.

Out west, Martha was the most caring person I had met. She was a big lady, too. She saw my swollen shoulder as soon as I walked in, even before Mr. Jeff could tell her my name, and got upset that I was injured. I said it wasn't hurting me, but Mr. Jeff knew lying. He told her his cousin had hit me with a nightstick, and she told Mr. Jeff that his ass wasn't going to sit at her table for a month. Mr. Jeff said that was too much punishment for the crime, laughed, and said he was starving from the aroma coming from the kitchen, which was making his mouth water too. When she said for us to get washed up, Mr. Jeff laid his hand on my shoulder and I winced and went to the floor. He gave me a good look of concern. "I'm okay," I said, "just didn't expect that."

Martha announced Mr. Jeff was taking me to a doctor after we ate. Mr. Jeff told her it wasn't anything a doctor could do with a broken shoulder any better than him. That was fine with me. I wasn't going near a doctor or a hospital as long as I could fight. After we ate, Martha wrapped my arm in a sling. When she finished, she kissed me on the forehead in front of Mr. Jeff.

It was only a peck above the eyebrows but still it floored

me. I had never been kissed before and felt embarrassed to no end. Mr. Jeff, who could read faces better than me, thought it was funny and encouraged her to do it again. I was fixing to run out the house when Martha noted how red in the face I was and said she had a cousin she wanted me to meet. That frightened me as much as if she had pulled a gun on me. I didn't know anything about dating girls.

I only knew what I had seen Bugdaddy do. I liked girls and I fantasized having sex with them when I masturbated but I didn't know anything about the responsibilities that went along with sex. Performance was it and nothing of the mind other than lust. I looked much older than I was, coming onto fifteen, but I couldn't mention that for fear Martha and Mr. Jeff would have to do something about it. I held a straight red face, nodded that it would be nice to meet her cousin, and felt not one piece of guilt about my lying. I was trying to survive. Mr. Jeff tried to hide his grin. I guess he saw through me but knew how to play along with Martha's big idea. But I had to come to terms with the problem. I had been through a lot and being with a girl wouldn't kill me. Ignorant about love and sex, I told myself, "You can do it," and only worried I wouldn't misfire too soon and about how Check would act. The gray dog with a soul had the power to take me where I needed to go and keeping us together was my highest concern. What would he do with a woman at my side or under me? I guess I would soon find out as Martha reached for the telephone. *Oh, Moses, deliver me.*

Mr. Jeff saved me from jail. Martha fed and mended my shoulder. Gave me my first kiss, too. I couldn't leave on foot and I didn't want to be rude to two people who really liked me. They were about forty, which was very old to me, and didn't have any children. A dog, named Ring, had been their child and that's why Martha said Mr. Jeff took it so hard when Ring died. I liked it there with Martha and Mr. Jeff. One reason was they spoke my language. The chance of meeting someone who wasn't worried about using incorrect grammar meant the world to me. In school I was afraid to open my mouth because of that. Not around Martha and Mr. Jeff. Mr. Jeff wasn't a showoff person and Martha was relaxed. She had a Ph.D. in economics and Mr. Jeff didn't make it through the third grade. I didn't know the title of doctor came before a person's name that had a Ph.D. until a man came to their house on business. I asked Martha about her medical practice because she'd done such a good job on my shoulder. She just said I was a sweetie like her husband, Mr. Jeff. If it weren't for Check, I would have stayed with them and been their boy. They made me feel good about myself, and that was a rare thing after being beat down. Martha said I was very handsome. I didn't see myself as that. When I stood in front of a mirror, I saw someone different from what other people saw. A stranger stared back without a smile. But Martha never mentioned that I was screwed up in the head. She just made me feel good when I wasn't in the looking glass.

When Mr. Jeff asked me about things, I knew he did it out of concern and not just being nosey. I really looked up to him as a father type, someone I was proud of because of his patience. After three days with them I was settling down some, but the longing to ride with the gray dog and my many unanswered questions were making me antsy, especially when Check and I were alone. Those yellow eyes of Check's were like bullets passing through my soul, making me want to get on with life, to find out where we stood, who I was, and what my new name would be. My emotions were running high. I was torn between the love of Martha and Mr. Jeff and the unknown world that waited for Check and me just down the road and over the next hill. I needed to see Chief.

I told Mr. Jeff something was wrong with my head. He said something was wrong with everybody's head. Mr. Jeff had a way of smoothing things and keeping people calm like he'd done with his two cousins, even with Check and that was really smoothing things.

Mr. Jeff was fixing a car for me out of all the cars he had in his junkyard across the road from their house. Martha said that he had a gifted mind because he could fix anything broken on a car and, if he wanted to, could make a car from scratch just as easy as she could bake a cake. But I was impressed most with

Mr. Jeff's strength. While working on the car, Mr. Jeff asked me to bring him a bucket of bolts. It was a ten-quart water bucket half filled. I said it was heavy as I crossed his shop. Mr. Jeff said it wasn't much more than a cork. "Watch this," he said as he opened his huge hand inside the rim, spread his fingers like his hand was a top, and picked up the bucket waist high. He said that was a good test to see if he still had the right stuff. Mr. Jeff was very powerful. That's why Check respected him, displaying at times a willingness to let Mr. Jeff get within five feet of him.

While Mr. Jeff worked, Check hung around our old car, making sure no one messed with it. I knew he'd be on board front and center when it moved the first inch. Mr. Jeff said that Check loved that car as much as he loved me and I had to agree.

Chapter 19

Martha made arrangements for me to meet her cousin the second day I was there. No disrespect intended, but I can remember their dog's name, just not that girl's. To Martha, men weren't supposed to invest much value in a lady's looks, as it was the personality that mattered most of all, the brain. That's what was wrong with Martha, the Ph.D. thinking as Mr. Jeff called it. I had a type of thinking too, but didn't know if it had a name other than plain scared. I had worried myself nearly sick about if I could perform sexually and not given one thought about what could be said to a girl. The girl was plain as a left work boot and silent the whole time. She was so shy that Martha spoke for her, Mr. Jeff spoke for her and, if Check had been at the table, he would have spoken for her too. I never thought it would be over. I think Martha got worried that she would turn me against women if she kept pushing the union another minute. I heard Mr. Jeff say later that night, when they thought I was asleep, that my date could have bored a cactus into growing up over night and running away. I thought that was the funniest thing I had ever heard but it was true. Mr. Jeff said if that girl ever got married he wouldn't mind putting on a monkey suit, a tux, for the wedding. Martha answered he'd only said that because the odds were a million to one.

The time was drawing near for Check and I to be on our way, southbound to Oklahoma. Mr. Jeff test-drove my new car up and down the highway, a 1948 Chevy. I started thinking about a job because, after paying him, we'd be just about out of money. He pulled the car in front of the mechanic's shop where his darling wife Martha stood, holding onto my neck so I couldn't run from her. Dust rose from all four wheels. The sedan idled as smooth as Mr. Jeff's handy work. Martha said, "It's your car, Johnnyboy. We want you to have it."

"I can pay."

"We know that. We want to do this for you, that's all. Now don't be stubborn like Jeff." Then she hugged and kissed me again.

Mr. Jeff handed me the keys and told me to try her out. As soon as I opened the door, Check scooted by me like a bullet and over the front seat into the back. They laughed. We had already transferred my stuff from the old car. They laughed, but I cried and had to wait a minute before I could see to drive. This was my machine into a future. I wish it was just for joyriding like other teenagers but it wasn't. Mr. Jeff and Martha knew that. A home and a den, a way to find myself, that's what it was. Mr. Jeff stopped Martha who was going to comfort me as I wept. He knew if she hugged me at that time it would have been too much for him to take. I finally got myself together, waved and drove away with Martha and Mr. Jeff yelling for me to come back sometime. I watched them waving in the rearview mirror until they faded on the horizon. Check was asleep on the back seat. I said out loud to Check like he was listening that I loved them and we would return someday to Martha and Mr. Jeff's . . . but we never did.

Chapter 20

My faith restored in humanity, Check and I left Wyoming and headed south toward Oklahoma. I was going by the map in my head but things didn't look the same at a steady fast pace, 45 to 55 MPH, on the rural stretches. I think it was the vantage point behind the wheel that made me feel I wasn't always on the right roads. Like a lot of men, I wasn't much on asking where I was or how to get to some place like Oklahoma. Gas, tires, and oil to keep the car going were my concerns and a few mistakes off track wouldn't bother Check or me a whole lot. We were happy just to be riding the first few days.

I thought how great a job Mr. Jeff had done with the car. It didn't bounce when I hit dips like our last car did. It didn't smoke or rattle, but just like the last one the radio didn't work. The vacuum shift worked. I could drive with one hand without much trouble. My arm was still wrapped like I was a half-clothed mummy. Down the road a good piece from Mr. Jeff and Martha's, I used my pocketknife to cut myself loose, throwing the sling in the back seat where Check felt obliged to tear it to threads. As far as pain, I couldn't tell any difference. My shoulder still hurt whether I moved it or not. Time would heal that or like Mr. Jeff had said, "Johnnyboy, it'll get well before you get married." Without a radio, the sight of Check slinging the bandages around was welcome and funny. Of course he might get carried away and start on the car's interior. It had happened in our old car. He'd just get worked up and wouldn't know how to stop. But I figured I could calm him down, if that ever happened again, by pulling off the road and letting him out to pee.

After the bandages were shredded and pieces of lint had drifted past my face, into my nose and out the window, Check went to sleep. I was left with amusing myself while I drove along. I was a little jealous that Check could fall asleep so fast when the car moved but, when I stopped to sleep, he was all action, ready to make tracks. I told him if I ever got a radio, I'd play it so loud he wouldn't be able to sleep.

In the rural countryside, most gas stations were open business hours. If we wanted to make tracks at night, we had to top the tank with gas by five. In big towns there were a few all-night stations, but out west I didn't see a lot of big towns. Some communities looked like everybody cut their lights off and went to sleep right after dark. I'd get edgy when my tank was down to a fourth, anytime, day or night, but especially in the middle of the night and it was cold. It would only take one wrong move and we could be in trouble. I had to be smart. I had the same forged license plates and, of course, no driver's permit. We would pull far off the road and make camp at night, saving as much gas as we could to reach a gas station the next day.

When I slept, Check stayed vigilant. That's the way it was and those were the rules according to Check. Sometimes, just playing with him, I called him Rock Head. If he didn't want me to touch him after I tested ever so lightly, he would show his teeth or move to the back seat where I'd cuss him a little. He knew I didn't mean it when I cussed him because he could see right through me.

One time a car full of guys pulled up beside us wanting to race. When I refused, they yelled and cussed me and said they wanted to kick my ass. Check took this personal. He didn't want anyone but me to cuss around him. I had to stomp on the brakes because Check was going out the back window after them like he could walk on air. I pulled over to the side of the road and figured five of them and two of us would be a fair fight. Check did too. As soon as they saw Check and me and our willingness to get it on, they changed their minds about messing with us.

Only a fool would go up against the gray might with bulging muscles and eyes that told the outcome before it happened.

Check was all business. He could do things that reminded me he was a regular dog, even puppy like. But that wasn't always the case. I had given him a tennis ball for a toy and he took to it. He loved it for a few days all to himself. Then he wanted me to play with the ball too. He wanted me to try and take it back so he could show me how fast he was and who was the rightful owner. I'd tell him to give me a shot at the ball and he'd back away a little more and stand motionless. Then I'd flinch like I was going after the ball on the ground and in a flash he'd scoop it up into his mouth where it disappeared completely. I'd complain. "Hey, Check, give me more room. Back away!" Check would drop the wet tennis ball and put his front paw on it. He'd look at me to see if I was ready to risk my hand, which we both knew he could take off. With Check, I had to know the rules of the game. I'd say, "Come on." Back away a bit more. He liked teasing me and I liked him going after the ball when I faked a grab, his muzzle slamming together a fraction from my hand. The only way I could beat him was to say something like, "Who's that coming?" and point in a direction over his head with my other hand. The second he'd turn I'd go for the ball. It worked every time. He never got mad at me for doing that and I'd never take the chance without distracting him first. I'd put his ball down and the game would begin again. This went on a long time. When he got tired of playing our game he'd show his teeth, which meant my ball and I knew better than to flinch or fake it. We were partners and I loved him for making me feel we were. Chief had said I'd travel with a great power. Check was it and I felt blessed.

The Sacred Mountain was far behind us and we had driven through hill country much too long. In the headlights I spotted a new state sign, New Mexico. I was off course. We were supposed to be in Colorado, Kansas, then Oklahoma, not New Mexico.

"Got-damn-it, Check. I thought sure I was on the right road." Check got up, stretched himself, made a few turns on the back seat and went back down like he didn't care where we were. "Why does this kind of crap always happen? No, don't answer that. I can see it on your face, boy. You can just sleep through tomorrow. I don't care."

I was tired so we pulled well off the road to hide the car. I'd been driving hard and the smell of oil and gasoline along with the engine's heat filled the inside of the car after I stopped. It was a pleasant smell. I thought about seeing Chief and that made me want to crank it up again and move on, but that wasn't smart. I worried about all sorts of things like not having money for our next meal. If only I could be like Check. I guess he trusted me and knew somehow things would work out. Check lived by a different set of rules, yet he accepted a very flawed human being as his partner. My mind was turning and churning up things that had nothing to do with getting sleep. Why couldn't I learn from Check that I could only deal with things when they happened and face the fact that there wasn't nary a thing I could do about the past? Stay hidden as far as I could from everyone. That was a good rule, yet I broke it over and over, and he put up with me. I broke a lot of his rules too. He wanted me to stay on the Mountain but I was driven. I needed to tell Chief what happened there and that I had the great power looking over me. Why else was I in the middle of nowhere, lost?

I drank down a hot soft drink and opened the back door to our rolling den to let Check out to take care of business. My aching body said we'd driven a long ways. I was too tired to go any farther and Check needed to sniff around. Sometimes I'd say to him that we would stay hidden forever, that I'd follow his rules and become what the Great Spirit intended, wild and free. No tomorrows, only the moment. This was one of those nights I couldn't sleep because stuff like that was on my mind. I should have been in Oklahoma, not New Mexico. I hated restlessness. Check did too because he stayed away from the car longer than usual. When I thought about what could have happened here and there, I'd just slip into thinking about the future, a week ahead, even a day. Then I'd think about the people I'd met before Check, people who were good to me like Simon and Minna, Mr. Jeff and Martha. Minna had taken me in, fed me and wanted to give me her son's room. Why couldn't I have accepted what they wanted to give me, a home with love? What the hell drove me down the road? Something was wrong with my head. My teachers were right on some of that stuff. I could hear one say, "What's the matter with you? No one can do a thing with Johnnyboy. He's wild."

One good thing about being on the road was I didn't have to put on the charm to keep everybody happy. Oh, Moses, that was an exhausting job in school. When I ran out of charm, I used to fear I'd be put on display as an idiot in front of the whole classroom. I couldn't let that happen again. I'd stay hidden with Check forever and no one would ever see my face. With what I was given on the Mountain, maybe things would change. I was tired of being in suspense about what the rocks and the trees and even what the water had said. I needed to know if I might be put on display again, because if that happened, who knows what I would do.

Check finally returned. He stunk so bad it made me sick to my stomach. He'd been rolling in something dead to hide his scent.

"No, Check, I'm not proud of you one bit, you asshole. You can sleep outside tonight," I told him. But I didn't really mean it. Funny thing about smell, it wears off after a while. It's strong to a newcomer but a person can get use to it. I said, "Den, Check," and he jumped in the car in his usual fast speed.

"We'll go east to Kansas tomorrow, boy. I overshot Oklahoma. Don't worry, it's only a minor adjustment."

Inside the car I liked using my bedroll for a pillow when it wasn't cold. I'd sleep with my head on the passenger's side so I could rise up quickly behind the stirring wheel and make a fast get-away if needed. This night I put my head down a minute or two but the stink wouldn't let up. I tried burying my face in the bedroll. That didn't work either. One of us had to leave the car. "Check, is this an old hunting trick of yours?"

I thought long and hard about why man didn't hide his smell with stink. Maybe he doesn't need to anymore. It was plain that men hid other things, like not letting others know their real intentions, and I wondered if that had something to do with hunting for food and women. If some guy knew where the food was and brought plenty back to camp, he got the women. Instead of using stink and food, now it's money. Get the money so you can have everything and have as many brats as you please. Not much different than any other animal on earth. Is that what life is all about . . . exchanging hunting tricks and forgetting about the stink? Do men use cologne to hide their smell or to attract mates? Chief could answer these questions. No doubt.

"Check, you're going to get the hell out the car. I can't take the stink." When he jumped outside, I closed the door. "Leave," I said. "I've got the money in my pocket. You don't."

Chapter 21

The next morning we didn't mess around. I had learned that even numbered highways, ones that can be divided by two, run east and west and odd numbers run north and south. So we turned into the first major thoroughfare I saw with an even number, right into the morning sunlight, and headed east. It wasn't long before we entered Oklahoma. We spent the next day riding in and around the town of Alva, but we couldn't find Chief's hacienda. I didn't have his address but I remembered what his neighborhood looked like, his yard too, with a few junk pickups close to the side of the house. I knew he didn't live far from railroad tracks because I had heard freight trains come through. Frustrated, I decided to camp well outside of town and try again the next day.

Luck was with me the next morning. Just like a wild bird flying back to its last year's nesting site, I pulled our car in front of Chief's. I told Check to stay put with the car. Neighbors stared from windows and doors. I felt like I was a target and that a bullet could pass through my body at anytime. I climbed the one-step front stoop of Chief's, rapped on the door, and waited and waited. No one answered. Standing on the outside, I started having doubts that I was at the right house. I leaned close to a window and peeped inside. This was the house all right, but Chief wasn't home or he would have answered the door. What to do? I couldn't stand there all day, so I went back to the sedan.

"Check, we'd better move on and try back later." I looked

around. A few dark-haired children playing in a yard two doors down were ordered inside. Maybe their parents thought I was a bill collector. I felt like trouble for them, knowing that Check and I were not welcome. But so be it. I needed answers, a new name. Chief was the only person who could help explain those things that happened to me on the Sacred Mountain, what they meant. I had crossed hell to get to his house and I'd go through hell again to get what I wanted.

"We'll come back tonight, I yelled. Mess with us if you want. Hey, Check, we'll give them a fight, huh." I drove away with dark eyes watching us from dilapidated houses. I have a sense for this sort of thing and knew, if I hung around, something bad would happen.

That night I drove back into the neighborhood soon after dark. Chief still wasn't there. The next day I went back again and started knocking on doors. I knew his neighbors were home but they wouldn't answer. After a few houses, I got the picture. I thought if they were real scared of me, they would have called the police by now. No, that wasn't it. They just didn't like me because I wasn't in their clan. I yelled again, "I need to see the man who lives over there," and pointed to Chief's house. After a long time standing in my tracks, a storm door creaked and an old woman nearly as round as she was tall came out a house where three kids had been playing in the front yard earlier. She walked up to me without expression. I couldn't tell if she meant me harm or was bringing me water for thirst. She held a glass the size of a flower vase. She strolled through her yard, then the gate, and into the dusty dirt lane. She stood two feet in front of me and held a blank face, one completely empty, not one sign of expression. I was uneasy. She must have known I read faces because she wasn't giving up a thing.

"I'm looking for Chief, the man who lives in that house."

In broken English she said he wasn't home so I asked where he was and she pointed over my shoulder in a westerly direction. I asked was he out west on spiritual business and she hissed with a spurt of breath between tight lips like I had asked about a town drunk. Then she laughed like I'd asked her something crazy.

Maybe she misunderstood me. I could feel everyone watching us from protected barriers. This wasn't a laughing matter. The gray power inside the sedan was stirring and I needed answers. "How long will he be gone?" I asked. She didn't know. I told her Chief called me Timekeeper, hoping that he had mentioned me in a favorable way. She smiled and pointed over my shoulder again. I felt like a ton of weight had been taken off my back. She meant me no harm.

As she looked at my hair, there were things going on in my head I didn't want to give up. I was tired of being different. I wanted my hair to be straight, long and jet-black like everyone else around me. I was sick of being rejected. I longed for a connection with a group of people, but I was always alone, always until Check had come along. Check watched for my movements. One wrong move and he'd be out the window and ready to fight.

"Lady, where did Chief go," I asked, looking in the direction she had pointed.

She yelled in her tongue back toward her house and someone inside with a feminine voice answered. She turned back to me without expression and said, "Arizona. Be back in two moons."

"Two moons." I thought a second. "That's two months," I exploded. My heart went to my throat. What was I going to do for two moons? I hadn't counted on anything like that. I couldn't wait that long to find out about my visions. I had to get things done. This was a bad dream, something like being alone in the morgue with dead people. She didn't know how much I needed to see Chief . . . about spiritual matters. Her face changed to compassion but it was the wrong thing because no one could help me but a shaman. She stood and admired my curly sun-bleached hair and that led to anger. I could feel heat rush over me. "This can't be happening," I shouted. "Isn't there anyone here that can help me find Chief?" Her eyes moved from my hair and met mine for the first time. I knew before she said a word what she was going to do. I stood helpless and absorbed the inevitable while whispering to myself, "Hell no, this ain't real."

The round lady raised her hand and pointed over my shoulder. I felt abandoned once more. I could fall spell to a Johnnyboy fit and release my anger, but that would mean someone would call the police and me going to jail. Everyone in the village would think I was a crazy man, breaking up stuff, anything I could get my hands on. I felt the urge but I stayed glued together, knowing I had the power riding with me. Check was my ticket to a future. Angry, I said the first thing that came to mind, something crazy to act the part. "Round-woman, do you know God?" She released my eyes and swept her hands, speaking in sign. She moved them all about as though she was gathering up the neighborhood, showing me where the Great Spirit dwelled.

"He's all around," I said, louder and with much force. I'd lost it and anything could come from my mouth.

"Round-woman, tell Him I said to go to hell." She pointed over my shoulder again toward the western mountains. It didn't bother me as before. I looked around for someone else to speak with. Curtains fell back in place and no one would show themselves. It was Round-woman and nobody else. *Okay, I'll go to Arizona, damn-it. I'll find Chief.*

Never mind the needle in the haystack crap. I had Check. He had the nose, the eyes and the heart to find Chief. He looked after me and I didn't have to ask. No wonder he hated the smell of mankind. At that moment, I did too. What a sorry lot of animals we were and it was me I hated most . . . the illiterate fool. I needed to deflect my feelings so I called on the gray dog. "Hey, Check." His head popped out the back window of our car. I wanted to say for everyone to hear, "Take a good look at Check, good neighbors. That's my dog." I wanted to say, "Hey y'all, I didn't come this far to chicken out."

I didn't know how far Arizona was and didn't care because I had Check and we would go there and find Chief even if we had to walk.

How about that, Moses? God thought something of you but He damned me from the beginning. Can't read, can fight. Something is wrong with my head and the minute I get close to fixing it, something goes wrong. Why didn't I just stay on the Sacred Mountain? In time I'd learn what my dreams meant. Hell no, I want everything right now.

Round-woman went back to her house and left me standing in the dirt lane. If it hadn't been for Check waiting in the sedan like a gentleman, I don't know what I'd have done. I was so angry with myself I wanted to die right there on the spot. I hated the God that had made me. I wanted to unleash the gray power and destroy the poverty-stricken neighborhood, wanted the frightened eyes hiding behind thin walls to scatter like rats from a struck corncrib. *Got-damn Johnnyboy, got-damn this clan and got-damn Moses too.*

That's how I felt. I counted my folding money without taking the first step back to our car. We had over thirty dollars, which would take us long and far, maybe to Arizona or hell, I didn't know which. But at that instant I needed a place to hide, a place where I could gather my senses. I looked toward the hills where the Round-woman had pointed and decided we would go there and stay a while. Maybe I could figure out my visions there. How crazy a thing to try . . . but nothing could be crazier than my life.

I called to Check that we would travel but kept where we were headed to myself, west to the hills and then onward to Arizona. I looked at Chief's hacienda. Then I rested my head on the wheel and something came to me. It was like a foolish dream, the kind that makes no sense. I was standing before a crowd of people and it didn't bother me. Being in front of a group of people had been one of my greatest fears. I was fantasizing I wasn't afraid, the aftereffect of the mescal?

"Check, let's get moving." I started the engine and felt lost except for the forward motion of first gear, then second gear and then third, driving speeds around a half-hundred.

Chapter 22

We went to the hills in the west, the ones Round-woman had pointed out, and made camp far away from everyone. Check got excited because he thought we would hunt and be natural. But I needed to think, to make sure I was doing the right thing, looking for Chief in a vastness of strange land. Usually I made my mind up in a snap but I was near exhaustion. Not tired of the road, but tired mentally. Tired of weaving the modern world.

Something had happened in my head and I didn't know how to relate to it. I could see colors like never before. The buttons did that. I appreciated the colors. Since the Sacred Mountain, doors had opened to me and, if I chose, I could cross the threshold and enter a new forest, a new world, a modern world. I started putting pieces together; the stuff teachers had tried to force on me. Now instead of rejecting them, they made sense and I saw value for the first time. The teachers had been trying to help me, for God's sake. I couldn't see that before, but now in our campsite that came to me. If I'd learned to read I wouldn't face a wasted life. From the mescal buttons, I would try again. I might be ignorant but I was never stupid. I'd learn about this reading world my teachers and even Chief talked about and become someone of high esteem. They would never make fun of me again.

Check was whole and didn't have problems like mine. He just needed a partner and being in the hills away from it all did him a world of good. It wasn't all that great for me because my mind wouldn't stop stirring. And now I had to hide out and kill time for two months. That proved impossible. I stayed in the hills as long as I could, about two days.

Two months is a lifetime when you're a teenager and on the road. But we could get back to Chief's hacienda. I had proved that. And that was a comfort beyond measure.

Check knew the value of the car for what it was, a rolling den for the journey of life. If it moved one inch or five miles, the desire to ride was the same. The car's motion sedated him into a calm, the kind I needed. All he needed was food and a pan of water. He could hold his pee all day if we were driving to some place. I'd learned from him the value of moving on. Being really pissed off about my illiteracy and Chief not being home would let up as soon as we were back on the road. I would be covering new ground heading west and that was the welcomed adventure Check and I both needed. I had learned to read some road signs and billboard advertisements. Comic books helped with reading the most. Words with pictures made it easer to understand.

We left our hideout and covered some long miles west. Close to the state of Texas, signs started popping up at road crossings. Texas would be interesting, I thought, so we made a turn and headed south until dark.

Chapter 23

As daylight faded into darkness, Texas looked the same as Oklahoma. We found a place to pull off for the night. It was an old dirt road, mostly overgrown by brush, but tire ruts guided us far enough away from the paved road where the police patrolled.

Check came to life because of brush sweeping the underside of the car. That let him know a campsite was near. Not wanting to get stuck, I watched carefully for holes and deep ruts. We kept going until finding a big house up ahead. Following the dirt lane, we came to a small circle that looked like it was made long ago, maybe by horse and wagon. I made a U-turn and faced us back out. I stopped the car and got out, Check clipping at my heels. The stars were bright and the moon looked like a golden brown pie just above the horizon, brightening more and more as it rose. Stretching and looking around, I saw we had parked near what appeared to be an old abandoned farmhouse. A windmill tower was nearby, the blades in a heap on the ground. My attention turned to the house, thinking it would be fun to go through it, but I needed more light than the moon to do that. The occasional puff of wind would have blown out our oil lamp so I had to wait until morning to explore. That was the safe thing to do.

I had gotten a fascination with oil lamps from Frank's mama who showed me how to take care of them, trim a wick and wash the chimney, stuff like that. Oil lamps will give lifesaving light when everything else fails. In rural settings most everyone had trash piles in the back of their houses. In one trash heap, Check and I came across a very nice oil lamp that I kept in the trunk of the car, wrapped in rags so it wouldn't get broken.

Our lamp gave off plenty of light. I'd open the glove box and rest the lamp on the lid. It was great with Check around. I could watch his expressions while telling him about the old days when Bugdaddy would come looking for me. When I got to the part where I'd holler, acting like I was in pain, Check was wide-eyed, ready to fight. I would laugh and get on a subject that settled him down, something like food we wanted, like steak that didn't take two rows of teeth to chew. When he was calm, I wanted to pet him. Sometimes I would try but he would show me his fangs and the many white soldiers standing guard in-between them. He didn't like me putting hands on him, but I could read his face. He loved me as much as I loved him. No one could fool me when it came to reading faces, especially Check's.

I decided to play and try to pet him. My hand coming closer only made him pissed off. With his awesome teeth shining in the lamp glow, he licked his nose, allowing him to smell me better, and growled his warning. He was telling me I wasn't at liberty to touch him this night. He seemed to be saying, "I'll fight to the death to save you from our enemies, but lay off the gray fur, Johnnyboy, or you'll pay with blood." I laughed and went back to talking about the old days, just to watch him revert to his old self. He'd watch me like I was a TV. In the back of my mind though I always hoped that some day I could pet Check and hug him around the neck. Under the lamplight, the entertainment was good enough until sleep hit and I'd blow out the light.

Daylight woke us. Now we would go through the house and its trash pile to hunt for treasures. The dumping ground was probably out back somewhere close by.

The house was a mansion much bigger than I'd thought. It was as big as some of the old hotels I had seen out west, three stories and deeper than I had imagined. We parked at the side of the building. After peeing on the bushes, Check was ready to follow me to wherever. No one was around or he'd be acting cautious and fly out of sight.

The windows were boarded-up. The weatherboards were weathered gray, the white paint long since gone. Blowing sand had cut away the paint in most places except the overhanging soffit. In front, the porch ran the entire length with some of the pickets missing from the hand railing. Looking up the eight or so steps to the porch, I saw that the front door was big and matched the structure's size. Check's toenails clicked as he climbed the steps in front of me onto the long porch. Ten feet down the porch to my left was a red and blue hobbyhorse that had once shone in deep rich colors but was now faded to near nothing. It cocked to one side because of a missing rocker. Farther down the porch were breaks in the flooring. A breeze suddenly came up and I flinched when an old welcome sign decided to break one of its chains and bang against the front wall just above my head.

I looked at Check, but nothing had changed. He was ready to go in. Someone cared enough to board up the windows but not enough to keep things up. Guess they didn't want vandals messing around. I looked at the once spacious yard and knew we were the only ones to visit in a long time. I turned the front door handle and the door creaked open. Check zipped by so he would be the first to cross the threshold. As soon as the door was opened wide enough, he was in and out of sight. Stairs were straight ahead, and big rooms were to the right and left. Check came from the one to the left. Wanting to do something new, he climbed the steps. I listened to the hollow sounds of empty walls as he went to the top. Any small game in the house would soon be found by gray, the awesome hunter.

The homestead must have really been something in its day. Nothing of use was left in the many rooms, only broken-down chests with missing drawers and scattered papers everywhere. On the top floor, peeping through the cracks between boarded windows, I could see for miles. The house faced the main road that was maybe only a mile away, but in Big Sky Country distance could fool me. The road was far enough away to feel safe and that's what mattered. Now the house could be whatever I wanted it to be. It was my house and we could stay a while if we pleased.

Check was nosey. Every time I went into a room, I could see he had been ahead of me. His paw prints in the dust showed he had entered and left for another. On the third floor at one end was a big room with windows facing three sides. That would be mine. I was the man of the house. Only I had to share it with the gray dog. Wealth has its privileges and Check could be the butler. That was make-believe and fun, but the tin roof overhead was real. Never mind room service. Check and I were satisfied with an able roof. We would stay for the day searching for treasures, sleep peacefully that night and stay another day because it felt good being there. One more night and all would be grand.

The next night, I would find something I didn't bargain for . . . the overseer of my handsome mansion.

CHAPTER 24

Relaxing with a cigarette, I peered out the master bedroom window. I wasn't looking for anything special, just having a smoke before bedding down. Suddenly, between two outbuildings, I saw embers of someone smoking too. My heart went to my throat. We were cornered. Someone was watching us. It was too late to blow out the oil lamp. This was the first time I'd been caught off guard without any warning from my new butler, Check. I could never sleep now.

Check picked up on my stress. "Someone's out back," I whispered. Check knew it too because the hair stood up on the ridge of his back and his body stiffened. I figured it wasn't the law and it wasn't a person hiding. Hell, whoever it was stood in the moon's glow having a smoke. A bad person who wanted to do us harm would never show himself. I ran down the steps as quietly as I could but, before I got to the next floor, Check passed me. When I got outside, Check had searched around our car for a scent. Nothing had been touched, so I put Check inside the car with a window down. He would stay put as long as I didn't yell for help.

I circled close to the building, my back close to the wall. I didn't have a plan. I just had to face whoever was out there. When I got to the last corner, I paused. My pulse was pounding in my ears. I was afraid because I didn't know how many had cornered us. It felt a little better not being trapped inside, but the pounding wouldn't let up. I told myself that Check would be here if I called. He was most likely near by anyway, hidden in a shadow. He'll protect me. *Oh, Moses, please don't let it be a mob of men wanting to lynch me like a criminal.*

I thought about that and decided to flank where I saw the fire. I did and surprised a lone man still puffing away. I hadn't meant to startle him but in the night there's not much else can happen between two strangers. Better him than me.

"Looking for someone, mister," I asked as peacefully as I could.

"Oh, you frightened me," he said, taking in a deep breath.

"I didn't mean to, mister."

I could hear Check behind sagebrush not more than ten feet away ready to charge the stranger with one distressful word from me. Because of that I was certain there was no one else around. I knew how it felt to be outnumbered and scared. I didn't want the stranger feeling that way. A scared person can be dangerous. They can hurt you.

"My name's Billy," I said peacefully. "I was using the big house for a place to sleep. Does it belong to you?"

"Yes it does," he said peacefully as well. "My name is Peter, but you may call me Pete." He stuck out his hand for me to shake.

Peter said he'd seen my lamplight in his grandparent's master bedroom. I told him about Check being close and couldn't shake his hand for fear of him attacking.

"Where is he," he asked, thinking Check was a man and would show himself like a gentleman. I said that he was a dog in the brush and that was the way he was. Pete said, "Okay." Unless Pete had a gun, I wasn't worried.

Pete was lanky and dragged one foot as he walked over to me. Maybe he'd had a stroke. I lit a smoke and could see his eyes were dark brown, kind and his skin was wrinkled deep. The crow's feet around his eyes had connected to his cheeks making them look like tiny dry river beds running down his face. He moved a little too fast for Check who sprang from the bush and got between me and Pete, ready to take charge. I yelled for Pete to stop jerking around so I could get Check under control. Pete was cool and understood, but I was still a little uneasy about him, even if he was old and friendly. I trusted only Check's judgment and this was at night. I figured we could talk a while near the house by my car. We walked around the building and I settled down so Check would pick up on that.

"Pete, we stayed last night in the old house," I said, to feel him out.

"Yes, I saw your light. You're not from these parts," he said in the same tone. He pointed toward our car. "Montana plates."

"That's right." I felt proud I'd done a good job on the plates. I told Pete we were just passing through and would be moving on as soon as I got packed up.

"What's your hurry? I don't get much company these days," he said.

I had two months to kill, so I said we weren't in a hurry. Pete invited me to his ranch house. He pointed and I didn't see anything but, with Check watching, I could play along. Without any warning, Pete turned and started walking away. I hollered, "Hey, how about we take my car?" He said for me to leave it and bring my keys. No one would mess with it.

I followed, not knowing what I would see. The land was foreign like walking on the moon. Pete's house lonely. Inside, the foyer had pictures hanging of his family, mostly from Europe. An old hand-painted oval picture of his great-great grandparents was the centerpiece hung among pictures of fancy framed deceased family members. I asked if they were royalty. Pete paused with that. I figured he was trying to figure me out to see if I was serious. He said no and continued through a door that led to the rest of the house. My jaw dropped when he lit an oil lamp and my eyes adjusted to the light. Every available wall space was covered with books. The room was dark because even the windows were covered over with books. Without the oil lamp, I'd bet I couldn't tell if it was day or night in the house once I'd gotten past the small entrance of pictures. I was in shock. Pete had more books than the Glen Allen School library. I said something like, "Holy cow," and started to touch some leather-covered books. Pete got nervous. He said not to touch them without gloves because they were extremely valuable.

What a knockout that was. I didn't know a book could be worth raising your voice over but, when he said he could buy a new car for the price of one book, I stood up straight and took notice. I said I couldn't imagine anyone paying more than a dollar fifty cents for a stupid book. And I was the guy who had just followed Chief's advice to find the Sacred Mountain. But the kind of money Pete had invested in a house of books was beyond my way of thinking, anything I could imagine.

Everyone I knew saved everything because they couldn't afford to throw it away. Pete threw everything away to make room for his beloved books. Nothing else mattered to him. He was very smart but also very strange. He was born wealthy and expanding his mind was his life's work. It didn't take but a day to see that he had plenty of book sense. He figured out things before scientists did because he put this to that like mixing up a cake and came up with answers. He said he loved other people's minds because they were like worlds in themselves. Knowing Check like I did, I had to agree. When he asked me crazy questions about the masters, the great philosophers, at first I thought he was talking about slavery. I told him I knew Chicken Bone's friend Herman who was born a slave. He just looked at me and studied my face to see if I were for real.

I said that my people were always poor as church mice and books were for folks with a lot of time on their hands. He laughed, showing brown smoke stained teeth.

Pete liked me right away. He said I was honest and kept things on my sleeve. He said his wife had died years earlier and, instead of saying how sorry I was about that, I told him he did right by living a simple life and getting smarter.

"You can trace your family way back," I said, pointing to his ancestors' pictures in the hallway. I bet they were all smart, but they'd never seen what Check and I had seen in America and Canada. Pete said long ago some of his kin had headed big institutions like colleges in Europe. That didn't mean spit to me. You'd think it would have bothered him when I asked stupid questions like, "What's a dean?" but he liked me asking so he could show off how smart he was. Pete liked telling me about smart people and interesting subjects in the books that covered his walls, and I liked listening. How could a man remember so much? He could recite long sentences before he picked up a book. Damn, I was impressed. Him being book smart was one thing I couldn't get over because my mind didn't work that way. I told him I was like my best friend, Frank, and I had all the damn education I needed. I didn't know Pete good enough to tell him that something was wrong in my head and that Chief was fixing to bring it all to light in the old Indian ways. I didn't mention mescal buttons either because Chief had said it was against the white man's law to do the drug, and Pete was a white man for sure, white as a ghost. He drank a lot of wine and shared lots of his smarts with me. I never had much wine before and got tipsy a few times, but it wasn't anything close to the buttons I ate.

In Texas, I'd come across hog heaven and stayed longer than I'd planned. Pete couldn't do anything with his hands so he paid me very well for my skills in repairing what needed fixing around his place. Check wasn't too happy though. He didn't like being away from our car and refused to come in the house at any time. He didn't like the smell of books, and who was I to fault him. I slept on a throw-down pallet while Check slept outside against the front door. Sometimes I would fall asleep by the fireplace while Pete read aloud in a rocking chair. That's where he slept most of the time.

I taught Pete about sardines and he showed me how to grill outside, Texas style. He was impressed with how I got things done around the ranch. When he used words like efficient, I had to ask if that was good or bad. I wasn't stupid but no one I knew used words like Pete did. He was very cool with that.

"You can fix anything broken," he'd say, "and not think twice about it." I told him I could even fix things while daydreaming about something else a million miles away.

Check peed on every bush, post and corner of the house. I think he was trying to show Pete how smart he was, but

Pete didn't know about insmelligence and I didn't bother to tell him. I was too busy working and having fun listening to Pete read about smart people. Pete would walk around reading aloud, stepping this way and that way like he was on a stage performing for a big crowd. What a sight. I thought he was from another planet because he could become the person in the book he was reading. Sometimes he'd act out all the characters, swinging a sword and then holding the back of his hand to his forehead like a woman suffering, ready to faint from something somebody had said. Him acting out the characters got Check's attention too. Pete was so good at this Check thought he'd become another man. Check would lift his head and take in a whiff of Pete to make sure it was still him. And when Pete got to yelling, I'd have to tell Check it was only Pete playing the part in the book. With the loud scenes, Check bristled, ready to take Pete on in a fight. All this was fun for me but confusing to Check who couldn't weed through what was going on. I didn't know how much fun could come from a book until Pete showed me. He was someone to look up to. He said I was very smart and meant it too. At first I didn't believe him but I wanted to. That coming from him made me swell with pride. I think Check was a little jealous.

There are no words to explain what Pete did for me. I didn't know how much I disliked myself because I had done so poorly in school. Pete turned that around when he convinced me that I was smart, even better than Frank. In my wildest dreams, I couldn't imagine anyone saying that about me, especially someone like Pete, the smartest man in the whole world. He said for someone who couldn't read I had done amazing things. Damn, that made me feel great. At the time I didn't have a clue that Pete had opened a door of opportunity for me. It just felt good and that was new.

Pete made me a keyhole gadget from a piece of cardboard. He cut a slit big enough to only see a few words at a time in a sentence. He said my mind moved so fast I couldn't stay focused on one line when there were so many on a page. He said I had an overactive brain. I didn't argue with him because he had me feeling so good about myself.

Because I was having lots of fun, I stayed a good while at Pete's house, more than any one place so far. After two weeks of him reading aloud and me reading in the evenings with the undivided help from Pete, Check was ready to go. Check didn't care that I had learned to sound out some words. He didn't care that I was reading, but Pete damn sure cared a whole lot. You'd think I became one of Pete's priceless books. I had to swear before God that I would continue to read to make Pete happy. Pete said some day I would enjoy a book like he did, but I thought he was foolish about that.

Check and I could ride in style because Pete had paid me a couple hundred dollars for my work on his house, enough money to buy four old cars if need be. We had enough money to last us three months if we were careful. Now we could hold out in the hills because the trunk of the sedan would be filled with supplies.

Pete was more than a good man. He tried to pay me more for my work than I was worth. I said, "No indeed." We laughed because I used indeed in a sentence, one of the words he taught me. I promised him that Check and I would be back for more reading lessons, and I really meant it. I liked learning about the great philosophers even though I didn't have a clue what the hell they were about. But Check was anxious to leave and something in me still needed fixing. Only Chief could do that. With our newly earned wealth, I wouldn't worry about food and Check could always find water no matter where. But I was pulled in two directions. One was staying at Pete's getting smart and the other was finding Chief to get my new name, new life. As Pete shook my hand goodbye, I patted my back pocket that held the big dollars and knew another pocket held thirty dollars more. We had a roof over our heads with the sedan and it was there, untouched, at the big house when we returned.

Check got in the car first and didn't show any signs of not wanting me to have my share of the front seat. He was ready to travel. Check didn't give a happy damn about a house of books but he knew the value of the journey. He was my kind of dog and he was asleep before I got back on the main road. We were west bound to Arizona to find mescal and perhaps Chief, if I had enough faith and good luck. I could trip again on the drug and find out all the things I needed to know about my messed up head. Something had happened to me at Pete's, my attitude toward books, but I thought I needed something more. Pete made me understand that books were valuable for the things they can give you. He said it took a lot of work to write one and the guy who wrote it had something to say for all times. For the life of me, I could see clearly what Pete had done. He had planted a seed of thought about reading. By God, I wanted the things Pete had, the pleasure of a great book waiting for me at the end of a long day. I wanted to have fun like he did, experiencing a person with pain, pleasure, and passion for this and that and all coming from a got-damn book.

What the hell am I thinking about? I'm a freeborn man, ready to have the new name coming to me. Hell no, I don't have time for books right now. Check is ready to roll and my hands will sweat from holding the wheel. Get your ass down the road, Johnnyboy. Come to your senses. Books, what a stupid ass I am.

Driving away, it never occurred to me how we came to Pete's house, that I needed to remember the route through a field of sagebrush and junipers somewhere in the Texas panhandle. Months later when I returned, I looked for him and the big house in Texas but to no avail. The big house had led the way to Pete's rancher. I remembered the smells in the big house, my lamp as I trimmed the wick and the dust that stirred when I flung open my bedroll and let it fall on the floor. Check had watched me light a smoke, which had a pleasant aroma. I guess he wondered why I'd never offered him any. Check and I knew the big house was safe because we were alone, and I was the master even if it was only for one night. Check had played the part of butler and I had spoken out one side of my mouth like I was a big shot. Check liked every thing I said.

I still dream about all that happened in Texas. I always go to the big house first for a good night's sleep knowing my friend, Check, will be standing watch over me and hoping I'll wake up soon to play. It's a good dream because I know I will see Pete the next night and his house of books. Again, while Check hangs out in the shadows of Pete's rancher, Pete and I will laugh and learn the educated ways of this world. And, sadly, again it will come time to leave. The golden eyes of Check stare at me. To relive this, even in a dream, becomes a sweet burden to endure, something like the mythological man, Sisyphus, had to do.

I don't understand anymore now about the man pushing a stone uphill, or life, for that matter, than I did then. I wish I could have found Pete one more time. Nineteen fifty-nine was a long time ago and Texas far away. But my mind is at peace because Check and I made tracks in Texas in a big house and around a house of books. Chief had said, "There is meaning in everyone we meet." I couldn't agree more.

After I left Pete's ranch and was many miles down the road, I had a strange feeling in the pit of my stomach. It dawned on me that Pete was part of Chief's vision, his prediction. How could I have missed that? Chief had said we would meet and part company too soon. I left Pete and the house of books and I grew to regret not staying longer. Pete was studying to find out what was wrong with my head, why I didn't cotton to reading. He said there was a reason. Pete looked beyond me not needing books and saw the good in me. That's what amazes me to no end. He said if I would stay a little longer he could help me, as a doctor would do. Like the journey of life, you go through one time, and Pete and I met and parted. But just like old Chicken Bone, I will keep a piece of Pete in my heart forever.

Chapter 25

A day later we were deep into New Mexico. Check got restless in the high desert wind. I thought he was worried about something sneaking up on us and not hearing it, but that wasn't it. He would raise his nose and sniff while his eyes searched frantically. Later I learned from mescal what made him antsy, spirits riding the air currents. You have to be close to your soul to know and see stuff like that. I used to think about a person's soul, where it goes when he dies. People who are dying have that far off look in their eyes because they see spirits, things never seen before. Check lived close to the edge of the doorway to life and death. He saw something in me on that matter and that's why he took up with me and nobody else. He would give me that far away look sometimes because he was looking into my soul. He knew everything about me so I didn't try to hide things from him like I did everybody else.

We were equals. Folks didn't understand that. They were used to a man being boss over his pet. Check would never be a pet. He was something special like a person who could do magic. With a person, I'd know it was a trick but Check's magic wasn't. I could never find words for the gray dog's gifts. When I was ever in doubt about what to do next, one look at Check fixed that. *Move on down the road, Johnnyboy. Get your ass a moving.*

Check didn't choose me because I had a good nose or any great hunting skill. He chose me because I was like the spirits passing our campsite in an endless search for cracks and crevices to rest peacefully in. I didn't know then that you only have a short time together here and that you should make the best of it. In my youth, life was forever. I didn't bother reading the signs like Check did. He was wiser to that. I'd fight up front before my opponent had a chance to hit me. Check would drop out of sight and only return if someone wanted to do me harm. Like the spirits in the wind, the bad guy never knew Check was there until it was too late. My job was stopping Check from finishing him off and sending him on to the next world. Some dumb men didn't know how to play dead and Check would rip flesh until he thought the threat was over. One time two bums tried to rob me, and Check thought they were going to kill me. He did them in real bad. I did what I could to stop Check but he wouldn't take orders at times like that. I would be yelling at my enemies to stay still. Check would stop but not until they played dead. One time a big man cried from the pain Check inflicted on him and I said crying wouldn't do him any good. He had to be still. Christian folks called it, "Putting the fear of God in a man," but I knew Check was taking them close to the spirit world. He wanted them to see what he saw and for them to find order in a short life here in this old world. One thing they learned for sure when it came to fighting, Check meant business.

The ladies saw something about me they wanted, but I was too young for that. The love of the gray dog was all I needed. Check would help me search for Chief and not complain one time like I'm sure the young girls would have. I'd never worry about a beating again as long as Check was alive. That was a great feeling and no sweet young lady could give me that.

Near the base of the mountain we made camp. That night Check's golden eyes flashed their black wetness as our fire whipped like a flag from the wind. Spirits roamed. Some spoke to Check when they went by. He would let them know by sitting bolt upright that he understood their place and would soon be following them someday in the endless search. He was here to watch over a lost soul's well being. Check knew his task and he would be patient until it was over and I had an honorable name. I would be treated with respect because Check would see to that with his life. I stirred our campfire with a stick. Embers rode with the spirits and faded in the dead ones hand as they clasped the sparks for fun. Check liked it when I played like that. He knew playing was the right thing to do until we got hungry and then we ate, face close to the food.

"Check, the Sacred Mountain opened up my head to things I don't understand. You could tell me about them . . . but I know that's not how it's done. You've given me so much, and I don't have that right to be asking for something you ain't supposed to give."

I messed with the fire to set free the sparks. "Don't worry, Check, we'll see Chief and he'll take care of all that. He'll have a fit when he sees you, but he'll give me my new name. Timekeeper, that's a hell-of-a name."

Sparks rose and caught the wind just above my head. Spirits took each one, and Check licked his nose for a better sniff. He was riding the wind too. Check was happy for me because things were going my way and I was getting to do what needed to be done, play. Bugdaddy had said the ox was in the mire and I had to get him out. Damn the old ox and damn the work too. It was time to play. Check knew I had to make up for lost time at that and nobody better mess with me when I was having fun. Check understood and saw to it that I was left with a free reign.

Chapter 26

Check and I hung out at the base of a named mountain another night. It was a volcano long time ago. We were at a good spot and I owed Check time because I had overstayed at Pete's.

Check had a way of knowing bad men. That was part of his power. There had to be some kind of odor coming from them that he could smell or he could read their thoughts like a telephone line. He had liked Mr. Jeff and Martha right away. Check liked women and children too. Sometimes when he disappeared, strangers would show up. If they planned to do me harm, Check would stay out of sight but make a high pitched shrill like he was telling me, "They are bad ones, Johnnyboy. Watch out." Check's shrill wasn't just for me. The bad men heard it too and it bothered some of them. The shrill messed up their concentration, made them nervous. I could see it in their faces. "What's that? I don't see anything. Maybe we're not alone," concerns like that. Check made enough weird sounds to throw them off course and give us the advantage.

To Check, you were either good or bad and bad meant it was a life and death situation. If there weren't a shadow for him to hide in, he would keep his head down on his paws. Nothing would move but his big yellow eyes, watching for our foe's first move. If the enemy got too close, he would bring him down.

I wondered how a person thinks he can come up and just take what belongs to someone else, something that Check and I had worked hard for. Doesn't he know sooner or later he'll get caught and maybe go to jail? Maybe the person is so stupid he doesn't think ahead. Whatever the reason, Check and I weren't easy marks when it came to stealing from us. We could fight with the best of men. One night Check jumped up and dropped out of sight. He had taken care of all his business earlier so I knew someone was coming. A few minutes later two men walked into our camp, one was holding a pistol. They said they wanted my money, money they had seen at the store when I bought supplies. I believed they were going to rob and then shoot me. Check thought so too.

With Check and because of youth, somehow I wasn't that scared. Things happened so fast I didn't have time to be. Some people think dogs don't understand what is said because they don't speak our language, but I believe otherwise. Check was listening in on what was said. Somehow Check knew what could harm me, the gun. He sprang from a shadow and bit the hand that held the gun while I went into the other man who gave up right away. I told that man to stay down and not move or the gray dog would eat him alive. He believed me because he saw his buddy wasn't faring so well with Check. The gunman's hand would never be the same when it came to shooting or holding a pistol. I had seen Check crush a ham bone that I could have used for a mallet. The gunman was pleading for help from his buddy. I told him the only thing he could do was play dead, not to move, to stay still.

"He ain't going to stop till you stop moving, mister. You had better play dead."

Funny how Check could learn who stupid people were quick as a cat could lick his paw. The man cried but didn't move. I called Check like I needed him and the man stayed still long enough for Check to think there wasn't a threat any more. If the man had made so much as a twitch, the gray might would gladly have gone back to work and I wouldn't have been able to stop him. That was the law, the way things were. I made that law clear to both bad guys while Check watched them intently.

I didn't like having to leave our camp but I knew it was the best thing to do. The two men could have friends who would come after us, and I couldn't take that chance. I didn't like driving at night, but this time we had to make tracks. I let the men know I didn't care for that one bit. I asked the smartest one, the one who wasn't bleeding, could he get his friend to a hospital and he said he could. I asked did he want me to turn Check loose on him and he started crying. I was thinking a man who lived on the edge of life and death had seen things. His face to the ground like he was talking to rocks, he said he had never seen a dog like Check. That made me smile with much pleasure inside my chest. *Maybe I should take Check back to Bugdaddy and see if he could tie a tin can to the gray dog's tail. If he drew back like he was going to beat me, Check would bring him down like a rotten branch, just as he'd done to the two bad men with their faces in the dirt, too scared to flinch.*

I was a little worried. If we stayed much longer, the stupid gunman might bleed to death. I yelled, "Den, Check." In a flash he jumped through the open car window and made a U-turn to watch the two men if they moved. I warned them, if they moved before I pulled away, I couldn't stop Check. I got behind the wheel, started the smooth engine, and yelled to two faces down in the dirt. "Hey, you remember the gray dog, hear?" Then we sped away. I'll bet those two dirty dogs didn't move until the sound of our car faded away.

"Check, you reckon they'll change their ways? If I didn't think so, I would've let you do more chomping. You've got the power to put the fear of God in 'em. Man, I can't wait for Chief to see you. You're going to like Chief. He's a mighty good medicine man."

We were forced to flee New Mexico because I couldn't take a chance the two outlaws would call the law on me. It would be their word against mine and there were two of them. I changed our course like Frank had taught me, from west to Arizona to north to Colorado. We were so close to Arizona, but anyone who figured out we were headed west would soon find us.

At daylight the next morning, we drove into Durango where I bought gas and then headed west toward Utah. I thought of my Aunt Midge who lived in Salt Lake City. Maybe I would go there because she always liked me. She wasn't ashamed of her

Indian heritage like Mama was. She had visited Mama back in Virginia and introduced me to her girls my age. They were okay, but I didn't care for girls at that time. Right away Aunt Midge, like Mama, said I took after their side of the family. She told me more stories about Grandma Flat Foot and Grandma Tippy Toe. I thought they had funny names but, after meeting Chief, I knew better. They were honorable names, ones earned from merit. Chief would give me my new name as soon as I could tell him about Check and me on the Sacred Mountain.

Chapter 27

Gassed up, we headed west until midmorning. Aunt Midge had told me about sights in Utah but nothing about Colorado. As the sun rose from behind, it lit up huge plateaus that didn't look real. They were far away but they looked like we would be at the foot of the mesa in a few minutes. After a long drive, we came upon an entrance to Mesa Verde National Park. I liked national parks because they were for everyone, not just the rich who had everything anyway. I always felt welcome at national parks but sometimes Check acted like he wasn't. He was lacking in social graces and had no intentions of changing his attitude about what he figured he owned anyway. If there was a shrub around, or a tree or even a fireplug that resembled a sawed off tree, he'd cock his leg and mark it with his scent, like it or not. I always thought he did that to mark his trail, so he'd know his way back.

There was a short line of cars waiting to go into the Park, maybe five or six, and the man with the Smokey Bear hat pulled the pipe gate open and waved friendly for us to come on in. He smiled until I passed, then Check lunged at him in the back window and showed his big teeth. I could never figure out why Check didn't like uniforms. Yelling at Check only made matters worse. I would have to speak to him like he was a runaway horse to calm him down. "Easy, easy, easy, Check." Maybe someone wearing a uniform had done something bad to him one time. Anyway, I smiled and followed the car in front of me to the top of the hill.

It wasn't an easy climb. Our car was heating up, but we made it without a rest. We twisted and turned on the edge of a cliff that rose into the clouds. At the top we found a parking spot away from everyone. Check and I were our own tour group and didn't need a guide to point out the things we wanted to see. Check figured I was too slow so he made tracks without me. I didn't worry because he was never so far away that he didn't know what I was doing. Those yellow eyes always had me in focus.

I was excited about being on top of a mesa. What a view. A lady working there said you could see a hundred miles. She was right. The panorama was unbelievable. About eighty miles away I watched a storm cloud with its lightning flashes. It looked like a miniature puff of smoke in a cartoon movie. I couldn't get over how far I was seeing and I wasn't alone with that. I was close enough to hear a group of excited people. Everyone was shocked as the park ranger explained the atmosphere and landmarks many miles away. This place was spiritual and I felt it as soon as I walked over to the edge of the cliff. The ranger talked about the ancient ones called the Anasazi. No one knows what became of them not even the native people. The Anasazi made their homes in the sides of cliffs on the mesa. I felt I had to go in those houses or bust a gut. A nice young girl, a part-time worker, took a group of six on a tour to the cliff houses. I followed from a distance so I could hear what she had to say. The more I tried to stay back from her little group, the more she would yell and invite me to come along and join them. She liked my shy ways and all. When she mentioned a kiva, I got even more excited because Chief had a kiva, where he gave me my ceremony. When she asked if anyone wanted to go down in the kiva, no one raised a hand but me. Speaking out in front of a crowd of people for the first time in my life I said that I wanted to go inside. "Okay," she said, but first she had to explain about the old people and what they did in the hole in the ground. The kiva was used for spiritual matters. I didn't tell that I already knew that, but listened out of respect. She said the kiva was the womb of the earth. I knew about the Christian rebirth so when she said a womb, I thought that's what I needed, to go down in the hole and get reborn. I didn't ask to go the second time. I just went and she didn't stop me. It was dark. It took my eyes a while to adjust to the dim light coming through a hole in the ceiling. The room was round, about six or seven feet across with a seat all the way around. My guess was about a dozen people could cram themselves on that seat.

I thought about Check, what he was doing outside. He could be rude to sightseers if he looked for me and I wasn't around. Also, the pathway was narrow in spots, just big enough to place your feet. If Check decided to follow me to the kiva he would go past others without permission. He would simply pass and if you were at a narrow spot you would be in trouble. In a while I saw his head poke in above and look down at me from the top of the ladder. He couldn't come down. I told him to get lost because I was about to be reborn, that I hoped he would like me when I was finished. Check didn't like that idea. He wanted to jump down where I was but I knew that would be a bad move. He couldn't climb ladders and, if he got down, I couldn't help him out. He'd be stuck then because he still wouldn't let me touch him. I moved under the ladder and he seemed okay to stay put.

Check was boss at the top of the womb and I was boss at the bottom. If someone else wanted in, that would be a major problem. I said for him to be a good boy and heard the guide answer for Check. My eyes were clear, yet I couldn't believe them. Check was letting her stroke his big brick head. Damn, I was jealous but relieved that he wasn't getting nasty with her. I told her he wouldn't let me do that and for her not to push things too far. The young girl's hair was in braids and her eyes were dark and kind. She asked me my name and I said without thinking, "Timekeeper." That knocked her for a loop and I couldn't believe I did that. I felt stupid but she seemed delighted that I was in the kiva and that was my name. She said that she would see that no one bothered us, that the kiva would be closed to others as long as I stayed. Then she hugged Check around the neck and kissed his muzzle. Damn, I couldn't believe he let her do that. After she scooted back out, I told Check I felt real good about the kiva and he should feel like royalty, but I was actually jealous. I guessed he figured I'd get over it in a while. He watched me pray.

The room was cool and quiet. Check's panting quieted. I began to chant like Chief did, working myself into a state of calmness. I wanted to do things different from the way I had been taught in Sunday school. I couldn't pray pretty like Mama and old Chicken Bone. It didn't work for me. I was disappointed with the outcome of my Christian life prayers because nothing much changed. God gave me the most undesirable father a boy could have and, if anyone was left behind any farther in this world than me, bring them on so I can see what they looked like. No, I didn't need the blessing of Moses' God because I'd had enough of that. I needed to know where I was headed in life. I didn't need to look back to that world I left behind because back wasn't a pretty sight. Back meant death as far as I was concerned. My freedom was everything and the kiva was a looking glass for the future. "Faith is everything, Check," I said chanting, thinking he could see the old people's spirits gathering around the Timekeeper. Two thousand years before, answers came while they sang in the womb and the Timekeeper would get help too.

My mind drifted back to unimportant things like, why was the dark-eyed girl with long plaited hair so nice to Check and me? I looked at my arms and saw they were strong. I stopped my chanting and said, "Check, maybe that's what she saw, my strong arms. How come she can pet you and you like it?" Check never moved, not even an eye blinked, just stared at me waiting for some miracle, something that would interest him like a beefsteak or the mention of a hunting trip. I figured he was willing to put up with me because I was calling on the old ones for answers. That much I knew, but my mind was stubborn.

"You like her more than me . . . and you and me are a pack." I complained knowing very well that's not the way you get answers from a prayer. "I've got to get a hold of myself. I like her too, Check. She sure is pretty."

In a while after the brooding was over, I got back to spiritual matters. I looked around and thought about the old ones, how they managed to make a living on the mesa. They were very smart to be able to farm and irrigate the land to grow the crops. They had it harder than me. *Maybe I should be thankful for them making the kiva for Check and me so we could ask them what to do next.* I'd be happy and chant long and soft just like Chief and the old ones would hear my prayer. I didn't need mescal for that. *Maybe what to do next will come to me in a dream like it does for Chief.*

Check looked content while I sang a song that made no sense of rhyme or reason. It was fun chanting. I spoke my heart to the old spirits and I believed they liked it.

The kiva was magical. I thought it was doing Check the same way it was doing me because he looked content. This new thing, with the pretty tour guide loving him like he was her dog, made me think the kiva had made Check docile. I climbed the ladder up to him and tried to rub behind his ear. As soon as my hand got close, he'd show his teeth, letting me know I was out of order. That knocked me out of the spell I had worked myself into.

"What does she have that I don't?" I asked. "I feed you and we live together. We're a pack, remember?" I could tell Check didn't want me to take it personal because he moved out of reach. After all, I was the one with the problem—I needed him more then he needed me. He had the power and I was being disrespectful thinking I could treat him like an ordinary dog. *But how can he let a stranger love on him? Maybe she has knowledge like Chief. Maybe she can help me find out what is wrong with me, why Chief called me Timekeeper. Maybe she knows about spiritual matters and that's why she gave me the kiva all to myself. I can read faces, she likes me. Maybe she knows Check is the power. I should watch myself and get back to business. The Anasazi will know my new name.*

Slowly I lowered myself back down to the bottom of the womb. This time I would be sincere about what was to be done, what I needed to sing. This time I would not look up at the gray power with yellow eyes that could strike terror with one glance. This time I would only ask for one thing, to find Chief. The pretty girl was a gift from the old ones and they would tell her what to do . . . to honor the power and let us sing our songs.

My emotions swung to this side and to that side but I didn't stop singing. I wasn't singing the tunes I had learned in the cotton fields but the ones I learned from Chief with no certain melodies. This was one of my gifts. I could hear a song and repeat it years later in the same key. The Ant People, the Anasazi, would know what I was singing as the sound was only a feeling to me. I was a young man who needed answers and didn't mind singing. I had gone too far to give up. If only I could keep my mind in order, then things would work.

Check may show his teeth sometimes but he's there when I need him, and he's willing to give his life for mine. I should be grateful for that, huh. Stuff like that was going on in my mind while I kept my head down singing Chief's song, the one I liked the most. Chief had said that people can call you a name and that name shows your nature.

I heard a soft voice from above. I knew it wasn't Check, although the thought did occur to me. It was the tour guide again. She said I had a beautiful voice. I looked around to see if anyone else was in the kiva. No. She was speaking to me. I thought what reason would she have to say that and then I remembered Chief warning me to pay attention when you first meet someone. She sat by Check and again hugged him around the neck and asked me to continue my singing. I felt a little shy, but her soft ways eased that. I started singing, but this time I changed it to a key that felt better. She rocked with the tune like she liked it and that only made me want to sing louder.

I wasn't jealous of her loving on Check because I was doing what I was supposed to be doing. Things felt natural. *Sing, Timekeeper,* I cheered myself on. *Sing the songs of peace, love and happiness, not resentment, fear and hurt.* Suddenly I couldn't sit still. I had to move around, move my arms like I was holding onto a lovely lady, and the girl above smiled and hugged the gray. She was so pretty holding onto Check. Check thought so, too. She broke the spell with, "Timekeeper, come home with me. I want you to meet my family." *How do I say no to a dark-eyed young girl with plaits in her hair? Check knows she's pretty, pretty, pretty. No wonder he let her hug him.*

I thought hard about the invitation. I was afraid I would do everything wrong, just like I'd done in school. When she said the second time she wanted me to meet her parents, that did it. No way I was going home with her. But I did agree to follow her off the mesa after work. She rode a shuttle bus to the main road that ran east and west. We stood by my car and talked until her mom picked her up. She told me her name and address and said for me to come by. I didn't tell her anything about myself but mostly talked about Check and Chief. When her mom pulled up, I was introduced from a distance. To remind me how she felt and what was waiting for me, she kissed me on the cheek and hurried away to her ride. She was the second woman to do that. I stood there breathless while her mom smiled at me. Our eyes were locked onto each other while her mom drove away. I saw her hand out the side window waving me goodbye.

"Check, she likes me more than you. Thank you, Moses for that." I tried to memorize the address she gave me but the excitement of the mesa, the kiva, the old ones and the singing, the address got lost in my head.

Farewell to the girl with the dark eyes, long plaits and pretty smile. She would be forever young, smiling above me in a kiva, and leaving me with a magical kiss, a tender kiss that has lasted.

I stood outside our car looking at the road that ran east and west. Everything was in place. Check was in the back seat waiting to see which direction I would take. I finally took the westbound lane and drove into the night. Hardly a car was on the road. I was a little low on gas so I pulled well off the highway where car headlights didn't reach and thought maybe I had made a big mistake with the pretty girl. I couldn't recall her name and address no matter how hard I tried. Fate would have to bring us together if I was ever to see her smiling face again. I thought about that and felt lovesick strike my heart.

She worked weekends and I would have to hang around for the following Saturday. I couldn't wait that long. I knew I would never see her again. I couldn't dwell on that magical moment too much because it would cause me to make a mistake, maybe land us in jail. It would get Check in trouble too and surely put to death because of his spirited nature. People didn't mind doing that to dogs in those days. No, lovesick or not, I knew what had to be done, stay on the straight and narrow, and keep a low profile, just like always.

Chapter 28

The next morning I started driving. I was still reeling from the dark-eyed girl and all that had happened, the kiva, and the kiss. But soon the salmon-colored canyon walls got to me, staring at me from all sides as I snaked deeper into Utah's Canyon Land. This was like being in a kiva while driving a car. I was awestruck with the canyon and kept Check awake with, "Hey, look at that." I couldn't believe there were so few cars on the highway. This was a majestic place and we practically had it all to ourselves. I pulled into a rest area, home of a two-seater privy, and Check ran around while I made up my mind about going north to Salt Lake City to look for Aunt Midge. I decided I had a better chance by far finding Midge than roaming around in Arizona like it was a department store. It made good sense. I rested against our car and watched Check do his thing like a puppy at play. The air was easy to breathe and I felt good with my mind at rest. Above I heard the shrill cry of a white-wingtipped bird, an eagle. The air was clean and the eagle's cry could carry far, maybe reflect off canyon walls. I yelled but my voice kept going and didn't echo back.

We hung around a while. It was a neat place, spiritual. I tried to figure out how we could stay a while. Beside the two-seater privy, there was a washbasin on the outside but no running water. Check could usually find water. But when he returned to the car to get water from his bowl in the back, I knew we were in a very dry place. His nose could find water miles away and we had been there long enough, maybe an hour. He needed a drink and lapped up a pan full. I had food and time to kill so it didn't matter what we did. My oil lamp was full and a gallon can of kerosene to refill the lamp was in the trunk. But water was the problem. I had a glass gallon jug, the kind with the one finger ring, only half filled with water. I told Check if he could find water we would stay. That was wishful thinking because his bowl, an old enamel washbasin, was empty for the second time and he wanted more. I knew he would rather drink water out of a mud hole any day than that washbasin. But we stayed a little longer at the rest spot because it was so enchanting. I opened a hot Pepsi in a long neck bottle. We belonged where we were and we both knew it.

Another old car pulled in and a longhaired man, a young American Indian, stepped out to stretch. I spoke first by pointing up with one finger when the eagle somewhere above cried out its call. The man raised his head slowly, letting me know he understood the big bird's shrill. He looked like some of Chief's people. He was friendly. Chief said his people were raised in close-knit clans and disliked strangers. I knew this guy was cool because Check didn't drop out of sight or bristle down his back. I wondered if he spoke English because we stood longer than normal before we talked. He was looking but probably couldn't figure out my nationality. My skin was darker than his, but he focused on my sun bleached curly hair. Everyone did. I said, "This spot is peaceful as a grave." He nodded but didn't add anything. I started to leave but then he said I had a nice dog. I thought he recognized the great power and had said the right thing. I told him Check and I had been to Canada but I didn't mention the Sacred Mountain. He didn't ask questions like what's your name and where are you from so I didn't either. We talked about the spiritual canyons until I said I wanted mescal buttons to help me get in tune with the eagle. He said he had plenty but they were used for ceremonial purposes. I told him that's what I needed them for. When he found out I was sincere, he got a brown paper bag from his trunk and handed it to me. He said he had just collected them and was on his way home. I didn't think to ask where he got the buttons because I was overwhelmed at the amount. It was ten times the amount Chief had given me. The lunch size bag was bulging, nearly spilling over at the top. Now I could kill a lot of time as soon as I got drinking water. He didn't have as much water as we did. He didn't want pay for the buttons but I insisted he take gas money and handed him ten dollars. With gas at twenty-five cents a gallon, ten dollars could carry him a long ways. He did the right thing by giving me the buttons and I was right giving him the gas money. Chief had said no one we meet is an accident, strange place or not. "We're directed by spirits and they watch to see how we react toward one another." Chief had said there is meaning when paths cross and, if you look for the meaning, you will find it. Two men with no names parted as friends. We lived by the same rules. Check had known that right away.

Life was wondrous and faith like that meeting had meaning. I thought if you don't believe in spirits that show you the way, you have had your mind closed. The gray dog had shown me much from that world. The man gave me buttons but Check gave me a future. Check was a part of my soul. Check would stand watch as I searched inside myself for answers, answers about the confusing world we traveled. The main question was, "Why am I different from others? What's my life about?" Check was the guard, the one loving soul who gave me time and, when I needed to eat buttons, no one was allowed in that ceremony but us. He got very protective when I ate the buttons. Without Chief, it was the only way I could find answers.

We covered a lot of ground. For two days I drove all over Salt Lake City but couldn't find my Aunt. I was frustrated. I was killing time but it would have been nice to see her. It would've been nice to talk to someone who knew me and I could imagine the look on her face if we'd walked up to her door. On her turf, we could have gotten to know each other better. I wondered if she had heard that I had left Glen Allen. I hoped so. If she had, she would know how Mama was doing. I could only imagine that too and it got to me. I couldn't do much looking back without getting sick to my stomach. I had to tell myself Mama was doing fine, knowing that was not so. My mind was in conflict and I turned to Check for support. "Check, we need to get the hell out of Utah."

With Check stirring in the back seat, I got tired of driving around the clean looking town. I headed south out the city toward the countryside, which was more beautiful. In less than one full day I had returned to Canyon Land with water and the gray might.

Chapter 29

I passed trucks hauling trees going toward Salt Lake City, but it wasn't Christmas. They made me think about a Christmas when Mama was giving birth to my brother, David. We worried she wouldn't make it back home in time to see the tree Newt had found in the woods. I was five and not long out the hospital myself with lots of closed-in feelings. I was staying outside most of the time and always without shoes. The cold didn't bother my feet one bit. I loved Mama so much and needed her so badly I went into her closet so I could smell her clothes. If Bugdaddy had found out, he would have beaten me, so no one said a thing about that. In our house everything was usually every man for himself, but us kids stuck together when it came to Bugdaddy. Mama did get home on Christmas Day and we were happy. Nothing else mattered. We had our mother and a tree decorated to the max by my two older sisters. That was a special Christmas for all but especially for me.

Driving in the majestic canyons, I kept on thinking about who I was. When I looked into the rearview mirror, I couldn't believe that I looked that old. I would've been twenty to match the face I saw. I didn't see Johnnyboy or the Timekeeper Chief saw. I only saw a man looking for a place he belonged. Sometimes, I'd think I saw another guy in my body, but I knew not to worry about that because Check was in the back seat. He wouldn't let another man get inside me or in our car. No way. It was me in the mirror looking road-weary, lost without direction. *Oh, Moses, this is the worst old feeling I've most ever had.*

Please, help me. If it weren't for Check at those times, I surely would have just faded into a canyon wall.

It was 1960 and the world seemed to move faster. I needed a jumpstart to keep up with things, but what was new. My head needed opening up and mescal would do the trick. We found a good spot in the canyons and made camp. The nights were cold, but Check snuggled up against me making things perfect. The sun poked through clouds during the day and made everything around us happy. Somehow I felt more protected in the canyons. Check liked it there, too, if only we could find water.

I chewed all the buttons I could get into my mouth. It wasn't the same as it was on the Sacred Mountain. I did more thinking about myself and that was the trouble. After going nearly out of my mind, I figured out I was being selfish. I didn't give a thought to anyone else who might have been in need, just my wants. Only when I thought about the gray dog with soul did things turn for the better. *This was the thing about life,* I thought. *You have to give in order to receive.* Chief would have straightened me out on this matter right away. But I had to find out the hard way after nearly killing myself with an overdose. I puked and puked, but at that point I didn't care.

Check was cool. He didn't need to take drugs to get knowledge. He already knew life's secrets and enjoyed watching me learn. Chief had said that all the animals knew more about life than man. Man had to learn on his own or from them. I couldn't ask Check about life's secrets because that would be wrong and, if he gave them to me, he would be deceitful to his kind. Chief was right. I had to earn the knowledge about the way of life and then live it. Just like he did. Who did I think I was? I wasn't the first lost person on this planet. I'd tell myself to be cool like Check. Just being around him gave me time to learn. I'd tell myself not to look back at past Christmases because they were over, be they good or bad. *Chew another button and be glad you have this time, this very minute. This is my life, only the minute and hope for a tomorrow, maybe that would come, maybe not.*

In one of my mescal dreams, a lady told me life was like having a baby. No one could stop it. The baby was going to come out. Even a man understood that. I needed to be satisfied but like most young people I wanted things to happen right then. The only way I could get things going was with Chief and he was in Arizona doing his Chieftain thing. I told Check as soon as I could get behind the wheel and drive we were going to Arizona and look for him.

Nothing could match Check and I going across America. I didn't have to worry about the horrible life in Virginia. No more lying about why I wasn't in school when my father took me to work with him junking cars, nailing boards, and fixing rich folks' houses. No worries about standing before the class while the teacher made a fool of me. No more worrying about the class laughing at the stupid, dimwitted idiot who couldn't read. I wasn't stupid and I had some sense of pride. I wasn't about to let anyone beat me down again. No one could do that when Check and I took on the road because we took on the world too. It didn't matter about reading, writing and math or a steady job. Hell no. We didn't care about the Dow Jones average. In fact, we didn't know the first damn thing about stocks and bonds. Never knew they existed until a few days before. Oh, but me behind the wheel and Check riding on the back seat like a king, the freedom of only one day was worth all the wealth in the world, all the education a man could have. Why should I worry about tomorrow? I could learn all the secrets about life when I came across Chief and that would happen soon enough. He would tell me smart things. I had learned more in the short time we were together than in my entire life, Frank and all. Chief was a friend in the plus column and I needed to keep things simple and not let myself get confused. I could count on Chief giving wise advice, and I could take mescal whenever I found a spiritual spot to keep in touch with the world of wonderment.

Driving along I'd sing made-up songs like Riding High, Alone, and Restless . . . I'd sing the world is a playground for those who like to play . . . Giving love a little, if any, watching good things fall by the way. Good things were the things other people valued. We didn't. I felt different in that sense. I didn't care about many things other people had. I had Check.

My column of good things could be added quickly, but they mattered the most to Johnnyboy.

We drove south through the Navajo Indian Reservation and on much farther to another national park.

"Look at that!" I yelled when I first saw petrified trees scattered over the landscape. Check acted like he already knew about trees being rocks. Nothing like that excited him, only food or a fight. I had to get out and touch things like the cactus, trees, and stones on the ground. It was very hot. "You won't find any water here," I said to Check. And we didn't.

We didn't stay there long. Instead we turned around and headed east toward New Mexico for no reason other than cooler weather. I didn't want any parts of the California desert. Also, someone had told me they check for plants in your car at the California border. The buttons in the trunk would have put me in jail. I couldn't take that chance.

CHAPTER 30

We were real lucky because nothing major went wrong with the car Mr. Jeff and Martha had given us. I did notice the generator meter needle ducked back into the no charge side now and then. Sometime later the generator stopped altogether and we were running off the battery. We could run maybe four hours before it went dead. I complained to Check that things like that seemed to happen when a person was in the middle of nowhere. From the terrain it looked that way. I'm not sure if we were in Arizona or New Mexico when the car started sputtering from lack of spark. I would cut off the key, shove in the clutch and drift as far as I could before turning on the key, engaging the clutch again. During that little time, the battery would gain enough strength to run the car a short way. We would get up as much speed as we could, turn off the key and repeat the drill. Somehow, the battery found the current needed to run the motor. This went on for about an hour until everything finally quit. We drifted to the side of the road. I didn't want to go back to thumbing and Check wasn't about to ride with anyone after being back-seat king so we had a problem.

I told Check that we needed to get a new battery or fix the generator. It didn't matter to him. He was happy as long as he had the car or was near when the iron beast cranked up. That's how Check saw it. I had to wait for someone to help me like another motorist or for a generator to fall out the sky, which was not likely to happen. I told Check to stay with the car while I went scouting. Nothing doing. As soon as I headed down the road, Check followed. He knew something was wrong or maybe he thought I was going hunting. It was okay because Check could always find water and it looked like we would need it before too long.

We didn't get a half-mile when Check suddenly dropped out of sight. I thought a bad man might be near. I listened hard and heard men laughing in the bushes to my right. When you are down and out, you have to do something. I headed in the direction of the men to ask for help or a ride to the nearest town. After several hundred steps, I could see men and machinery on a railroad track. In those days six-volt batteries were plentiful, especially in commercial machinery. The new cars had twelve-volt batteries, starting in 1955. Anything before that had what we had, a heavy-duty six-volt battery. I walked straight up to the group of men and asked when they were going to lunch. They asked why I wanted to know, and I told them point blank that I was going to take one of the many batteries they had in their strange looking rail machine. I said that I would leave them mine, that it only needed charging. I could get my car's generator fixed in the next town going west, which was a lie. They started laughing like I was just joking. After all, what kind of man would have the nerve to tell them he was going to steal something and mean it? I said, "Okay, wait and see."

Check and I were going to get a battery. I only hoped it would go down like I planned. If they didn't leave for lunch, all I had to do was start a fight and Check would finish it. But we would be in trouble and I would go to jail. Thinking about how faith and patience was always the key, I joined Check in the woods where we would wait for our chance. I looked at him and knew it would be all right as he was around. The crew left, most likely thinking I had pulled a prank. But as soon as they were out of sight, Check and I ran down and twisted two cables loose from a battery and snatched it from the rail machine. On the way back to our car, I felt I had misjudged how far away we were. My arms were nearly gone by the time we got back. I popped the hood, but I had to move fast and not think about cramped muscles and an aching back. I changed batteries and took off. We stopped on the side of the road where I thought we'd come out the bushes so I could leave the rundown battery. If the men tracked me, they would find a battery that only needed charging. Maybe I should have taken my battery and put it in their machine but that would have been another chance of getting caught. If they hadn't laughed at me like I was stupid, I might have taken the chance. But now, if they were not stupid, they would find my old battery and that was good enough for me to leave with a clear conscience. Check agreed.

I didn't stop driving until I saw a junkyard of old cars a few hours later. All I needed was a handful of tools and I could fix our car. The man loaned me what I needed to change the generator I had bought from him, and then we were on our way, far away, from the battery crime scene.

I never feared that Check would leave me stranded in the middle of nowhere—not as much as he loved to ride. Faith has everything to do with how well a man travels and how he deals with obstacles in his path. I worked but Check called the shots on that. What a dog, a mystery at times, but always willing to move on. That feeling couldn't be duplicated with anything. To ride with the gray power had brought meaning to my life. Everything worth the effort was doable. Check was quiet in the back seat but could explode into action to defend our way of life. It was my job to keep the four-wheel den rolling—his was to look over me. Every ten minutes I'd glance in the rearview mirror to see if he was there on the seat. Check made me feel like I had things put together. Failure wasn't part of life anymore. We were on the highway of freedom and good things were just ahead. While Check slept, my hands on the wheel, I only needed my new name as we left New Mexico and entered Texas.

Chapter 31

I have reworked this over and over in my mind a million times. I think if it had gone this way or that way, things would have turned out differently. But the facts remain, you can be in the wrong place at the wrong time and I was the one who chose the service station with the cheaper gas. The car's gas tank was half full so I'm sure I could have gone on to another station. That's what haunts me. Why didn't I just go on? A chain reaction of life shaking events happened seconds after I turned off the key and got out to gas up. A man, not wearing a station's uniform, greeted me sheepishly. My back was to the station but I knew something was wrong. Check got agitated and started working himself up into one of his bad attitudes. I didn't calm him down because I knew he had this gift to know bad people. I was scared to take my eyes off the man posing as the station attendant who said that I needed to pay before I got gas. I answered I wanted to pump my own gas because of Check. Meantime the gray might was trying to work his head out my window, which was rolled down a few inches to let him have air but also to restrain him inside the car. Because of Check's protection of the car, I always rolled the windows mostly up so he couldn't take bites out of the attendants. I knew I had to play along with this guy, so I handed him a ten-dollar bill and told him to check my oil while I filled my tank. He took my money and I could read his face that he thought there was plenty more where that came from. Also, I could see he was nervous. It wasn't long before I found out why. His buddy was inside, robbing the station. To Check and me, to be a victim in a robbery was as bad as being the robber. The law would investigate and having a car with made-up license tags would end our journey. I wouldn't see Chief and learn what was wrong with my head and get my new name. At this point, I was like Check. Things were all or nothing, a life or death situation and nothing in-between. The man went under my hood. He saw I noticed what was going on inside but pretended everything was normal. I knew he wanted to add me to the robbery but was worried I could take him. I was scared he had a gun like his buddy who was waving it inside at the real attendant. Check was getting crazy trying to get out because he had picked up on my stress. Things were getting out of control.

I was still pumping gas at the back fender when the gunman came out the station toward his partner who was under my hood. Suddenly, the pretend attendant was brave and came toward me real confident. When he passed Check's window, Check lunged. It startled the man, making him throw up the hand that held the rag he'd used to check oil. I didn't think Check had made contact until blood spewed from the man's hand during our tussle that followed. Check had the rag in his mouth and was flinging it around in the car to satisfy his anger. The bad guy and me went crashing down on a pyramid of cylinder looking oilcans that were stacked between two gas pumps. Some of the cans got punctured, making it near impossible to stand, much less fight on our feet. I saw the face of the gunman and knew he was going to shoot me. Check did too. Check figured there was enough window open for him to go through. Check could only get his head through but it was enough to keep the man with the gun at a distance. Whenever I was down Check was insanely protective of me. Now he had worked himself up into madness seeing someone trying to harm me. I could hear Check biting and digging at the window to make a way out while the man with the gun tried to get at me. He stood in front of our car waiting for his chance but I kept my man between us.

Things were happening so fast. I wanted to leave. I wanted to get away from there and nothing else mattered. Somehow I worked my hand close enough to unlatch the car door. I felt relieved. But when I released one hand to free Check, the bad man stabbed me with his knife. Not a bad exchange when another man held a gun over me. I'm sure he would have shot me if I'd given him the chance.

The oil didn't seem to bother Check's footing as he went to work on the man holding me first. I remember thinking it wasn't a big deal being stabbed because I came back with a right punch to his nose and got up while Check went after the gunman who tried to flee. I got behind the steering wheel and backed away and then pulled out to the edge of the road, not even looking down to see where I had been stabbed. I only wanted my partner and to get the hell gone. I yelled like never before for Check to come to the den. My voice must have sounded stressed or maybe the bad men were down because he came flying to an open door and sailed over me like a bullet. I drove off. Later I had time to think about what had taken place. I was involved in something bad and the police would be looking for me to get my side of the story. But I had to hide. We were on the run and all because of my bad decision. My tank was near full but my mind was running low on what to do next. Check snatched the oil rag up from the floorboard and jumped in the back seat to fling it around. To my horror, something flew out, a piece of a man's finger. Now I knew why I had blood all over me. Check had bitten off the bad guy's finger at the first knuckle just above the nail. Later, when I reached to get it from the floor to throw it out the window, Check got a little crazy and took possession. He thought I wanted his prize so he swallowed it.

I should have stayed longer to see about the guys inside the station, if anyone needed help. That was another mistake, but instinct to run overruled my better judgment. I knew I didn't fare well with authority, the reason I was on the road in the first place. Okay, I'd made a bad judgment to run but the other choice was jail. The station man would have to take what life had brought him, just like me. All I could think of was hide, hide, hide and let time make things right. Check could find water and, if I was smart, we could stay hidden maybe two weeks. About fifty miles backtracked from the service station

I pulled well off the road and cut bushes to hide the car like a thief on the run.

Check wanted to look for water. He hadn't eaten much dry dog food but did lap up what little water was left in the washbasin. He seemed real thirsty, not acting the same. Maybe he was still pumped up from the action. I let him out to search. Alone with my thoughts, I completely forgot to check on my stab wound. I usually kept my big belt buckle to one side because it was cool looking, like having my smokes rolled up in my shirtsleeve. My buckle on the side may have saved my life. The knife blade got caught in the buckle and couldn't go but so far. The blade did break the skin but it only looked like a scratch, maybe a half-inch wide and not much blood. I didn't know how deep.

Later into the early night, even though my car was warm inside from the heater, I felt cold. Something was wrong. I didn't get sick on the road. That much I had learned. But now I was running a fever and felt myself plunging into a frigid realm. My teeth chattered. Even when I had fallen into cold water one time in Canada, I hadn't had this feeling. This was like being helpless, no way to warm up to the freeze. At the time I didn't know the bad man's knife had punctured my intestines. That's what I think happened. The stabbing sent me into a fever with horrible dreams, trying to find the light switch in the morgue of Medical College of Virginia.

Check was not the same toward me when he returned. He licked my face and pawed me to get me to sit up. I did and he laid his head in my lap, something he had never done before. He had been running a long ways because his body was hot, yet it didn't warm me much. I was so glad to have that warmth but fell into morbid dreams like being locked away in a jail cell, not being able to breathe. Nothing could be worse in a dream and nothing could be worse on the road. Being sick.

I was in deep trouble. The nights were cold and I used nearly all our gasoline the first night trying to keep warm. Check stayed different toward me, showering me with affection because he thought I was dying. I loved and welcomed it.

I lost track of time, not by the hour, but by the days. I came back to life when warm sunlight glittered through shrubs I had used to hide our car. It felt like my face was soaking in warmth from every ray as I kept my eyes closed. Check wanted out so I lifted the handle with my boot to open the door. He walked on my legs to get out but I still didn't open my eyes. I just wanted to lie there and not go back into nightmares because each time I fell asleep that's what happened . . . in a jail cell, in a morgue. Why couldn't I dream something pleasant? Hell no, life is not that way but maybe Chief could explain why. I had to get back to him. Check wouldn't let me die. He had the power and, from the way he was nursing me, showed he loved me a bunch. I was down and he really cared. It felt good when he licked my face like a mama dog licks her puppies. He was tough but he had a heart and brought me comfort. I knew I would get better with his help but the winds came.

The wind blows harder in the fall of the year because the spirits that ride the air currents are excited about the coming of winter when old folks die more readily. That's what Chief had said. He said winter winds are angry and take souls ready or not. He said most folk in the modern age don't take the time to listen to the wind and learn what's to come. He made me aware of all the signs but especially of the winds, and I'd sit and listen to a breeze like someone listening to the radio.

Chief had taught me about spirits. Before I got my first car, Check and I would wrap up in an old wool blanket, one I had found on someone's trash pile. I'd sit against a tree facing a cold night wind until I fell fast asleep, the cover over my head, and wake up just before daylight. It would be deadly quiet because the winds would pause. Why were the winds quiet? Had the spirits taken someone's soul? Was the person ready to go? I hoped they were. I remembered a change in temperature. One night it got so cold I didn't want to get up to pee. Check was close and his body heat had kept me from freezing. As soon as the sun broke over the horizon of a new day, the wind picked back up again looking for somebody.

Don't run, I said to myself like it was Chief speaking to me.

Stay and learn what the spirits are stirred up about. Is it my soul they want . . . or is it Check's? I'll listen. I'll listen, I swear. I'm not afraid.

I'd pulled the blanket over my head and held my water. When Check got up, it would be time to leave. Without his body heat, I had to move around. Check was always a little nervous when the wind blew because he could see spirits. Most were good, but now and then he would flinch from a twig snapping or a whiff of something I couldn't smell. Bad spirits did those things to him. Anyway, it was fun watching his ears twitching around listening for bad spirits. When the wind made him nervous, I'd say, "It's okay, boy," like I could protect him from the things I couldn't see. Those were the good times because I knew I was really the one protected.

With the fever still running, I asked Moses to hold off the cold night. The sun's rays warmed my face, yet chills ran through my body. My mouth was dry, and I didn't want to un-ball my arms and lose any heat to get something to swallow. I just lay there and worried about the robbery, the empty gas tank, how we would freeze when night came, had Check eaten and was he now out searching for water? Would I fall asleep and go into another nightmare? I had to get better. I asked God for my kidneys to stop hurting because I didn't want to get up and go outside to pee. I could hardly stand. The last time I tried, I had puked my guts out.

Chapter 32

I don't know how long it took before I felt better. When I finally sat up behind the wheel, it was pitch dark. Check moved close to me and put his head in my lap. I did what I always wanted to do, stroke him. I felt his front paws and his pads were worn down badly. He had traveled far to get water. I felt grateful to be feeling better, not to be shaking inside. My tongue was thick so I reached under the seat for a soft drink, bit off the cap and started sipping. The Pepsi tasted unbelievably good so I snorted the fizz back up my nose to have every drop. With Check looking after me we had made it, and now we would work out our problems at first light. I found a can of sardines and another Pepsi. Nothing could have been better.

I found my smokes and burned maybe three or four cigs. Somehow I felt rested and wanted to go, but Check was settled in. Each time I moved around he'd snuggle up closer to me. Maybe he needed to keep warm. My desire on one part was to fling away the branches that covered our car and flee but that could wait until morning. I felt well enough to tease Check that he had softened because he was acting out of character. Maybe it wasn't the stab wound that had made me sick. Maybe I had the flu and now he had gotten it from me. I told Check to rest up because if he had what I had, he was really sick. I went to the trunk and got the oil lamp that puts off heat as well as light. I would burn the lamp as long as I was awake and I was wide-awake. Check would be ready to go in the morning and, being young, I believed he would show me the direction. Maybe we had to hang out a few more days to let things cool down. Then we could return to the station to see if any of the good guys got hurt.

The bravest dog alive laid his head in my lap. I lifted his tired head and kissed the top of his muzzle. His golden yellow eyes gleamed in the lamplight. But he needed rest and I knew how it felt to be sick, really sick. I would comfort him like he did me. We were pals, partners for life. I would gladly lay down my life for him just like he showed he would do for me. All I needed to do now was to wait for first light and the gray might would be ready to do.

But I grew stronger while Check's breathing became labored. "What's wrong," I asked calmly, not wanting to excite my friend. But when Check didn't respond, I panicked. He was shivering cold and I didn't have much gas, gas we would need to get the car back on the road. I turned the key to warm the night air so Check would stop his shaking, put some rags in front of the radiator to make the heater hotter, and let the motor idle. With the heater fan on high, the inside was very hot but Check still shook. Maybe he got into some poison. Maybe he had the flu. Maybe he took the sickness from me to save my life. Why else would he be so sick?

When the sun's rays seeped through the brush on the windshield, Check's labored breathing got worse. I didn't see any bullet holes in him and I wouldn't think a lump in his chest just under his front leg was one. My mind was on him getting better. Did Check take a bullet meant for me? He would do that without a second thought. As he panted harder by the minute, blood came out his nose. I sang to him in a low hum to let him know how much I cared. "Look at that," I said about the sun streaking the morning sky. Check didn't look but took in a big breath, held it a few seconds and then let it out.

"Oh, Jesus, oh my God, no!" My partner was dead at sunrise from a gunshot wound and I was alone in a misery, to hum, to cry, to moan a broken heart. I couldn't believe he was dead.

"Check, we've come too far for this to happen. Breathe! Raise your head. Look at me, please!" But he didn't take another breath. My friend was always ahead of me. He died for me. I couldn't face he took the bullet meant for me. He took the sickness upon himself to save my life. What was I to do? Where would I go without him? Life wouldn't be worth living without Check. He taught me so much and now my overseer was gone, his body turning colder by the minute.

"No! Hell no, got-damn-it! This can't be." I screamed like God was listening. "No! Hell no! I can't make it without Check, God! Bring him back! I don't want to live without him. Bring him back, please! Please! Have mercy on me, Jesus!"

I pulled open one eye and instantly knew he would never return. The power was gone. The eyes that had struck terror in bad men's hearts were no longer fearful. In a fit of rage I got out the car and kicked out some of the windows, which left me breathless. I wiped the tears from my eyes with my shirtsleeve so I could see. I screamed and cursed God for taking my partner. I told God that I would always hate Him for doing that. I meant every word. I begged God to strike me dead to make it fair. Then suddenly, as natural as the rising sun before me, a thought came to mind. I knew what to do. I wasn't afraid of anything like going to jail or of being trapped in a room not breathing. I had something in me that was stronger than all that. I snatched the oilcan I used to fill the lamp from the trunk of the car. Nearly blinded with tears, I moved Check to the back seat and doused the interior with the oil. I stood outside by the steering wheel and lit a cigarette asking myself over and over, why, why was Check gone? How could I make it in this confusing world without him?

While I smoked, I talked to Check like he was alive. I told him I was fixing to set his soul free. I told him that I would tell Chief we had been on the Sacred Mountain. I told Check I would never be afraid of being closed in anymore. I told him I was so sorry that I never said I loved him before but I did, and I had ever since the first night we stayed in the old barn somewhere in Louisiana. I told him the second his head rested on my leg in the barn I knew we were partners because I could feel his love for me.

"I'll miss you and I'm sorry I went in the wrong service station, Check. Please forgive me!"

With all that behind me, I tossed a lit match onto the front seat and soon had to stand back from the blazing heat. The flames went about thirty feet high and, in one of the sparks that rose, I pretended the ember was Check's spirit rising high to catch the wind where he could roam freely. I stood there numb, without a soul, because my soul for a while went with Check. I dreamed we were riding the upper air currents searching for a place to hunt, a place to camp. Sometime later I snapped out of this, maybe because the nice car Mr. Jeff and Martha gave us was black from tire smoke. I spat on the ground and stomped my bitterness until I was engulfed in dust. I was out of breath and numb. I stood a while looking at the car that had made us so happy. Then, like the sun had moved on, I turned and walked away, listening only to the sand crush under my boots.

CHAPTER 33

I was no longer scared of the same things and had a new attitude about life. But I was uncertain what would become of me. I decided I'd do the things I'd learned from Check. I'd stay out of sight until I was cornered and then I'd come out fighting like it was life or death. My mind wasn't on jail cells because I had lost my fear of being closed in. I had more determination than ever. I needed Chief's advice. He was all I had to go by and life really didn't matter now that Check was gone. I felt dangerous like the power from the gray dog had slipped into my body and toned my muscles. I thought it was silly at times, but at other times it was the only thing that made any sense.

I can make ground move under my feet, catch rides and explain to the many so willing to help where I'm headed. Just don't ask me where I'm coming from because that's behind me and long, long ago. Don't ask me how to spell anything. I'm not like you. I can't read but a little and I damn sure can't write nothing but my name and that don't amount to spit. No, God thought it right that I'd be that way. Hey world, no need in feeling sorry for my sorry ass because I'm damn sure not stupid, and you can bet your ass on that.

My attitude wasn't a good one. And when I spoke to someone, I did like Check had done, looked them straight in their eyes. They could see where I was coming from and that I meant business. No foolishness about Johnnyboy.

Now I had a one-track mind and I was going to Chief's house. If he wasn't home, I'd wait outside in his yard a month if that's what it took. His unfriendly neighbors could call the law and have me put away but I'd be back the minute I got out. I was down to one hope. Maybe Chief would show me how I could get Check back and why I was living on the move. There had to be a way through magic to get the dog back. Chief had knowledge of the old ways and maybe he would do that for me. Chief and I would eat buttons together and he'd speak his tongue and bring us all together. He had to see Check, the power. Chief had said I'd go to the Sacred Mountain with a great power. He'd seen everything in a vision and Chief knew much more than he'd told me. As soon as I found Chief, he'd have to tell me everything. I'd see to that. When he looked into my eyes, he'd know what to do because he'd see a man with a broken heart.

In my journey to Chief's house, I made sure I remembered every footstep Check and I took. I retraced them over and over, just like memorizing a road map. Chief would want to know everything. I'd tell him where I went wrong, that it was me who used the wrong service station that led to Check's death. It was my fault that he got shot and I had to live with that. I'd tell Chief what I couldn't face, that maybe Check took a bullet meant for me. I'd need buttons to see myself through all this.

Chapter 34

This time Chief was home. He met me a few miles before I got to his house in his old truck, just like before. Like in a dream, his noisy truck came from behind. He pulled off the road and I wanted to tell him everything right away but he stopped me, waving his hands downward in sign language. It wasn't the place, he said, his eyes showing a ring like the winter's moon. "Not here. Get in. We talk hacienda."

He said I needed food and handed me a strip of dried beef he always carried to chew on. So I didn't talk on our ride to his house. It felt strange him not uttering a sound but I figured he was thinking real hard. I thought he was disappointed with me and, when we were inside his house, he would let me have a scolding. But Chief wasn't like that. He was a good listener. He parked in front of his house and I got out the truck first while he gathered his things off the seat. I looked around and saw window shades close when my eyes panned his neighbor's houses. I wanted to see if Chief's people were still standoffish. This time they moved behind their curtains faster like they were shields of armor. Their rejection of me just set me up for hurt feelings and that activated anger. With my anger rising, I imagined that Check was near and the tribe feared his power. Then I felt that power quivering through my muscles, muscles that were ready to fight. It was as though I became the gray dog and the people in Chief's neighborhood could see him and his frightening war stance. Chief spoke to me calmly because he knew what was happening. He asked me to forget his neighbors and told me to go inside the house. He said he didn't want me to get on the wrong path.

Inside he made a pot of hot coffee. The smell eased my bad feelings, my anger. He poured two mugs, nodded for me to sit, and slid out a second chair at the small kitchen table made for two. "Timekeeper, it is time to talk. Speak from your heart, not your head."

I started out telling him about the first night . . . Check sleeping on the other side of the giant live oak tree and me not knowing it. I said the gray dog followed me all day. I explained how Check could disappear in a flash when someone came into our camp. Chief never asked one question, just sat there like a stone statue listening to everything I said, like my words were money and it was raining the stuff, filling up his tiny kitchen with riches. I could read faces better than ever, and I could see Chief was very pleased with what I was telling him. I continued telling how we started out making friends, me offering Check my food, him eating it when I turned sideways. I told about the next morning after learning that Check had slept by me and how he let me see him drink water down stream, his eyes searching my soul. Chief got stiff and sat up straight when I told him about the night of the lightning storm in the barn filled with animals, and about when I first saw the wet yellow-gold eyes which allowed me a glimpse into another world, one wild, free and without time. I could see Chief wanted to ask me a question but he sat motionless for me to go on. I said he was right about the Sacred Mountain because I had found it, and Check and I had dined with wild buffalo. I explained that I couldn't have done it without Check, the great power Chief spoke of. For the first time Chief leaned forward and nodded in great pleasure, his face stern as a rock.

I talked on and on. Sometimes excited, I jumped ahead of myself. But it all had to come out and Chief, like a good grandfather, listened to everything. I blamed myself for Check's death and he didn't flinch. I had retraced our footsteps and did something I hadn't done in front of someone in a long time. I cried aloud and felt the tears stream down my face, and I tasted the salt in them. Chief grunted and slid his chair away from the table to get a can from a wall cabinet. I couldn't see clearly what he held but it looked like a flour tin. He said something in his language and then in English, saying that he was going to help my broken heart. Then he waved a handful of flour above my head. I looked up and the flour rained down, sticking on the wet rivers on my face, neck and chest. He told me to go outside to the dirt lane and come back. I did and everyone looked at me, the ghost man, without hiding their faces this time. They respected the ghost, that much I could tell. I wasn't one of them but they knew I was special, not like anyone they had ever known. When I got back inside, Chief handed me a looking glass and I saw who I really was, and nothing could have braced me for that. That's what Chief said my vision quest was about. I wasn't the boy playing on the bridge or the child in school who never learned to read. I was a man with a soul like Check's, wild and free.

Chief yelled, "Wild and free, Timekeeper," then he spoke in his native tongue and with much strength in his voice. He moved about the room, something like Pete had done when he read from his books, but Chief used his arms and hands in signing along with chattering in his strange language. He did this a while until he settled back down at the table, arms folded at his chest, a man swelled with pride. He said it would be a perfect time for him to part this world. I didn't understand what he meant, but he said his life was fulfilled and he was ready for the next. He said I would learn all he spoke of in due time, not to be in a hurry because it would come to me.

It was Chief's turn to talk in my language, and I held back my tears and listened real hard. He said that he had seen the gray dog in one of his visions. He said Check was very old and had hunted with peoples of long ago, that Check was the first dog to do that. He said I was honored to have him look over me as long as he did, that the wild dog was known to move on quickly. He said we would have to be in a different time than in his kitchen to see more. "This is what it's all about, Timekeeper." He said it takes a lifetime to understand a friend. He said that's why he named me what he did because I had the rest of my life to learn about what my friend Check had showed me.

"Timekeeper, man who searches his soul," shouted Chief.

I got angry because Check was real and not a mescal dream like I believed Chief thought. But Chief was patient with me and didn't show any fear of my anger. He soothed me by chanting an after-hunting song, one where the hunter did good. My mind went back to my Sunday school class. I was a small boy singing *Row, Row, Row Your Boat* to a nursing home bunch and, when they got to the part "life is but a dream," an old man with skin stretched tight across his bent nose, his mouth gapped open like a wren's nest, yelled as though he had seen a revelation. The old man shouted, "That's right! That's right! Life is but a dream. That's what it is," he repeated until they took him away, his voice growing weaker by the minute. Someone said he'd died later that night and he'd repeated those words to the end.

I wasn't satisfied with what Chief had said. I didn't want to spend the rest of my life searching for the meaning of my journey and an honorable name. That would be hell. But Chief was truly wise. He chanted until I fell asleep at the table. The last conscious word to enter my mind was Timekeeper. By then it sounded natural, so peaceful was Chief's voice.

Chapter 35

So it was me now, the Timekeeper, and all would be forgotten if I didn't hold my friends close to my heart as years went by. Chief said he named me right the first time, but I still wasn't pleased about that. I had wanted a new name and I didn't want to stop until I got the right one. Got-damn-it, I had been through so much and thought I deserved a new name.

Things didn't turn out like I thought they would at Chief's place. Maybe I was oversensitive because of the loss of Check. I couldn't deal with his death like Chief did. It appeared Chief was cold because he wouldn't talk about it any more. I needed to get back on the road and I said so. Chief welcomed me to stay, but at the same time he was proud of my stamina. I was really let down he didn't give me another name so I gave myself one I could spell, Montana Red. I remembered the name from our old license plates, the ones Check and I forged.

I liked the sound of Montana and folks would think I was from that state. I'd used lots of different names to fit many occasions. One day I made up my mind I'd say a different name to everyone who gave me a ride. One guy asked me how to spell the name I gave him and I said, "Hell, I don't know." We both nearly laughed our guts out. It was so funny, the man had to pull over and hold his side. I just laughed at him, laughing.

Since he was in such a good mood, I asked him did he have any whiskey, saying that I needed a drink to wash down the trail dust. The bad thing about thumbing, you got rides with the down and outers, the crazies. Misery is joined to misery,

I always believed, and the laughing man seemed pleased that I couldn't spell the name I gave him. He looked at me with a stupid grin and reached under his seat and pulled out a pint, a flat bottle that could fit in a back pocket. He handed it to me and I broke the seal and threw the cap out the window. He went into another laughing fit from that. *Laugh all you want, but I'm damn sure going to take a big swig of your whiskey.* In my way of thinking, the little pint would be passed back and forth until it was gone and that was maybe two drinks apiece.

My first swallow didn't water my eyes and that seemed funny to him too. After he stopped laughing, he took a taste and said he didn't want anymore. Okay, I'd show him how Montana did it. I turned up the little bottle and didn't take it from my lips until it was empty. I wiped my mouth with the back of my hand and said it was mighty fine, mighty tasty whiskey. He was thinking I was going to pass out so he stopped his cackling to check me out. Maybe he was thinking I was a bit crazy, but I didn't care. I was worried about my next ride and the new name I had to come up with. I wouldn't choose one until a new driver would ask, "What's your name?" I couldn't see myself using Virginia as a name because that's feminine and, if my mind weren't working off the effects of spirits, I could always fall back on Montana. That cut down on one question I got tired of answering, "Where are you from?" If I was in a bad mood, I wanted to say, from hell, but I never did. People most likely wanted something but it wasn't abuse from me, that was for sure.

Chapter 36

I was reading on a second grade level but I couldn't write a sentence no matter what. But the seed Pete had planted in me about books was growing while the desire to roam withered. I didn't have the urge to cut and run when things didn't go my way. Who had time for that? I couldn't figure myself out all the way but no one else could either. It looked like Pete was on the right path about why I couldn't read and that caused me to think about him and all he had done in his old age with books. With his books he had been roaming the same places I had. It didn't seem fair that everyone else could get joy from pen and paper while I felt misery. I could still remember seeing the agony on Mrs. Heenon, my third grade teacher's face when she lost control and jerked me from my seat. Being a little older I could set aside the embarrassment because now I could see her side of it. She had tried to help me the only way she knew how. "I'm losing you, Johnnyboy!" she'd yelled. Mrs. Heenon had taught my brother Newt and two sisters before me without any problem. But I wasn't like them. I was Johnnyboy and something was wrong with my head. Suddenly, I could see how hard she had really tried. I didn't feel that way with any of my other teachers. My last teacher had heard all the horror stories about how I acted in class. She didn't really care about me and didn't go to any trouble to help either. I wished it wasn't so but it was true. Maybe I had gone too long without any improvement in my reading for her to do anything. I wasn't worth the effort. Except for my third grade teacher, Mrs. Heenon, each teacher passed the same story on to the next: Johnnyboy can't read.

I was okay with my teachers, but not how they treated me. It wasn't their fault I couldn't read but it wasn't mine, either. Pete made me feel good about myself. He said I was smart and when I felt that way to pick up a book and read, that I could figure out things on my own because my pride wouldn't let anyone help. Surely I wouldn't let another teacher take a shot at me saying I was stupid when it came to reading. I would teach myself and they would be sorry someday for giving up. The desire to learn was there because my attitude had changed, thanks to Pete. That feeling he gave me grew inside with each new word I learned.

I could always go back and see Chief. He thought the world of me. How about Mr. Jeff and Martha? What would I tell them? That I burned up the car they gave me? I'd love to see them. Maybe they would understand. Old Pete, I'd bet he was reading one of those fancy books and getting smarter and smarter every day. But could I find his place without Check's help? I looked and I looked. How stupid of me not to remember his address. He could teach me how to read. He'd never make fun of me. He'd said he had read about boys like me. No matter what I asked him about, he'd find it in one of his books. I liked that a lot. Yeah, if I got enough money I'd look him up if I had to search every mile of Texas. Damn straight, that's what I'd do.

If I had spent any length of time with them, my mind drifted back to faces I had met on my journey, their eyes. Then came the what-will-you-do-now question. *You can't read shit, Johnnyboy. You'll be exactly what the teacher said you would be, a common laborer. You like that? Well, you'd better get used to it because she said you'll work the rest of your life educating other people's children with tax money coming out of your little paycheck. To hell with that. I'll learn to read . . . and write. No matter what I've got to do, I'll do it. Why should I pay for what was cheated me? I've got to find Pete. I've got to see Pete so he can say I'm special. I'll work long enough for road money. That's what I'll do.*

I bought a junk car in Arkansas and was ready to travel. Now I had deeper matters to tend to. I needed lots of help with my studies and I knew where I could get it . . . at Pete's place and, off to Texas I went.

Chapter 37

Nothing stays the same. I could read well enough to find Pete's address in his local post office. I hadn't bothered to do this before. The postmaster said his house was empty but, if he'd gotten mail, he'd forwarded it to his administrator. He said I was five months too late. Pete had had a stroke but they didn't find him until a few days later. The postmaster knew something was wrong after his books came and Pete didn't pick them up. He sent someone out to his place and he found Pete sitting in the chair I knew well. His oil lamp had burned empty and he held a book in his lap. He said that's the way he wanted to go and I agreed. I told him I was just a friend he'd helped one time. I told him how sorry I was I didn't get back to Pete sooner. I said to give my best to his family. I smiled but my heart was suffering the loss. There wasn't anything I could do to change one thing. Once you're gone, that's that.

I had one hope left, Chief. I could go and see him. I hoped he hadn't died too because he had looked a lot older than Pete. Before I left the post office I asked the man what happened to Pete's books. He said he left them to different ones and they were being lapped up quicker than ice water on a hot Texas day. He had mailed them to Pete's friends all over the world. He asked me my name again, making out like Pete may have left me one. Still shook, I forgot what I had called myself when I stayed with Pete so I said Johnnyboy. He said, "That's too bad. No books for Johnny." He said he did have one for a Billy Barlow in Virginia, no address. He said he was trying to get Billy's address. I told him

Billy was my name, too, but he said I had to prove it. Things were looking foolish because I said I couldn't prove it, but I wanted to know what book was left to Billy. He said it wasn't anything valuable. Said it was well known that Peter had expensive books but this one wasn't. He said it was a book on phonics. I didn't know anything about that subject so I thought no loss.

I left the post office down low in the heart. I had a sick feeling in the pit of my stomach. But I was proud Pete thought of me in his will. Yet I felt guilty I didn't find him in time. I kept telling myself that I couldn't read a signpost back then, but that didn't stop my guilt feeling. I needed a drink of his wine to relax and reflect on my dear friend. I planned to honor his life at the old three-story house where Check and I slept the night before we met Pete head on.

Nothing stays the same because the big house was gone too. If it weren't for the postmaster sending me on the right road to the old house, everything could've been in my imagination. They had burned everything down, out buildings too. I stood in the ashes of the big house for a while wishing I could go back in time. A foolish thought, as I stirred the ashes with my boots looking for a connection. I looked up and saw where the flames had scorched the trees that surrounded the old house, leaving only green leaves on the outer side trying to survive the once inferno. I knew they wouldn't and that saddened me to tears. I was feeling sorry for myself for losing a friend, being selfish. Somehow I needed to honor Pete's life.

Pete would have helped me further my education. Now learning how to read would have to wait. He had set me on the right path and for that I owed him. Chief helped me too but I was from another culture, one like Pete's. I needed to learn how to live a whole life and to taste the things Pete tasted from his books. I had seen how he lived and he didn't have to run all over hell like I did. He'd enjoyed his old age through reading and expanding his mind, getting smarter each day. He knew how smart I was, how I needed to read and someday write. He believed I could become somebody that added to the understanding of education if only I could learn how to express myself with prose. I wasn't stupid and the only way to break the label that was placed upon me by the academic establishment back in Glen Allen was to beat them at their own game. Pete was smart enough to know that I'd figure out how to do that some day. I'd show them. They wouldn't make fun of me again because I'd have a Ph.D. like Martha. Doctor Johnnyboy, but it didn't sound quite right.

The daydream felt fine as I stood in the ashes of Pete's old home place. But soon came reality and it hit me like a glass of cold water in the face. Why couldn't I put the pieces together, the sounds of words? I'd read a comic book and struggle with a word as if it were a big stone the Greek man pushed uphill forever. Standing there, I was less connected to the world than ever before. I felt just as beaten as if it were done by Bugdaddy's hand. I needed answers to life's problems. I needed a name more than ever. I felt lonely and forsaken by Moses and by God. He'd dropped me off on this planet. I was so different; I just didn't belong anywhere. *Jesus, help me. Where can I go?*

I needed someone who was willing to stand by me while I figured out a new direction. The only living person who really understood me was Chief. I knew I didn't belong around his people but at this juncture I was more like them than others. After being away from Chief a good while, I thought he might be wiser but I was too. Go here, go there, for answers that might work, but I didn't know any other way. I couldn't stand over a pile of wood ashes for long hoping a spirit would rise up and lead me someplace.

I thought about the night Check and I had slept in the old mansion. Check went ahead of me making sure nothing could harm us. *Oh, Moses, I wish Check were here. Oh, God. Please take me somewhere that will make a difference.*

I couldn't stand still but so long when I was conflicted. I needed to be a part of something and that was pulling me apart. Searching for identity was a living hell. In a pile of ashes, I gathered the bits and pieces of my life and made plans to head to Oklahoma for one last time.

As I expected my homecoming wasn't welcomed by Chief's

neighbors. They said he had moved away and didn't know where, but they didn't want me hanging around. This was hard to face, me not seeing Chief ever again. My emotions ran from self-pity to blood curdling anger. Why did these people hate me? Was I so damn different? Of course I was. Hell, I wasn't like anybody. *I'm Johnnyboy, the stupid kid.* Maybe it was because my hair was too light and curly. *Face it, Johnnyboy.* Chief had said I wasn't part of the clan. Maybe they thought I'd steal from them. I don't know. I tried everything to find the whereabouts of my friend but his neighbors wanted me gone. I'd have to live with the name, Timekeeper, for the rest of my life. Hopelessness fell upon my soul.

I knew I was down to only me so what did I want to do with myself. Eyes peered from all directions. The tension was high enough to explode.

How stupid to think you were going to make something out of your life after getting to Chief's house? You're a stupid ass breed, Johnnyboy. You ain't going nowhere in life. You're nothing but a damn loser.

I couldn't help believing what I was told back home in Glen Allen. Facing unfriendly people was my lowest point. I told myself not to get shook and spoke to the ones I thought could hear me. Some had sticks in their hands like they would beat me away. "Hey, it's only me, Timekeeper." They didn't acknowledge I had spoken. That's where I stood, alone, and with people that were afraid of me. I'd be on my way except I didn't know which direction to take. *Maybe I should make a scene before leaving so they can see the man with no direction. That's the worst thing that can happen to a soul. Not having a place to go, a goal in life.* I stood there in danger hoping something good would bring insight. "Leave or we'll call the law," someone yelled. I didn't want to go to jail so I turned and left without a crossword. *You'll be sorry some day. Maybe I should put a curse on you people. No, that's not right either.*

I thought about Chief. What would he have me do? I had to find something new. New, new, new, so I could have a new outlook, a new attitude.

Chapter 38

With Chief's people behind, I headed out west to see what was hip on the coast. I went to a free beach when I got there and could see California was years ahead of folks back home in Virginia. I didn't fit in with the beach scene, but that wasn't a surprise. Maybe if I returned to the Big Easy, things would go good. I had enough money to hold me a few months if I didn't drink too much. The alcohol put me on a short mental vacation from a confusing life. That worked, but only by the hours, and that was no way to live.

Still in Los Angeles, I bought a cheap guitar for about five dollars at a junk shop. The man who sold it to me showed me where to put my fingers to tune one string to the other. I had wanted to take music in school but in those days, if you didn't make good grades, you couldn't take band. Here's the deal; if everything came as natural to me as playing and singing, I would be a brain surgeon. In less than a month I was picking and singing. I sang one night at a bar where this black lady was playing piano. I stood by and sang to her melody. She was so impressed she asked her boss if I could do a few songs with her as a team. This was a fancy place in Santa Barbara and I wasn't dressed for the club. Her boss liked my stage presence, and the pianist and I did our songs like we'd been doing them all along. I came back the next night with my guitar. I didn't make them jump out their seats but they damn sure could feel what I was putting down. I sang the blues because that was what I felt. I could only play what I felt. If someone asked me to play a certain tune, it confused me and I lost track. Sometimes I was this way with a song of love and sometimes I was that way with a song of soul, the blues. I could sing the blues when I was on top of the world because I had seen the bottom. The blues set me free and that's what they were supposed to do. Sometimes I sang to hide from the pains of life as I'd learned to do in the cotton fields back east. Black folk taught me how to moan, how to switch off the hurt and switch on the joy. That's why I sang. Not just to me, I had sung to Check and to Chief and Pete without a guitar, and folks knew where I was coming from. I sang the songs about lifting up your hands and touching Jesus. I moaned an old Hank William's song, *Moaning the Blues*. Johnny Cash's *Big River*, and *I Walk the Line*. Did Elvis' *Hound Dog* too. If I could've learned reading and writing as easy as music, I would have had that Ph.D. before I was twenty.

But music didn't help me find where I belonged. I continued searching for that. I had a lot of made up names but I didn't belong anywhere. Timekeeper haunted me. Chief seemed to know this name from a vision like he knew more about me than I knew about myself. He said I had to go the distance from mountain to mountain whatever the hell that meant. I think he knew my new name when I came back from the Sacred Mountain but chose not to tell me for some strange reason. He took my new name with him and left me roaming an American hell.

I headed east, leaving Santa Barbara, but not the music on my mind. Music was stuck to my soul. My new used car had a radio and I played it loud. I could be completely immersed in a song and the world around me faded into void.

* * * * *

I had car trouble in the desert. I'd wanted to cross the desert at night and spare myself the heat of the day. A loud noise rose above the radio. It was in the rear of the car so I pulled into a service station rather than risk being let down in the middle of nothing but sand and heat. I knew the dangers of the desert so I made plans to sleep until the station opened the next morning. I stepped outside my car to stretch and relax. It was cold, but I loved the desert night sky. Searching the heavens, I thought about the night skies, the moon and stars, things Chief had mentioned. Being restless, I'd search the heavens like I was looking for some kind of doorway to a better life. Roaming had to end someday. Maybe that's where I would land, among the stars. The wonderment of stars seemed to soothe me this night, like it was something out there far better. And yet the endless space between them humbled me, making me feel small like a speck of dust floating in an unfriendly atmosphere, waiting to land and become stone with no real value. If there was a God up there, He wasn't hearing my heart. But I found comfort in other things in the sky. I knew the moon's faces like old friends. I'd learned stuff like that early on from Frank. Feelings were somehow magnified in the desert night sky. The stars became eyes that looked into my soul. They hung like ornaments from a great ceiling beyond reach. But my round face friend, the moon, was rising to give me comforting light. I always took pleasure in the moon's glow.

I whip-eyed around me. Behind the station was a city of junk cars, row after row as far as I could see, like the cotton fields back east. For no reason a breeze came upon me like an unwanted guest. It touched my face. Seeing the cars, my shelter, made me feel better. Seeing the field of junk cars eased my mind too. I could get used parts. I went back to the car and took a few big swigs of whiskey from a bottle I had under the front seat. I knew better than to drink and drive but when I was stressed out about something, like my broken-down car, I'd take a nip. As soon as I wiped my mouth with the back of my hand, the breeze picked up, a bad sign. It was so strange how things like that happen. The wind was gentle and soft at first but I could tell it was going to build bringing cold air that would take a bite out of my flesh. I leaned into the back seat and got a jacket. Whenever I went to the back seat, I'd think of Check. With thoughts of my friend, I put on the jacket and waited to see what the spirits in the wind had to offer. Another drink of fire water and I'd listen to hear who the night wind called for, to take them to the other side. Maybe it would be me, I didn't care.

"Come on, death, I'm ready," I said to no one I knew. I was enjoying the effect of the alcohol. But what was it about the wind that made me so uneasy? Maybe I was afraid Check's spirit would come and blame me for his death. *Bad Timekeeper.* I took more swallows of whiskey and wished I had mescal, something cleaner to get my head screwed on right. Then something like I had left the radio on . . . I thought I heard a voice from the direction of the junk cars. I listened real hard. *Timekeeper, you're imagining things.*

The wind picked up, got stronger with each minute and I felt someone was speaking to me from the other side. That went on awhile as I sat on the edge of the front seat with the door opened, my feet on the ground. I wouldn't lie down and try to sleep because I had more whiskey to drink. I needed restful sleep, but I heard someone speaking from the spirit world and that kept me on edge.

I managed to get a few hours shut-eye before a man came to open the station. He was Native American and wore a headband with his uniform. He took my car in right away but the part I needed, the ring gear in the rear axle, wasn't in the whole damn junkyard. He said he would have it the next day and offered me his home. I was a little agitated so I asked if there was a bus heading east. He said there was but it wouldn't come through for several days. I was stuck there so I told him to order the part.

As the sun rose higher, the temperature did too. Sweat evaporated as soon as it popped out my skin. I liked that because back east clothes got wet from sweat and stuck to my skin. I drank lots of water to stay hydrated and a coke or two as well. The soft drink machine was at the outside corner of the station so I dropped in a dime for a drink. When I did, I thought I heard a voice in the junkyard like I had heard during the night. I listened real hard for a while but dismissed it as the hot wind blowing through wrecked cars.

Heat can play tricks on a mind. Later that evening, the manager offered me his home again but I wanted to stay with my car. He was concerned about me getting cold in the night. He backed my car outside the stall after I told him I'd slept in it, that I was used to it. I liked him because he respected me. Not because I was spending money at his place, but as a person connected in ways beyond any spoken word. I didn't say anything about the voice I had heard in his junkyard. No, that was too risky, no matter how nice he was.

After he was gone, about an hour or two later into the night, the wind breezed up like the night before. It got stronger as the sandy land swallowed the sun and the stars became eyes. Most times the wind dropped out when the sun went down but this was in reverse. That's what spooked me. Not long into the night it got cold so I wanted a whiskey to help fight off the chill. I walked to the corner of the service station and got a coke from the drink machine for a mixer. After I dropped my coin in, I heard a strange sound again in the back of the station where the junk cars were. This time it was clearer like it was riding on the wind, a man's voice, but it didn't make any sense. Now I knew someone was in the junkyard and the cold wind was carrying the cries.

I wasn't stupid to go stumbling through the junkyard in the dark and get hurt. A near full moon would be up in a while and it would give me plenty of light to see my way through the wrecked cars. After a stiff drink, I made plans to check out the commotion that sounded deep into the lines of junk, a place no one should be. I left the shelter of my car a few times, waiting for the moon to rise, and poked my head at the side of the station for sounds. Again I heard something. "I'm not crazy," I told myself. "Somebody is out there."

The derelict cars went on forever like the cotton rows I chopped as a boy. Every few hundred feet was an opening like a highway intersection and I'd look both ways. The wind blew harder with the rising moon and I found myself fidgety just like Check used to get in a night wind. My head would snap from one direction to another. I started to go back, but without a doubt it was the voice of a man coming from straight ahead. My heart was pounding. Maybe he was a bad man trying to lure me into his trap. He could be waiting with an axe or a long knife that was sharp as a briar. What should I do? No one was around and, if things went wrong, who would know?

I heard the sound stronger, and thought I'd just walk close enough to hear a little better. After a good ways into the junkyard, I stopped and listened. There it was, a man's voice, strange as though it was calling my name, "Timekeeper." Maybe he was hurt and needed help. I lost some of my fear and moved faster, deeper into the junk cars until I was at last at a chain-link fence.

There the apparition was next to the fence. *Native American*, I said to myself. The old man had a tiny fire in the middle of a big farm tractor tire and the flames reflected a white face, like the one I had when Chief put flour on my face. I was too wise to think he was a ghost, but he looked that way because of his face. I spoke to him, "Hey, mister, you all right?" The old man acted like I wasn't there. *He didn't hear me.* I yelled and he still didn't react. *Maybe he is a ghost.* Why wasn't he freezing? His arms were bare and his blanket lay loosely around his bottom. The fire wasn't for warmth. He'd put something on the fire and chanted the way Chief did, but with the oldest voice I had ever heard, weak, yet it carried far, riding the night wind. I decided to make his fire bigger. I looked around for fuel and could only find stuffing from the seats of old cars. I put seat stuffing on his fire. As the flames rose, the old man looked blind.

What a hellhole of a place to be in his condition. I thought of old Chicken Bone, but this poverty was much worse than anything I could imagine. I ran back to my car and got my bedroll and my whiskey. Maybe he needed a drink to warm him. I returned and threw the blanket around his shoulders, but he flung it away like it was nasty. He wasn't blind and he wasn't deaf. He couldn't speak English but I knew to back off. I had invaded his space. After he settled down, he began his chanting again. He took something from under the blanket and put it on the flame in the middle of the big tire. The tractor tire was so big he had to lean over nearly on his chest to do this. He sat back up straight and held up his arms like he was asking the moon to help him up off the ground, something like toddlers do when they want their mama to hold them. I sat down to watch the show and planned to stay out of his way. I took a drink of whiskey and offered him one but again he acted like I wasn't there. After a while and because I wasn't moving around, I got cold and started shivering. It was still breezing up as the moon got higher. I feared the old man would freeze before the sun rose. I looked around his campsite and couldn't imagine how he had lived through the heat of the day without water. Not a drop was in sight but then he reached under the blanket and came out with a button. *That's how,* I thought, *mescal.* I wanted a button or two and I moved his blanket aside and saw some feathers and a leather pouch, which held about two handfuls of buttons. I picked it up and he didn't object so out of respect I tossed it back in place. For the first time, he acknowledged me. He picked the bag up and offered it to me. Even with the smeared white paste on his face, he showed me kindness, like a priest would do on the streets of a small town. I said, "Old man, you know you'll die out here soon, huh?" He held up the buttons until I took the pouch from him. At that point it was no doubt he wanted me where he was. I tossed in all the buttons my mouth could hold and chewed. They were very bitter like they had been picked too soon. It had been a while since I had eaten mescal. I was concerned it would make the whiskey in me angry but that didn't happen. I handed the pouch back to him but he gave it back for me to eat more. I chewed and spat out the pulp after my tongue extracted all the juice, then I reloaded my mouth.

    I felt good, very secure, so I sang a song like I had heard on the radio, *I'm So Lonesome I Could Cry*. The old man liked it. As the drug took me further and further into where I needed to be in the old man's world, he chanted away. His voice faded out at times but his jaw never stopped moving, even when the sounds were gone. I didn't know what he was singing about but at the time it didn't matter. I'd show him respect and a thing or two about the Timekeeper. I'd sing the song Chief taught me. I began and his eyes opened wide from excitement. From the flickering flame, his eyes looked old yet they sparkled. Skin on his arms hung down when he raised them toward the moon.

It was good not feeling any pain so I tried to make him happy with my songs. If a smile came upon his face, I'd see it and that would mean overwhelming pleasure. I wanted very much to make him happy because this was a place only a few could withstand, the harshness of the desert, much less the horrid sight of a junkyard cold and unwelcoming.

I had another reason for him to be happy. I wanted him to be Chief and in some way he looked the part. If that were true, then the old man could give me my new name. It was the mescal making me see things this way. Never mind the crazy stuff going on around us like spirits grabbing at the tiny fire, trying to take the flame with them. They might come after me if the flame died. The old man didn't look concerned about that and that eased my mind. He would be happy if I danced for him and for the dead. Chief had told me the old ones danced for the dead until the white man outlawed it. The whites were afraid to learn about things in the spirit world and not need the steeple buildings anymore. I'd dance for the ones on the other side because I was still wild and free, living on the edge. The old man would be pleased with me and maybe Check would come by in the cold wind and show me the yellow golden eyes with the wet black spot in the center that would reflect the light from our fire. Yes, me and the old man and Check were of the same mind, the same spirit. I'd show my heart to the heavens and let the wind blow. So I danced, and dust stirred up around my feet thick as a cloud. I must have looked like I was on a cloud. With more effort, I chanted and danced and finally the old man smiled. It wasn't a broad smile, like after a good joke is told, but one like two friends shared with one another when they meet. Him smiling that way made me feel good, and I knew from reading his face he had lived a kind life. He was a good man and had no worries parting this world so I danced harder for the ones scooping up the tiny flames and trying to steal our fire.

The old man smiled again and added more stuffing to the fire. He was very pleased with me and I was too.

Most of the night I tripped heavily on the drug. As it withered away, sadly I concluded I wasn't like the old man but had a closer connection with him than with anyone else. Mama's Cherokee blood ran in my veins and I'd heard her say many times that blood was thicker than water. But I was water in the desert, and water uncared for in the desert dries up fast.

I was young, just starting in my life's journey, and the old Indian was on his way out. That was the difference and yet that was the connection between blood and water.

Could the old man help me find my new name? He couldn't speak my language and I couldn't speak his, but we were brothers in the dance for the dead. All are brothers on the other side, the spirit world, and we stood in the doorway that passes through to eternity. There, amid a timeless heaven, he could give me my new name, I believed.

"Hey, old man, what's my name," I asked. I didn't really think he would answer. It was just a selfish impulse of mine. But the old man's smile broadened and he began to chuckle, his slender frame moved jelling up and down with the joy he felt inside. I didn't see anything funny about my question and I needed to be in on what was making him laugh. To let him know how serious I was, I yelled in anger. "Hey, old man, what's my name?" My question seemed to set him off and give him renewed vigor. I could only guess what was going on inside his head, the laughter. Maybe he saw Check licking my face, trying to get me up off the ground and on my feet. *Oh, Moses, he sees someone we both know. Please let it be Check.*

"Have you seen the great power," I asked like a child in awe of the moment. He nodded as though he understood me. He pointed over my shoulder at the rising moon. I turned and looked that way. The golden glow of the moon could have been one of Check's eyes. "You see him, huh?" The old man grew serious, yet he smiled. "Check is here, isn't he?" I asked with much fire in my voice.

I could feel the gray power watching. "Check, I know you're out there. Tell the old man my new name. I've got to know it, boy! You can do that now."

I turned to the fire and the old man's face, which was set like stone. I yelled. "Old man, what's my name, got-damn-it? Now, tell me!"

Never taking his eyes from mine, his hand went straight up toward the heavens and came down ever so slowly until he pointed to his wrist where a watch would be worn. I stood before him feeling Check breathing on the back of my neck. I said, "You're talking in sign, aren't you? That could only mean one thing, Timekeeper."

The old man smiled and tapped his wrist over and over, nodding that I got it right. Good God, what a moment, a shock for the ages. The old man took the guesswork out of my quest. With that, I fell into a deep sleep.

As the sun brightened the eastern sky, the dancing was done and the mescal had faded. I could have danced to exhaustion but settled with what I had been given. Although Timekeeper never left his lips, there was no doubt he spoke the name in sign. I wasn't looking for that name and it was unwanted, something like calling me a bad word. Maybe I would never find myself. My emotions swung wide. Check's spirit slipped away with the wind and darkness as the morning light rose. That aggravated the bad side of me. Somehow I felt stuck between two worlds. With the drug gone from my brain, I became agitated about first one thing and then another, not one issue that would matter to a healthy mind. This had to stop, me taking drugs. I had to look at someone else's life, not mine. *Isn't that what one does when their life is hopeless, focus on others.*

Someone had left the old man to die. Not just to die alone but to die in a hellhole of junk cars. I got self-righteous from that thought. Someone should have danced and sung for the old man. I was ready to take action. I was ready to fight for the old man's honor.

When the manager opened the station, I practically started

a fight with him, blaming him for the old man's plight. The manager said he knew the old man was there. I demanded that he take him to a hospital, that the old man would die from the heat before noon. The manager didn't get excited like me. He stayed calm. He said the old man would be fine. I yelled, repeating his words, "Fine! Not where I come from! Where's the telephone? I'll call emergency."

He spoke calmly, saying I was involving myself in something I knew nothing about. He explained it was the right of his people to do what his grandfather was doing on his final vision quest. He said over and over that he would be fine and could withstand the elements. About ten minutes later when things sank into my hard head, I felt better. When I knew my car would be fixed that morning, I settled down enough to ask the attendant what his grandfather was singing, what he was saying in his chant. I told the manager that I had danced for him and I knew more than he gave me credit for. The manager looked surprised. I told him I had danced for the dead most of the night. He was really taken aback, lost for words. Oh, how he searched my face. But I was water with sun-bleached hair.

I asked, "So, what's the old man singing about?"

The manager looked relaxed as he got in my face to make sure he wouldn't have to repeat himself and so no one else could hear. "He's thanking the Great Spirit for beauty all around him."

I thought a long second looking at the hellhole of cars and finally had to shake it off with thinking somebody had a big stockpile of buttons. The easygoing manager backed away and I asked, "Does the old man think beauty is here?"

The manager said, "Yes." He told me to look for beauty and I'd see it too.

I didn't see beauty then, but years later in a dream I recalled seeing beauty in the smiling face of the old man. The cold wind blew but it didn't bother us because we shared life without a common language. I danced for the dead but it was the old and the new beginning I was dancing for, one coming into the world, the other going out. Yet we were the same in spirit. The big moon and the tiny fire without warmth gave enough light to see all the lines in the old man's face. I was young enough to recognize the wonderments he had seen in his journey through life. I could read his joy when my dancing feet brought a cloud up from the ground. Things were good and beauty was all around us. I just didn't see it then because of my quest to have a name. My search for a name took a long time. Only when I had crossed mountain to mountain, from youth to old age, would I see myself in the mirror of life for who I am. Chief had seen me from the beginning as I am now. He saw me like I saw the old man on the desert at his end. Life has to be part dream when you enter the spirit world.

In the fall Chief and the old man without a name ride the winds and they get excited. The spirits talk to one another, not with words but with signs of how it is with the ways of the world. A twig snaps, a tree falls, the spirits are running with Check, and they become wind. When I've become the wind, I too will play tricks on the unsuspecting traveler. Ones who are bad will be frightened, but innocent hearts will know it's the one Chief called Timekeeper.

John Atkinson is diligently working away on the sequel to *TIMEKEEPER*. This follow up novel will be available in the not so distant future. To be kept up to date on John Atkinson's future publications, send an email with your request to orders@fisherkingpress.com

Timekeeper's Acknowledgments

The author would like to thank David Carr for insisting I write Timekeeper. Also, I'd like to thank Mary Ann Carr, David's wife, for her encouragement.

I will be forever grateful to Pat Adler and Janine Burns for their editing.

My best friend, Richard Bailey, (Rick) in a most kind way, taught me to never introduce eight people in the first sentence. Rick has the patience of a Saint and shares his skills freely in his writer's critique group. I'm grateful I've been a part of that group for ten years. I've learned something from each member.

In another critique group, I think of them as my girls, I'm the only guy, and from the first day I joined they've welcomed me. Thank you, Barbara Shine, Margaret Sibley, Linda Bartlett, Debra (Debbie) Miller, Sharon Baldacci and Reneé Atkinson, my wife and toughest critic.

The author sends out a special thanks to Jackson Fisher, editor and friend, for making me feel great through every step of the publishing process. Jackson has a gift for that. I have no doubt the Great Spirit crossed our paths.

Also from Fisher King Press

Available Spring of 2008

The Promethean Way:
A Jungian Perspective On Sin And Guilt

by Lawrence H. Staples, Ph.D.

Our hunger for the forbidden fruit grows as we get older and our need for it increases. By midlife, we often sense that something important is missing. Then the "unacceptable," "sinful" parts of ourselves that have been rejected begin to clamor with ever greater insistence to participate in our lives. Promethean guilt is the guilt we incur for the sins that we need to commit if we are to achieve, both for our selves and for our society, some of the social, political, economic, scientific, psychological, and other changes and developments that we most deeply need to sustain and nourish us. Myth tells us that Prometheus stole fire from the gods and made it available for human use. He suffered for this sin, but human society would have suffered if he had not committed it. There indeed are sins that are destructive to society, but the paradox is that there are also sins that inure ultimately to society's benefit. Those sins that benefit us could not be committed without a creative, Promethean spirit that is supported, when necessary, by an obstinate and irreverent insolence toward authority (political, theological, pedagogical, and parental) and that is informed by a love for freedom. Life inevitably confronts us with the Promethean dilemma: Do we live our lives without fire and the heat and light it provides or do we sin, and subsequently incur guilt, in order to obtain for ourselves and for society those important changes and developments that we need.

Available from your local bookstore, a host of on-line booksellers, and directly from Fisher King Press:

The Promethean Way
ISBN 978-0-9776076-4-8
Publication Date: Spring 2008.
To order your copy call 1-800-228-9316.
International orders call 00-1-831-238-7799
www.fisherkingpress.com

Have you read the Malcolm Clay Trilogy?

Who is Malcolm Clay, you ask? Well, he's a lost in life sort of fool who's just trying to find his way. He's turned his back on the conventional life and set out in search of . . . well, he can't say for certain what he's seeking, but my guess is, it's himself —all the lost pieces of his soul that were scattered along the wayside while trying to somehow find his place in this crazy world.

Come along on the journey of a modern day Perceval who stumbles into adventures and misadventures while searching for the Holy Grail. You never know, you just might reclaim a lost piece of your own soul!

You don't have to read *LeRoi, Menopause Man,* or *SamSara* in any particular order, they all stand alone. However, these books are about the transformation that takes place within the protagonist, Malcolm Clay. Plan to read more about Malcolm in the future. Four additional novels by Mel Mathews will be published over the next few years. To learn more about Malcolm Clay, be sure to visit www.malcolmclay.com

LeRoi – ISBN 978-0-9776076-0-0
Menopause Man – ISBN 978-0-9776076-1-7
SamSara – ISBN 978-0-9776076-2-4

Available from your local bookstore, a host of online booksellers, and directly from Fisher King Press:
To order your copy call 1-800-228-9316.
International orders call 00-1-831-238-7799
www.fisherkingpress.com

"An Important New Coming of Age Novel:
An Important New Author."
—*WNBC* & *BloggingAuthors.com*, by Grady Harp

"'It's more humane to face a firing squad than a classroom, humiliated because of illiteracy.' This opening sentence of TIMEKEEPER by new author (to this reader) John Atkinson begins a journey so deeply moving and profound, yet so utterly simply told that the book suggests Atkinson may enter the echelon of writers known for important Coming of Age novels. Such writers whose message and transference is tangential include James Joyce's 'Portrait of the Artist as a Young Man', Betty Smith's 'A Tree Grows in Brooklyn', JD Salinger's 'Catcher in the Rye', Robert McCammon's 'Boy's Life', Cormac McCarthy's 'All the Pretty Horses', Sue Monk Kidd's 'The Secret Life of Bees', Jamie O'Neill's 'At Swim, Two Boys' – a rather disparate group of books in style but related in topic - and I'm sure every reader has others of equal impact. Time, of course, will determine his longevity of importance, but at the moment John Atkinson appears to be a new voice whose book should find a very wide audience.

"Johnnyboy is a 14-year-old sensitive, handsome, sadly illiterate half-breed Indian who flees his severely dysfunctional Virginia family – his helpless but loving Cherokee Mama and his physically abusive father Bugdaddy – to find his place in the universe. His journey on foot and by car introduces him to Chief, a wise old Indian who sees into Johnnyboy's soul and with the aid of hallucinogenic mescal introduces the now named Timekeeper to the ways toward the path of life. The book is a road trip peppered with people, both kind and wise and evil and ignorant, who offer Timekeeper valuable lessons, both occult and temporal, as Timekeeper searches for his true identity and purpose. His constant companion is Check, a gray dog who seems from another time plane but who becomes Timekeeper's confidant and protector. Timekeeper's search reaches a tense denouement and a poignant climax as the now solitary lad accepts his place and purpose in the windswept soul of the Universal spirit. It is a journey fraught with hardship, danger, comic relief, heartwarming encounters, and above all the discovery of a boy becoming a man who accepts the gifts of the people who touch his life.

"John Atkinson is able to relate this story in the first person, and as Timekeeper is illiterate and nearly childlike in his beginning, the style of writing fits the character like a glove. As Timekeeper matures during his journey, so does the writing style, becoming far more rich in the etching of atmosphere and the terrain of the country Timekeeper and Check traverse. That is a difficult feat and Atkinson proves it can be done. This is an important book from an important writer. It will be very interesting to see where he goes from this auspicious debut."

In addition to the USA Today, WNBC.com, and BloggingAuthors.com, Grady Harp's reviews appear on Barnes & Noble, Soapadoo, Powells Books, and he is an Amazon.com Top 10 Reviewer!